Prairie Sonata

a novel

SANDY SHEFRIN RABIN

 FriesenPress

Suite 300 - 990 Fort St
Victoria, BC, V8V 3K2
Canada

www.friesenpress.com

ISBN
978-1-5255-7636-2 (Hardcover)
978-1-5255-7637-9 (Paperback)
978-1-5255-7638-6 (eBook)

1. FIC019000   Fiction, Literary

Distributed to the trade by The Ingram Book Company

This book is dedicated to my parents,
For all the gifts they gave me.

Part I

CHAPTER I

Qu'il est doux, qu'il est doux d'écouter des histoires,
Des histoires du temps passé,
Quand les branches d'arbres sont noires,
Quand la neige est épaisse et charge un sol glacé.

How sweet it is, how sweet it is to listen to stories,
To stories of past times,
When the branches of trees are dark,
And the snow is thick and covers the earth with an icy glaze.

—Alfred de Vigny, "La Neige"

And I would go back there if I could. Despite the freezing winters and piercing winds. If I could be in the same house and look out of the same windows at the long, arching tree branches laden with snow and watch the feathery snowflakes waft down from the sky like fairy dust. And if I could hear my mother in the kitchen, the rhythmic tapping of her wooden spoon against the sides of the bowl as she turned flour and shortening into a delicious cherry pie, so delicious it was almost like a miracle.

SANDY SHEFRIN RABIN

Yes, I would go back there if I could. Despite the short winter days and long winter nights. Despite what I learned about the teacher who moved to our community when I was eleven. Despite what I learned about *Chaver* B.

I grew up on the Canadian prairies, in Ambrosia, a town in Manitoba. Although many people might consider the prairies monotonous, I never found them to be so. Undeniably, the land was as flat as a placid lake on a windless day. The weather was predictable, and I concede that in that predictability, there was a sense of dreariness. Always cold in the winter. Biting cold. And you could regularly count on some hot, humid spells in the summer, though for the most part, summers were dry and punctuated with thunderstorms.

But there was also some excitement. Occasionally there would be hailstones large enough to rival those that descended punishingly from the heavens during the Ten Plagues. Not to mention blinding blizzards with fierce, icy winds whipping across the fields and down the streets, making it impossible for us to go to school. But because snow was a certainty, streets and sidewalks were cleared in an expedient fashion. No icy slopes to contend with when getting about. No hurricanes or tsunamis to worry about since we were inland. And even though we were on the plains, no tornadoes. Just a lot of pesky mosquitoes in summertime.

In turn, the weather and terrain led to a strength of character and an openness of heart. Enduring the extremes of weather created a certain fortitude that enabled us to deal with the vicissitudes of life. And with those vast sweeping spaces, golden fields, and azure sky, how could anyone's heart be anything but open, unguarded, and gracious?

And so, I believed that the world of one's childhood was the way the world always should be. That is, of course, if we grew up when times were good. But everyone lives in his or her own reality. If we grew up when times were bad, then we hoped, anticipated, prayed that things would become better. As for me, my world was an untroubled one, and in my naiveté and innocence, I assumed that it was the same for everyone.

Some of us have a year or summer or singular experience that changes our perspective or trajectory in life, or even how we view things that came before. I had one of those experiences, an experience that for me was both magical and horrific, perhaps a microcosm of what life is. But what I learned provided me with no great epiphany. I was left with only questions, questions without answers.

Still, I would go back there if I could. Despite what I learned from my teacher. Despite what I learned from Chaver B. And *because* of what I learned from him.

CHAPTER II

When I dipt into the future far as human eye could see;
Saw the Vision of the world, and all the wonder that would be.

—Alfred, Lord Tennyson,
"Locksley Hall"

I grew up on a gracious, wide, tree-lined boulevard. The tall elms formed a green leafy canopy in summer and a labyrinth of dark branches outlined with snow in winter. I dreamt of fairies and witches inhabiting the trees, all dressed in the same nightgown I was wearing, going in and out of doors carved into the trunks, flitting from tree to tree, whispering secrets amongst themselves. They always seemed to be involved in some clandestine intrigue, but by morning, I could never remember what scheme they had been up to.

Our house stood on the edge of town, and from my second-storey bedroom window I could see row upon row of sunflowers stretching into the distance, their golden yellow heads swaying in the wind, turned upwards trustingly as if smiling at the sun, like a young child looking up lovingly at her mother. The fields seemed to extend to the ends of the earth, and I was captivated by the mesmerizing magic of the seamless blue sky as it greeted the horizon. It all lay before me, like the fabric of a dream. Looking out that window made me feel that life was full of limitless possibilities, like the limitless land itself, and I was overcome with a certain lightness and sense of freedom.

My name is Mira, or Miraleh as I was called growing up, as an evocation of endearment. (In Yiddish, the suffix *leh* is often added to a name as a diminutive form and to connote a feeling of warmth). My mother, Claire, father, Reuven, little brother, Sammy, and I lived in the medium-sized town of Ambrosia, in the heart of sunflower country. There were two movie theatres, and for Sammy and me, these were the most important buildings in town. We would save up our weekly allowances—a shiny, silvery nickel with a beaver engraved on one side and a portrait of King George VI on the other—until we had the twenty cents needed to watch the double feature on a Saturday afternoon.

Even now, after all these years, it still surprises me that Chaver B arrived here in 1948, that of all the places in the world he could have gone to, he chose our community. What siren's voice had called him to us, and why?

To be sure, Ambrosia had everything we needed, including a small Eaton's Department Store outlet downtown, drugstores, dress shops, and a shoe store where we made our twice yearly pilgrimages—in the fall to buy warm, fur-lined boots to prevent frostbite in the winter, and again a few months later for rubber galoshes to navigate the slippery, wet slush as winter gasped its final breaths.

There were hardware stores, restaurants, a bank, a bookstore, and the bakery with its splendid, comforting smells. Each Friday evening, my father would stop there on his way home from work to bring us a loaf of braided *challah*, sometimes adorned with sesame seeds, sometimes with poppy seeds, and sometimes just plain. On our birthdays—in June for me and in October for Sammy—we'd buy cakes, vanilla cakes with snow-white frosting and blue, pink, and yellow flowers, the icing sweet, smooth, silky, and sumptuous.

On the periphery of downtown stood a two-storey medical office building adjacent to the hospital. That's where my father had his medical practice—Suite 207, Dr.Reuven Adler, M.D., General Practice. Sometimes my dad would let me accompany him to work and watch him as he applied casts to broken bones and sewed up lacerations on foreheads, cheeks, forearms, and legs. I would sit beside him, biting my lower lip and gripping the arms of my chair, my eyes fixated on every movement of his deft hands, feeling faintly queasy as I watched, but at the same time marvelling at the adroitness of his fingers and the depth of his knowledge.

But these trappings were hardly enough to have enticed Chaver B to our fair land. Presumably he'd come because of our Jewish community, a community founded by immigrants who many years earlier had escaped pogroms, poverty, and intense restrictions in Russia, in what was called the Pale of Jewish Settlement—the largest ghetto in the world—and who had come to the Canadian prairies searching for a softer, kinder existence. They'd dreamt of the *goldeneh medinos,* the golden lands across the Atlantic, but, like so many other millions of immigrants, had very little knowledge of what to expect when they arrived.

They moved to towns and cities with Cree names like Winnipeg, French names like Portage la Prairie and Beausejour, alliterative names like Flin Flon, and funny-sounding names like Plum Coulee, Moose Jaw, and Medicine Hat. Some were tempted by the Canadian government's promise of free agricultural land, and many did attempt farming, though they had no prior agrarian skills.

Despite having come from Russia, even they were ill-prepared for the brutal winters with the stinging, searing winds sweeping unimpeded across the plains, wreaking havoc on their crops, and many farms failed.

Some of these immigrants came to the small Manitoba towns and worked as peddlers or opened small stores after hearing of the Mennonite population who spoke a Low German that was similar enough to Yiddish to facilitate communication, and which was obviously good for business. After all, many of these immigrants had been peddlers in the Old Country.

My mother's father—my *Zaidi* Harry, *alev ha'sholem* (may he rest in peace)—had been such a peddler when he first came to Ambrosia, driving his horse and cart throughout the countryside, selling everything from eggs and vegetables and live chickens squawking in their crates to various notions and sundries, like sparkling necklaces for the ladies, lotions that promised perpetual youth, balsa wood kits to build model airplanes, and dolls with round faces, long eyelashes, and flowing dark curls; gyroscopes and magic lanterns, and once, even a rocking horse. People were always happy to see my zaidi with his horse and wagon, wondering what riches he would have for them that day. "Hey, Harry," they would cry out as they stood beside the road, the younger boys running alongside his cart, shouting to be heard above the clopping of the horse's hooves on the ground. "Got any treasures for us today?"

In the evenings, my mother would run to greet him when she saw him as a speck in the distance, gradually becoming larger and larger as he came nearer and nearer to home. When she reached him, she would jump onto his cart, sit on his lap, grab the reins of the horse, and guide them the rest of the way home.

Zaidi Harry's customers were loyal. He eventually opened a general store in Ambrosia, but when his store burned down, for unknown reasons, within twenty-four hours the townspeople had collected enough money for him to build a new one and start afresh.

When he was only sixty, long before I was born, he contracted pneumonia and died within two days. We only had two photographs of him—both as a grown man—so that was how I envisioned him, along with my mother's stories and any other imaginary fantasies I chose to attach to him.

But my grandmother, *Babbi* Rachel, still lived in town with my mother's sister, Miriam, and her family, just a few blocks away from us, and I saw her often. Babbi Rachel was like a queen. Whenever I visited her, there she would be, sitting in her comfy, dark green velvet overstuffed chair in her living room. Each *Purim* she would make me her special cookies—not the triangular-shaped, fruit-filled ones that everyone else made to symbolize the three-cornered hat that evil Haman wore —but her own secret confection. She would throw in a handful of this and a cup of that; she'd shape the dough into long, thin strips coiled up like snails and finally dust them off with coloured sprinkles. Although she never followed a written recipe, they tasted the same every time. "A cookie for a cookie," she would say as she handed me one. They were delicious.

So, why did Chaver B come to join us, here, on the Canadian prairies, I often wondered. Was he also escaping from something, just like the immigrants before him, and if so, what was he leaving behind and what had he expected and wanted to find here? Relief and revelation? Comfort and closeness? Or isolation and bone-numbing cold? He had obviously come to teach in our Jewish day school. Such a school had been established in Winnipeg, and our community decided to follow suit. The school prided itself on being secular or nonreligious, which coincided perfectly with my father's philosophy on religion. He never *davened*, or prayed, in *shul* and hadn't even had a bar mitzvah. Chaver B was somewhat more religious—on the outside at least—but what he really felt on the inside, I was only to find out later.

The school had a dual curriculum: English studies for half the day and Jewish studies for the other half. The latter were mostly conducted in Yiddish, with a smattering of Hebrew that increased over the years.

My school was named after I. L. Peretz, the great Yiddish liberalist and writer. Every day, Sammy and I would walk to school in one direction, while the other children walked in the opposite direction to the local public school.

One morning, one of the girls from the neighbourhood summoned her courage and asked me, "Hey, what school do you go to, anyway?"

"Peretz School," I replied quite proudly, chin tilted upwards and chest puffed out.

I'm sure she thought I was going to a school for birds.

CHAPTER III

Lomir zingen, lomir zingen,
Lomir zingen a lied tsu der Yiddisher shul,
Vos is alemen azoy lieb un azoy tayer.

Lomir zingen mit freyd, un mit hofening ful,
Oyf a velt a bafrayter, a nayer.

Let us sing, Let us sing,
Let us sing a song to the Yiddish school,
That is to all of us so loved and so dear.

Let us sing with joy, and with hope,
For a freer world,
A new world.

—Yiddish Folksong

And there we were, a community rising up like Shangri-La in a distant land or like Brigadoon from the mist. An irregularity on a smooth surface. There we were. A Yiddish world. An anomaly in the middle of the Canadian prairies. An anachronism.

Even though January was officially the beginning of a new year, for me the New Year always began in September with the first day of school, and that year, grade six, was no exception. I eagerly put on the green and blue plaid skirt and long-sleeved white blouse I had selected the night before. After buttoning my cuffs, I examined myself in the mirror hanging above my dark wooden dresser and tried to decide what colour my eyes were that day—grey or green—as they seemed to change with the surrounding light.

Today they're green, I said to myself, just like a cat's eyes. Definitely green. Then I brushed my long, chestnut brown hair into a ponytail and tied it with a royal blue ribbon.

Sammy and I quickly ate our breakfasts, left the house, and walked together down our tree-lined street. As we approached the single-storey, red brick school building and climbed the seven wide steps that took us to a broad landing and two tall glass front doors, I was filled with the anticipation of a new class, new teachers, new things to be learned, and a new level reached in the hierarchy of school dynamics. The shorter days and longer shadows were antithetical to my inner excitement, and my mood matched more closely the colours and vibrancy of the changing leaves. It was also the beginning of the Jewish New Year—the Days of Awe, as they were called.

My English teacher that year was Mrs. Pirsnansky. Unfortunately, or fortunately. It wasn't that she was a bad teacher, but she seemed to have very little tolerance for children, which made me wonder why she'd chosen to be a teacher in the first place. In particular, she became frantic when she saw a sea of hands waving in the air, each hand seemingly attached to a jumping bean waiting to pop out of its skin, each bean writhing, wriggling, squirming, breathlessly waiting for Mrs. Pirsnansky to call on one of them.

Upon being confronted with this spectacle, she would screw her eyes shut, clench her fists, flex her thick arms, and pump them up and down in short, staccato beats synchronous with each word that she would then proceed to utter in a most impatient and irritated voice: "Put those hands down!" To this day, her behaviour has remained an enigma to me. Aren't children raising their hands to be called upon rather than shouting out supposed to be a teacher's delight? Go figure, or *Gey veys*, as they say in Yiddish.

That same year, we had a new Yiddish teacher. "*Kinder, dos iz Chaver Bergman,*" announced the principal as he introduced Chaver B to the class.

It was customary for us to address our male teachers as *Chaverim*. Although *Chaver* is the equivalent of Mister, it's actually a Yiddish word that means friend. It's also important to know that in Yiddish, the *ch* is not pronounced like the *ch* in children, but like the letter *h* preceded by a guttural sound, as though you have something caught in your throat and are trying to clear it.

"Chaver Bergman has been living in Europe and just came over to Canada two weeks ago," continued the principal. "He is going to be your teacher."

We looked at him intently. He was of medium height and had thick, black, wavy hair and deep brown eyes. His was an interesting face—sensitive, in a sad sort of way, and not unkind. As Chaver Lieberman introduced him, Chaver B stood silently at the front of the class, arms hanging quietly at his sides, eyes directed down at the floor, then intermittently looking upwards to Chaver Lieberman and then to us, collectively as a group, not engaging any one of us individually. He didn't smile, and his demeanor bore a hint of darkness. His jacket was ill-fitting and baggy, grey tweed with brown patches at the elbows, and it was obvious that it had belonged to someone else before it adorned the slight frame of Chaver B. In short, he looked like someone uncomfortable in his own skin, a formula for disaster in a classroom.

Flashes of utter chaos darted across my mind. Last year in "English class," as we called it, a new teacher had been hired—Mrs. Campbell. From the perspective of a ten-year-old, she looked to be eighty, although she was probably no more than sixty. Her hair was thin and grey and tied into a tight bun at the nape of her neck. Her face had more lines and wrinkles than a shriveled prune; in other words, she was *tsekneytsht*. But despite the years of teaching experience we presumed she had, Mrs. Campbell was totally unable to control our class. We talked incessantly amongst ourselves, and without her permission, chose to arrange our desks in groups of four in order to work together, which was actually quite a forward-thinking idea at the time.

There was rarely a moment of silence in her class. Hard as it is to imagine, this din and clamour went on for two months before anyone in the administration took notice. And then one day, Mrs. Campbell was gone—that is, gone from our classroom—and Mr. Koschuk appeared, and things were restored to normalcy. I felt bad having taken advantage of Mrs. Campbell's ineptitude, for she had never been mean to us, but I often thought that she would have been better served taking lessons from Mrs. Pirsnansky, whose reputation as a battle ax was legendary and whom no one dared cross. Here was a prime example of Survival of the Fittest.

So, although Chaver B emanated vulnerability on that first day, I knew that he would not suffer the same fate as Mrs. Campbell. There was something affecting and melancholy about him, engendering *rachmonos* (pity) rather than gleeful mischief. He seemed fragile and delicate; even a child could sense that this was a man who needed kindness.

CHAPTER IV

My religion is very simple. My religion is kindness.

—Dalai Lama XIV

Without any forethought, we all began calling Chaver Bergman, Chaver B. One of the boys referred to him as such, and the name stuck. He was younger than most of our other teachers, and despite his rather serious deportment, it seemed to suit him better. My parents and others usually called him by his first name, Ari, at least when they thought we weren't listening.

One week after school started, my mother invited Chaver B over for Friday night *Shabbos* dinner. My mother was a *balabusta*—a perfect homemaker—and she had a special knack for making people feel at ease around her. That evening she wore a dark-green silky dress belted at the waist that highlighted her still shapely figure. A strand of smooth, milky-white pearls encircled her neck. Her neatly coiffed, short brown hair from weekly visits to the beauty parlour, and her long, slender fingers with their cleanly clipped and unpainted nails, made her the epitome of practical elegance. So it was only natural that she would lead the way in welcoming our new teacher to our community. Also, we had a kosher home, and my mother assumed that Chaver B kept kosher as well and would welcome the invitation.

In accordance with the laws of *kashrus,* we purchased all our meat at the kosher butcher shop. We didn't eat any pork products or shellfish, although in the middle of Canada there wasn't much shellfish to be had. And we kept two sets of dishes—*milchik* and *fleyshik*—one for foods containing milk products and the other for meat, and never the twain did meet.

When Chaver B knocked at the front door that Friday evening in September, Sammy and I raced downstairs from our bedrooms to let him in. Although Sammy was three years younger than me and at least six inches shorter, he was a fast runner, and by the time we reached the front hall, his blue shirt had escaped from the back of his pants, and my just brushed hair had become disheveled, quite a contrast to Chaver B's appearance. Chaver B was dressed very formally in a dark grey suit, a white shirt, and a navy tie. My parents greeted him warmly as he nodded his head in a somewhat obsequious manner and stiffly handed my mother a bouquet of purple and white daisies.

"*Ah dahnk,*" she said, thanking him, her voice rising and falling like the melody of a song. "They are beautiful, and it's so thoughtful of you, but not necessary. Why don't you and Reuven sit in the living room, and I'll just go put these in water," she added as she went into the kitchen to retrieve an intricately carved crystal vase from the cupboard. She put the flowers in it with some water and set it down in the center of the delicate white lace tablecloth covering our mahogany dining room table.

My father and Chaver B sat down on the ginger-coloured linen sofa in the living room, while Sammy and I sat in the two matching peach and green floral wingback armchairs opposite them, intent on every word they spoke. They both looked very distinguished, Chaver B in his suit, and my father with his thinning black hair parted at the side and his intelligent dark brown eyes behind black rectangular glasses that reminded me of a wise Solomon. In addition to being much taller than Chaver B, my father looked much older, and he was. I'd heard my mother say that Chaver B was only twenty-seven years old. My father had just turned forty-two, but despite his lean build, to me, he always looked "old." He already had deep lines on his forehead and around his mouth that I assumed were the result of him worrying so much about his patients.

After several minutes, my mother called to us, her brown eyes bright with the excitement of the evening, "Come, everyone. Dinner is ready."

We walked from the living room through the archway that opened into the adjoining dining room and gathered around the table. My mother handed dark blue velvet *yarmulkehs* to my dad and Chaver B, and she gave Sammy a bright purple one, his favourite, that he promptly placed on top of his shiny, straight black hair. My mother and I each covered our heads with a white chiffon prayer shawl, and she proceeded to light the Shabbos candles, following which we all sang the *brachos,* or prayers, over the wine and challah. These weren't rituals that we regularly practiced, but my mother did it out of deference to our guest. One might consider this one of my mother's religious idiosyncrasies; lighting the candles was supposed to welcome the Sabbath Queen, she explained, but since we didn't keep the Sabbath, she felt hypocritical lighting the candles.

As we sat down, my mother returned to the kitchen to complete her final preparations for the meal. While we were waiting,

Chaver B kept glancing at the bookcase along one wall of the living room, each shelf lined with the brown, black, green, and navy spines of novels, medical books, and my Zaidi Harry's collection of Yiddish literature. There were a dozen slim, cream-coloured portfolios of art reproductions that my father had purchased from the Metropolitan Museum of Art in New York—works by Degas, Renoir, Rembrandt, and Van Gogh—some of which my mother had removed and which now hung framed on the walls of our living room and along the staircase leading to our bedrooms. Had Chaver B noticed a specific book from this distance? I wondered.

My question was answered when he asked in a hesitant and almost hushed voice, *"Ver daw in shtub shpielt fidl?"* Who in the house plays the violin?

So, it was my violin case resting on a shelf that he had caught sight of.

"I do," I said, believing that my perfunctory reply would satisfy his curiosity. But Chaver B persevered.

"And how long have you been playing?" he inquired.

"I started four years ago, but my teacher moved away last year, so I haven't had any lessons for a while."

"Well, you will play for us after dinner," he stated matter-of-factly with seemingly newfound confidence.

Since I hadn't practiced in months, I was hoping that he had sensed my discomfort at his suggestion—or rather command—and would not pursue the matter. I'd actually started playing violin by happenstance. My initial inclination had been to play the piano, and I would pretend play on our dining room table, "accompanying myself" as I sang all the songs I knew.

The decision to play the piano had been a well-thought-out and calculated one. My father's parents, Zaidi Max and Babbi Hannah, lived in Winnipeg, where my father had grown up. Next door to them lived the Gilbert family, whose daughter, Sylvia, played cello in the Winnipeg Symphony Orchestra. Occasionally when we visited, her string quartet would be practicing in her living room, and we became inadvertent guests at what seemed like a private concert just for us. We would all gather on my grandparents' veranda, listening intently, hardly saying a word other than to remark on the beauty of the music that permeated the air and enveloped us with its entrancing melodies and satisfying harmonies.

But in kindergarten, our teachers had played piano, accompanying us as we sang Yiddish songs and danced and twirled around the classroom. I became enthralled with the idea that the piano, a single instrument, could play all the melodies and harmonies that it took the four instruments of the string quartet to do. The idea that the piano could stand alone and be independent, creating all those pleasing and complete harmonies without help from anything else, was very intriguing.

I desperately wanted to play the piano, but even though my father was a doctor, we didn't have a lot of money and were saving up to buy a piano when my mother spied a used violin at a school bazaar for only five dollars.

That was it. Violin became my new instrument, and Mrs. Morgenstern became my violin teacher. She was very traditional and followed the Royal Conservatory of Music program. And I liked her well enough, but after three years of lessons, she moved to Montreal to live with her sister. Since then, my violin spent most of its time languishing in its case.

My thoughts were interrupted when my mother called me into the kitchen to help her serve her wonderful chicken soup, each bowl filled with her aromatic golden broth, carrots, and *kneydlech*. I served Chaver B first, since he was our guest, and then my dad, followed by Sammy. Finally, my mom and I each carried our own bowls into the dining room and sat down.

Our dinner conversation mainly consisted of accolades for my mother's wonderful cooking peppered with questions about what Chaver B thought of Ambrosia. Chaver B wasn't particularly loquacious, and my parents seemed to virtually ask the questions and answer them, too.

"So, how are you finding your way around town?" my mother asked, then added. "Well, Ambrosia is rather small, so I'm sure you're not having any difficulty. Would you like some more challah, Chaver B?" she said while holding up the silver tray on which it lay.

"No, but thank you," he replied, between spoonfuls of soup.

"And it goes without saying that the teachers have been very helpful, too," she said. "I'm sure of that."

"Oh, yes, yes," he agreed. "I have two more invitations for dinner next week—one from Chaver Lieberman and the other from *Lererine* (teacher) Malka and her husband. I am very grateful for everyone's hospitality."

"Well, if you need anything at all, just let us know," my mother said as she returned to the kitchen to begin serving the main course of juicy roast chicken, *knishes* filled with mashed potatoes and fried onions, delicately sautéed green beans, and because of our guest, my mom's special sweet-and-sour meatballs. After we finished, I stood up to help her clear the dishes from the table, but my father reminded me, "Miraleh, why don't you play violin for Chaver B?"

I had never enjoyed performing for others, but it had been so long since I'd played that despite my initial qualms, I could hardly be nervous. I walked over to the bookshelf in the living room and carefully removed my violin from its case. I tuned it as best I could, rosined my bow, and began to play a song I had memorized from my early grades. I'd already resigned myself to the fact that I would sound off-key and scratchy. But Chaver B was very polite. He clapped when I finished and told me that I had promise.

I was about to return my violin to the bookcase when Chaver B looked at me for a moment and then quietly said, "I used to play the violin. Would you like me to be your teacher?"

I was surprised by this revelation and his offer, but not wanting to seem rude, I quickly answered, "Sure," although I was weighing in my mind if I really wanted to resume lessons. "If that's alright with my parents."

"Of course," they replied instantaneously, clearly pleased that a music teacher had fallen into our laps like manna from heaven. "Can you start this Tuesday, Chaver B?" suggested my mother. She was clearly not going to let this golden opportunity vanish. "Five o'clock?"

"Very good," he replied, turning towards her. Their eyes locked, almost as if they were engaged in a secret dialogue. All the muscles in his face seemed to relax, and the glimmer of a smile appeared at the corners of his mouth. He looked the happiest I had seen him.

On Tuesday after school, I set up my music stand in front of the sofa in the living room. Chaver B arrived at five o'clock sharp. Empty-handed.

"Where is your violin?" I asked him. Mrs. Morgenstern had always had her violin with her. In fact, it had been almost like an extra appendage. I didn't recall ever having seen her without it.

"I don't have one," he said. "I don't play anymore. I injured my left arm, so I can no longer play."

"How will you show me things?" I asked, confused.

"I will tell you," he said. "I will tell you what you should do and how you should play, and you will listen and do it."

That is going to be tricky, I thought. But Chaver B was true to his word. He would never play for me, but instead he used words to describe the sound he wanted me to produce.

"Music is filled with interesting characters, like a painting with many colours," he would say in a voice much too serious for such a beautiful sentiment. "Sometimes the music can make you think of a lark singing. Other times you might imagine people having conversations with one another. When you hear a minuet, picture noblemen and ladies dancing in the king's court."

He told me to imagine leaves swirling in the wind when playing Vivaldi's "Autumn" from *The Four Seasons*, each little leaf being carried aloft on a current of cool air. Or water gushing down a hillside after a rain when playing the "Spring" movement. I became so captivated by the tableaux he created, that once, forgetting what he'd told me about his arm, I asked him to demonstrate a particular passage on my violin. He again claimed that he couldn't play because of a problem with his left hand, though I never noticed him having difficulty with any other tasks.

First he gave me a serious lesson on how to hold and position my bow on the strings.

"You want to keep your bow between the bridge and the fingerboard and keep it parallel to the bridge," he told me. "If you want to play louder, go closer to the bridge." We practiced songs that I'd already learned while focusing on my bow arm. I could hardly play two notes without him reminding me about something or other, but after a few lessons and much repetition, I was finally able to discard some old habits and incorporate much of what he was trying to teach me.

Next came scales, those interminable, incessant, relentless scales that went on and on and on and on. He explained to me the difference between major and minor scales. "Minor scales sound sadder," he said. "A lot of Hebrew prayer music is written in the minor key, like '*Kol Nidrei*.'" The scales were tedious. "Even I hated practicing scales," he confided, "but it is a necessary evil if you want to play."

And I did want to play. Chaver B made the music so much more interesting than Mrs. Morgenstern had that I actually looked forward to lessons, and although I loathed to admit it, even practicing. After all these years, the violin and I were unexpectedly becoming fast friends. And although he was an adult and I still a child, Chaver B and I were becoming friends, too.

CHAPTER V

This is my tune for the taking
Take it, don't turn away

—Paul Simon, "Song for the Asking"

In addition to the weekly Shabbos dinners at which Chaver B became our regular guest, a different kind of event took place every Wednesday night in Ambrosia that carried with it almost the same sanctity as did the Sabbath.

As if performing a ritual, once a week the ladies of the neighbourhood gathered together to play mah-jong, a Chinese game of ivory tiles embossed with special Chinese characters and patterns accompanied by a laminated card of winning hands that was updated every year. A game of calculation and chance, it was the closest the ladies ever came to gambling, with the stakes no higher than fifty cents. Each week the game was held at a different home, and on this particular week in mid-October, it was my mother's turn to be hostess.

At eight in the evening, the ladies arrived in their finery, removing stylish coats and colourful scarves to reveal beautifully knit sweaters adorned with gold necklaces and jewel broaches, and matched with wool skirts beneath. My mother's group of four included Auntie Miriam, my good friend Annie's mother, Pauline, and our next-door neighbour, Clarice. As soon as they were seated comfortably around the bridge table and had laid their tiles on their respective racks, I assumed my usual perch at the top of the stairs, surreptitiously out of view.

"Four bam," said Pauline, announcing the opening discard as the game began.

"Five bam," countered Miriam, placing her tile in the center of the table.

"How are Mira's violin lessons coming along?" asked Clarice after she had completed her turn.

"Very well," replied my mom. "She seems to like Chaver B, and he's a good teacher. I've already noticed an improvement in her playing."

"And how is Ari doing?" asked Miriam. "Is he settling in?"

"As well as can be expected," said my mom as she took her window of opportunity to pick up Clarice's discard and then throw her own tile. "Nine dots," she called out.

"I think we should find a nice girl for him," suggested Pauline. "It's lonely here living as a bachelor. Mrs. Goldberg's daughter, Nancy—you know, the one who works at Eaton's in ladies' dresses—is available and looking."

"I think we should give him more time to settle in before pushing a woman on him," offered my mom without being too specific. "He seems shy, and it might make him uncomfortable."

"How much time does someone need?" asked Pauline. "This is Ambrosia, not New York City."

"Pauline's right," said Miriam. "He sometimes has Shabbos dinner with you, doesn't he, Claire?" My mom nodded in assent.

"Why don't you invite him and Nancy at the same time? That way it won't seem too contrived." Everyone laughed.

Against her better judgment, my mother went along with the plan. The next Friday Chaver B arrived for dinner, and a few minutes later, Nancy Goldberg rang the doorbell.

I had never met Nancy before, and I was surprised to find that she was actually quite pretty. She wore a fitted navy-blue dress that followed the curves of her slim figure, and her light brown hair was done up in a French roll.

Chaver B seemed to brighten a little when he saw her. He stood up when she entered the living room and was introduced, and he held her chair for her as she sat down at the dining room table. I'd suggested placing them opposite each other, but my mother said that might be awkward and too deliberate, so instead she had Nancy sit at the end of one long side of the table and Chaver B at the short end that was perpendicular to her and directly opposite my father.

But my mother was right. Although Chaver B behaved like a gentleman, he was very quiet, almost timid, and barely spoke to Nancy or asked her any questions. His answers to *her* questions were mainly monosyllabic—at most a few words. After the meal, we retired to the living room for coffee and apple pie, but Chaver B rarely looked at her. Nevertheless, at the end of the evening, he helped her with her coat and very formally said how nice it had been to meet her, almost like a previously learned recitation, a vestige from his past. Although his pronouncement lacked warmth, at that moment he seemed almost elegant, like a gentleman from another world, as though he had just stepped out of one of my storybooks. I wondered how old I would have to be before someone treated me with such courtesy and grace, and I felt almost jealous at this little bit of attention that he had bestowed upon Nancy. When she offered to drive him home and he declined, I felt a sense of relief.

After that evening, I began paying attention to the little things Chaver B did. How he organized the papers on his desk at school. The way he held his pen when he wrote. Although right-handed, he grabbed the pen from above, like someone who was left-handed would do. When he ate dinner at our house, I noticed how he tilted his soup bowl to finish the last drops and how he laid his fork and knife across his plate when he was done. And I tried to emulate him. When I learned that he didn't like asparagus, I decided not to like asparagus either. When he put on his coat to go home, I watched how he wound his scarf around his neck to keep warm and how cold it would have to be outside before he would put on earmuffs or a hat. And I tried to do the same, much to my mother's chagrin.

I wondered if the skills my mother and her friends demonstrated playing mah-jong, the ability to strategize and scheme, had transferred over to matchmaking. Had the chance that two souls might connect, one searching for companionship and love and the other for something as yet ill-defined and elusive, materialized into something real? Had the ladies of Ambrosia been able to capitalize on this window of opportunity and call a "mahj?"

According to my mother, the week after the dinner at our house, Nancy had asked Chaver B to go to the movies with her, but he had said no. A few weeks later, she went to Winnipeg for a vacation and met a nice lawyer. They were married the following summer.

CHAPTER VI

In the sufferer, let me see only the human being.

—Maimonides, "A Physician's Prayer"

Despite the mah-jong misadventure, Chaver B seemed to be slowly adjusting to his new environment. He'd garnered the students' respect quickly, not only because he was very knowledgeable about a wide range of topics, but also because he never seemed to lose his temper. One of the other male teachers would pull a boy by the ear and throw him out of the classroom if he misbehaved, but for whatever reason, the usual troublemakers didn't act up in Chaver B's class. He was strict, but kind. And while some teachers would humiliate or scold us if we didn't know an answer, Chaver B never did. He would just move on to the next student.

Our classroom was situated in the middle of a long, linoleum hallway and was sandwiched between Sammy's grade three class, taught by Mrs. Walker—a willowy blond, tall and slender, who moved as if floating on a cloud—and the grade two class, commandeered by Mrs. Moskowitz, the Yiddish teacher, who had her students memorize a poem a day—in Yiddish—quite an undertaking for a second grader.

Mrs. Walker would frequently appear in our room at lunchtime, carrying extra school supplies—like construction paper or coloured pencils—that she thought Chaver B might need. Mrs. Moskowitz usually visited at recess. She generally brought in books of Yiddish poetry; she would turn to a specific page and say, "*Chaver Bergman, ich hob aych gebracht a buch fun poezye vos ich meyn vet zayn gut far ayereh talmidim. Ich vel dos iberlozn far aych.*" I've brought you a book of poetry that I think will be good for your students. Here, I will leave it with you.

"*Ah dahnk,*" Chaver B would reply. "*Ich vel dos leyenen. Zay gezunt.*" Thank you. I will read it. Be healthy.

Yet, despite Chaver B's popularity, he rarely smiled, either at school, at my violin lessons, or when at our house for Friday night dinners. And when he did smile, it was a tired smile, like the smile of a weary traveller after reaching his destination.

At the end of October, while I was playing tag during recess, I scraped the palm of my hand against a tree trunk, and a huge splinter pierced it. I called my mother from school to let her know I would be walking to my dad's office instead of going directly home. Sammy usually walked home with his own friends, so she didn't mind.

My father's office always smelled like it had just been scoured with strong ammonia, which maybe it had. There were a lot of "germs" going around, and people were being more fastidious than usual.

As I walked in, I was greeted with a huge smile from Mrs. Rempel who worked as my dad's nurse and receptionist. I always liked seeing her in her crisp white uniform with her starched cap sitting atop her short, curly red hair.

"Mira, what a nice surprise, and very timely," she said. "I just put out a fresh bowl of chocolates. Would you like one?"

"You know I love chocolates, Mrs. Rempel. Thanks."

"What brings you here today?" she asked.

I turned my hand over and showed her the large splinter on my palm. "That looks nasty," she said with concern. "The skin around it is already turning red. Why don't you soak it in some warm water while you wait? I'll bring you a bowl, and you can sit here at my desk beside me." She went into the adjoining room and came back with a red-rimmed, white metal bowl full of tepid water and put it in front of me. "I think your father is going to be with his patient for a little while longer, anyway, and he's expecting another patient when he's done."

After twenty minutes, the door of the examining room finally opened, and Chaver B walked down the hallway and into the waiting room. I was surprised to learn that he was my father's patient, and he seemed equally surprised to see me. He appeared more downcast than usual, his dark eyes brooding, his expression more distant, his grey tweed jacket still drooping off his shoulders, and his sleeves slightly too long for his slim arms. But he was very polite, asked me how I was, and then awkwardly said goodbye and made his way towards the exit.

"Do you want to make another appointment, Mr. Bergman?" asked Mrs. Rempel with her usual joviality.

"I will call," he said, turning part way around to look at her. "Thank you." And then he left.

"Does he come here often?" I asked Mrs. Rempel.

"Oh, once in a while," she said. "We all need a doctor at some time or other."

The next patient was late, so my father ushered me into his treatment room while he was waiting. "What's wrong with Chaver B?" I asked him. "He looked so upset."

"Nothing to be concerned about," my dad answered somewhat dismissively. Then he paused and in a more serious tone of voice, turned to me and added, "I can't tell you what's wrong with him. What happens between a doctor and his patient is private. You shouldn't ask me again."

"Well, then you better not tell anyone I had a splinter," I retorted, feeling somewhat hurt, as if I'd just been scolded for doing something that I didn't know was wrong, but also feeling bad because I was being deprived of valuable information.

"Ouch!" I screamed as my dad prodded at the splinter. Finally, it was out. He applied some ointment and covered the area with a bandage.

"I have one more patient," he said. "Why don't you start doing your homework, and when I'm done, we'll go home."

I left the room and sat down again beside Mrs. Rempel, opened my math book, and began working on the problems Mrs. Pirsnansky had assigned. While I'd been with my dad, the next patient had arrived.

"Mrs. Singer," called Mrs. Rempel, standing up and grabbing her chart. "The doctor is ready for you now. Come with me."

Mrs. Singer, with the assistance of her cane, hobbled into the examining room. A formidable character, she was rather corpulent, and her forehead seemed to be fixed in a perpetual frown. With Mrs. Singer, there was no need to be concerned about privacy. Her booming voice told her story in almost operatic style, and by the time she was done, I was certain that everyone in the building knew about the pain in her right knee, her back spasms, and the burning jabs in her left foot, all these complaints explained in graphic detail between repeated bouts of coughing and punctuated with perfectly placed moans to enhance the experience.

I couldn't hear anything my dad said to her, but by the time she emerged, her voice had gradually quieted, and she seemed much calmer. After she left the office, Mrs. Rempel made certain that my father no longer needed her services, then put on her coat, and departed for home. My dad finished up some paper work. We shut off the lights, locked the door, and made our way down to the parking lot.

The sun was setting as we drove home, wispy clouds painted in varying shades of pink and warm gold stretching across the pale blue sky. My head was still ringing with Mrs. Singer's medley of vocalizations, and I thought what a great doctor my father was to have been able to tame the beast, so to speak, at least to some degree. He must have a golden touch, I thought, which really needn't have surprised me. After all, he was my dad. But again, my thoughts turned to Chaver B—quiet, kind, sad Chaver B. My dad seemed to have soothed Mrs. Singer's stormy spirit. I wondered if he could do the same for Chaver B.

CHAPTER VII

Falt a shney, falt a shney,
Falt a vayser shney.
Alleh tog di kinderlech
Shpielen zich in shney.

Snow falls, snow falls,
White snow falls.
Everyday the children
Play in the snow.

—Yiddish folksong

Winters were long, but the days were never empty. The cold drove us, or I should say, often forced us to stay indoors. Sometimes when leaving the house, I would be confronted by a blast of cold air, almost like a wall that took my breath away. But we did not become hermits, and wearing warm coats, boots, woolly mittens and hats, and scarves tightly wrapped around our faces, life went on.

Walking to school almost felt like an adventure. It was three blocks away, and the crunching of snow underfoot seemed to provide a musical accompaniment and make the time pass more quickly. In the evenings, the fragrant smell of burning wood from the shacks by the skating rinks would diffuse through the air. Saturday afternoons were spent sitting around the kitchen table, reading the coloured comics, everyone fighting for the last piece of one of my mother's delicious cherry pies.

Our first snowfall usually coincided with Halloween, and after that, the earth was invisible until the following spring. Holiday lights in various designs and patterns were hung across the streets, and the roofs and doorways of stores and homes were outlined with little coloured light bulbs that remained up until after Christmas. This made the town very festive, and each year my father would take me for a drive in his car to enjoy the artistry.

But the most memorable thing about winter was the view from my window. The fields stretched like a vast white void, unsullied and pure, and on sunny days, the sun glinted off the snow like thousands and thousands of jewels were dotting its surface. At night, when the sky was clear, the luminous light of the moon and the twinkling stars winking down at me added their own magic. I felt unencumbered and airy, and I was overcome with a sense of all the potential inherent in life.

Winter provided plenty of opportunity to practice violin, and as the snow became deeper, Chaver B's expectations grew higher. A few minutes before each lesson, I would stand by our living room window and watch for his figure in long, dark grey coat and brown fur hat to emerge from the whiteness, the street lights blinking alongside him as he made his way down the sidewalk. Despite the cold, he never walked at a fast pace, and sometimes he would even stop for a few moments and gaze up at the sky before resuming his trek.

But winters were also prime time for school projects, which meant frequent trips to the library after school and on Saturdays. The library was located next to the high school, and its appearance evoked all the majesty appropriate for a building that housed so much knowledge and information. Constructed of dark brown bricks, it had two white columns flanking the massive double doors at its entrance.

Once inside, I felt as though I had entered a place of reverence. With its rarified atmosphere, it had its own unique smell of old paper and musty books, and without even opening a volume, just being there seemed to transport me to other realms.

That year, Mrs. Pirsnansky assigned us a project on the moon. Even though we were nowhere near an ocean, we were to understand the phases of the moon and how that affected the ocean tides. My best friend, Annie, and I worked as partners.

I had met Annie on our first day of kindergarten. Immediately intrigued by two bright red barrettes fastened at the sides of her head and holding back her long black curls, I'd boldly walked over to her and asked her if I could wear one of them. Without hesitation, she unclasped a barrette and handed it to me. We tried in vain to clip it on to my fine brown hair, but it was too large to stay in place. I was so overcome by her generosity that I didn't mind, and although I was only five years old, one thing I knew for sure: Annie was a friend to be treasured.

As soon as we walked into the library to work on our project, Annie and I set our notebooks and pencils down on one of the round, wooden tables and claimed it as our own for the afternoon. We looked up information on the moon in the *World Book Encyclopedia* and took out some books from the shelves that had more pictures. We divided the books between us, painstakingly wrote down notes of all the important facts, and later compared what we had read.

The moon seemed to be a fitting topic for other reasons, since the Jewish calendar is a lunar calendar that follows the phases of the moon.

I wondered if I could find out anything else interesting about Judaism and the moon. Surprisingly to me, the library had a section on religions, and I discovered a book discussing Jewish thought. I went to the index and found several passages referring to the moon.

I walked back to the table where Annie and I had organized our books and turned to page ninety-two. According to the *Chumash*, or *Torah*, also known as *The Five Books of Moses*, God created the sun and the moon at the same time. But the moon complained that there was not enough room for both of them, and as a result, God told the moon to shrink itself. Because the moon's only purpose was to reflect the light of the sun, it was given the Hebrew name *levana*, which comes from the Hebrew word *lavan* meaning white. I'd read in my science book that the colour white reflects all other colours. Levana seemed to be the perfect name for the moon.

In another chapter of the book, the rabbi wrote:

"The waxing and waning of the moon is much like the history of the Jewish people whose fate has waxed and waned over centuries. Despite the setbacks, we have always been able to renew our faith and determination," he wrote. "Whereas in Ecclesiastes it is said, 'There is nothing new under the sun,' there is always something new under the moon. The moon itself is reborn every month."

It was a revelation for me to learn that there was, in fact, a blessing for the moon. Once a month, when the light of the moon appears anew in the night sky, Jewish people are supposed to recite the *Kiddush Levana*—Sanctification of the Moon—and tell God how grateful we are for all he has given to us. Some say that the new moon is like God coming out to greet us.

My father didn't believe in God. Yiddish culture was his link to the Jewish people. But my mother believed in God, and my father let her run the household and raise us as she saw fit. I guess my brother and I believed in God, too, but we didn't spend much time talking about Him or invoking His name, except when I would tease Sammy and right afterwards trip on the sidewalk. "See, God punished you for being mean to me," he would say. We also didn't say many prayers, except during the times we went to synagogue and sometimes on Shabbos. But if I could say only one prayer, I decided, I would choose the prayer for the moon.

Annie invited me over for dinner at her house that night. Her father had flooded their backyard with water that quickly froze and turned it into a skating rink. So after dinner, we put on skates and glided across the ice, carving intricate patterns into its smooth white surface as the cold, crisp air made our faces tingle.

Annie's dog, Fido, a reddish-brown cocker spaniel, followed us outside.

In those days, Fido was a popular name for dogs. The original Fido lived in a town near Florence, Italy. A local brick kiln worker named Carlo had come upon him lying injured in a ditch, and believing the dog was homeless, he took him home and cared for him until he recovered.

Once he was well, each morning Fido would accompany Carlo to the town square where he boarded the bus for work. And each evening, Fido would wait patiently for him to return, tail wagging expectantly, ears perking up when he saw the bus lumbering around the corner, bringing Carlo back home.

But it was World War II, and two years later Carlo was killed when the factory that he worked in was struck in a bombardment. When the bus returned to the square that evening, Carlo did not emerge.

Devoted and loyal, each evening Fido waited patiently in the town square for his master to come home, but to no avail. Although Fido was loved by many, his affection for the one being he cherished the most could no longer be requited. His disappointment and grief must have been cavernous and as bottomless as the dark night sky.

There was something about Fido's story that was both heartwarming and heartbreaking, and thinking of him made me think of Chaver B; there was something heartwarming and heartbreaking about him, too. He was so comfortable to be with—no artifice, no posturing—and I never saw him become angry or heard him complain; he was so different from my other teachers. They were all *nice* people, very nice people, in fact, who tried their best, even Mrs. Pirsnansky, despite her eccentric and sometimes gruff manner. But there was an inner goodness in Chaver B's eyes, eyes that looked at you as if they were on the verge of saying something, but then holding back. Eyes that sometimes looked lost and faraway. That vulnerability evident on his first day in our class had not left him. Someone or something must have broken his heart.

Annie's Fido was as equally devoted to her as Carlo's was to him, and he followed her everywhere. He immediately began tearing around the ice, ears flapping wildly, and before we even had a chance to gain our equilibrium, he crashed into us, knocking both Annie and me on to our backsides. We began laughing uncontrollably, but unharmed, we quickly bounced back up; this time we decided to skate arm in arm for better fortification.

"Have you read the book *Cheaper by the Dozen*?" asked Annie. "It's about a family with twelve children."

I nodded. "Can you imagine being in a family with twelve children? I think my mother has her hands full with just Sammy and me."

"I don't know," said Annie. "I think it would be fun. Ever since my brother started high school, I feel like an only child."

Almost on cue, Annie's older brother, Kenny, joined us outside. He braved the cold wearing only a navy-blue wool sweater and a red and black striped toque covering his dark brown curls. Annie and I decided to show off, although our only skating skills were skating forward and a little backwards, and doing a rather stilted figure eight. Kenny had come to play with Fido, anyway. Barehanded, he whipped a rubber ball to Fido who yelped and barked in sheer happiness as he chased it to the other end of the rink and then returned it to him for another round. I wondered if Chaver B had any brothers and sisters, and if so, where they lived. He was probably an only child, I thought, since he never mentioned other siblings. That must have been lonely.

After a short while, Annie's mother appeared at the back door and called out, "Miraleh, it's time for you to go home, dear. School tomorrow."

As I walked home, there was the moon looming white and large, not quite full, but I could still see its silvery light reflecting off the snow and its inscrutable face looking down at me. What was he thinking? I wondered. What secrets did he know?

I arrived home exhilarated, but exhausted. My mother was out attending a school committee meeting, and Sammy had already gone to bed. My father welcomed me at the door and then rushed off to the kitchen to make me some hot cocoa before I went upstairs. I took off my warm winter coat, hat, and boots and lay down on the sofa while I waited, but by the time he returned, I was fast asleep. He gently nudged me, and through cobwebs of semi-slumber, I climbed the stairs to my bedroom, my dad walking behind me, making sure I wouldn't fall.

Even though my eyes were half-closed, I was able to find my room. My dad put me under the covers, clothes and all, kissed my forehead, turned off the light, and went back downstairs.

CHAPTER VIII

Ah, music, he said, wiping his eyes.
A magic beyond all we do here!

—J.K. Rowling, *Harry Potter and the Sorcerer's Stone*

It was just before the Christmas holidays, and Mrs. Pirsnansky seemed to be in a particularly cantankerous mood. The sky had been overcast for several days, and we were approaching the winter solstice, the shortest day of the year; the sun didn't rise until almost eight thirty in the morning and set at quarter past four in the afternoon. Her dark mood clearly paralleled the dark days outside.

It was the last day of class before the winter break. We had just completed a lesson on calculating mixed fractions, and afternoon recess was about to begin. Mrs. Pirsnansky stood in front of us, and although she was neither a small nor a delicate woman, her tall imposing figure appeared larger than it actually was and seemed to loom over us.

"Class," she announced, "because it is so cold today, thirty degrees below zero, we will be spending recess in the classroom." Just then the bell rang, and we immediately began tucking our books into our desks and taking out our snacks. The noise level crescendoed as everyone began chattering at the same time, clearly forgetting that we were still indoors and that Mrs. Pirsnansky had remained in the classroom and was sitting at her desk. As the boys started to tussle with each other, and paper airplanes and marbles whizzed across the room, I could see Mrs. Pirsnansky's face growing increasingly red, her eyes narrowing, her facial muscles tensing, and the veins on her temples becoming larger as if they were about to burst.

"Settle down, settle down!" she shouted above the clatter, arms flexed and fists pumping wildly in the air, her short iron-grey curls bobbing up and down, as she tried to abort the pandemonium that seemed imminent. This amount of distress seemed uncharacteristic for Mrs. Pirsnansky who was typically and impressively masterful at controlling the classroom despite the constraints of the weather or any other unforeseen circumstance. Annie was the first to spot her frantic gestures, and she methodically moved around the classroom bringing Mrs. Pirsnanky's desperate movements to everyone's attention.

"Quiet, everyone," she said. "Mrs. Pirsnansky has something to tell us."

Gradually the noise dwindled. Having witnessed Mrs. Pirsnansky's crazed gesticulations over the past few months, we all felt that at any moment she might snap and drop dead right in front of us if we didn't behave.

"I want to tell you about the Manitoba Music Festival held in Winnipeg each year," she began in what seemed like a final attempt to quell the masses and allay her own agitation. "It takes place at the end of every February and is a forum where students can perform and display their talents. Now, I know that some of you take private music lessons. There are several categories for all the different instruments."

"I played in it last year," one of my classmates Karen blurted out, without waiting for Mrs. Pirsnansky to call on her. But Mrs. Pirsnansky allowed her to continue, probably seeing her as an ally in her struggle to keep things calm. "In my category, everyone played the same song on the piano. Can you imagine?" Karen asked incredulously. "There were one hundred four students all playing the same piece. I don't know how those judges stayed awake!"

"Good," Mrs. Pirsnansky said. "If you want to know more about it, you can ask Karen. In the meantime, I'm going to pass around sheets of paper that have the festival contact information, if you're interested."

The music festival sounded exciting, and I was always happy to find an opportunity to visit Winnipeg. Since I'd started taking violin lessons from Chaver B, I seemed to have lost my aversion to performing and would routinely entertain my relatives when they came over to our house.

When I arrived home from school, I showed the festival information to my mother and filled out the application requesting the syllabus. One week later it arrived, and I reviewed it with Chaver B. "I think this would be a good category for you," he said, pointing to a page with the heading Open Choice. "You can choose your own song, and there is no winner. Just a written assessment from the judges." It was clear that Chaver B didn't believe that I was a budding prodigy, but I didn't care. I had no such illusions myself.

He turned the pages of my music book and opened it to page seventeen. "This would be a good piece for you. You have just over two months," he said, "which is not a lot of time, but I think you can do it."

The piece was "Humoresque" by Anton Dvorak, also from Czechoslovakia, where Chaver B was born. "Make it playful," he would say, "like children skipping down the street on a summer's day. Then you become so hot in the afternoon sun. Your throat is dry, and your whole body feels heavy. You stop for ice cream at the corner store, each mouthful creating feelings of pure joy. You regain your energy and resume skipping along."

For the next two months, "Humoresque" became my obsession. I would practice as soon as I returned home from school and again after dinner, always with the images Chaver B had created floating through my mind.

Finally, the day arrived. I put on my best dress, the crimson velvet one with long sleeves, rounded collar, and white cuffs. I brushed my long brown hair, parted it at the side, and tucked it behind my ears. Since my section took place on a Saturday, Chaver B was able to come along. My dad drove us—me and Chaver B—through the waning, morning darkness to the festival. My mother stayed home to look after Sammy.

Because it was so cold outside, my father had bought little kerosene hand warmers that I put in my pockets to keep my fingers warm, limber, and supple. I knew ahead of time that there were forty-three children in my category and that no one was playing the same song that I was.

The concert hall, a three-storey, slightly weather-beaten, beige stucco building, was unimposing from the outside, but easy to find since it had MANITOBA MUSIC FESTIVAL written in large black letters on the marquee in front. As we walked inside, an usher handed each of us a program; I saw that I was listed as number thirty-one. We'd arrived on time, which meant that we had to sit through thirty other students before it would be my turn. As I waited and listened to each performer, my hands became increasingly warm and damp, and I wondered if with all those other melodies milling around in my head, I would remember how to play "Humoresque."

Finally, my number was called. I walked towards the stage and climbed the five steps leading to the black platform. The accompanist smiled at me, and with her help, I proceeded to tune my violin. I hadn't rehearsed with the accompanist ahead of time, but Chaver B had said not to worry, that she was very experienced and would follow my lead.

When we were both satisfied, I turned to face the small audience, which consisted mainly of the performers and their families, and paused. Despite the plain exterior, the inside of the building was breathtaking. I had never been to, let alone played in a hall so grand. The ceiling was high, and the walls were covered with ornate carvings and gold-threaded tapestries. The audience area was deep with a balcony and loges. I was so overwhelmed by the grandiosity of the surroundings that my anxiety miraculously dissipated. The accompanist cleared her throat, I'm sure as a reminder to me that I had come here as a participant, not an observer. I turned to her, nodded, and began.

As soon as I started to play, I was immediately taken aback. The sound I produced was so resonant and rich that I became completely enthralled by it. I was so fixated on this strange sound, which seemed hardly to be coming from my own violin, that I was almost in a trance; my fingers automatically moved to their respective places as my bow glided over the strings. Before I knew it, the song was over, and I felt like clapping for this unknown performer who had just played with such a clear and pure sound.

Everyone applauded, and when I returned to my seat beside my father and Chaver B, they were both beaming. I was elated. The judges' comments were enthusiastic and encouraging, but I doubt they ever said anything demoralizing about anyone. Nevertheless, I took their words at face value and vowed to continue my rigorous practice schedule.

Chaver B must have thought I had a flair for Eastern European music, for after the festival came a steady flow of Hungarian Dances by Liszt and Brahms, Slavonic Dances by Dvorak, and the song, "Csardas," by Vittorio Monti.

To prepare me for these pieces, Chaver B regaled me with stories of gypsies. The music was lively and rhythmic, and the melodies were "catchy" for classical music. As the passages became faster and louder, he would say, "There is energy in the music. You have to move with this energy, flow with it. Let it carry you along with it until the music can no longer contain it, and it explodes."

Lessons continued every Tuesday at five o'clock. The lessons were supposed to last a half an hour, but Chaver B was generous with his time and taught for however long it took. At the end of each lesson, he would conclude by saying, "*Zeyer gut, zeyer gut.*" Very good, very good.

For some obscure reason, he didn't have any other violin students, and not because no one else was interested. I knew that at least two students in my class had asked if he would teach them also, but he'd graciously declined, stating that he didn't have time. I wondered what he was so busy doing.

After my lessons were over, Chaver B usually stayed for dinner. I would go upstairs and start on my homework, while he and my mother chatted in the kitchen until my father came home from work. They spoke in such low voices that they seemed to be whispering.

Conversations at the dinner table were always general. Chaver B and my dad discussed politics. My mother usually talked about matters pertaining to the school. One evening, I decided to ask him if he had any brothers and sisters. The adults looked very uncomfortable after I asked what seemed to me to be an innocuous question. My parents cleared their throats and shuffled in their seats, but Chaver B just straightforwardly answered, "No, I do not."

"Were you a teacher before you came here?" Sammy asked innocently, not sensing the uneasiness in the room.

"I did a little teaching," said Chaver B, and then my parents quickly changed the topic.

After dinner was over, Chaver B and my dad would retire to the living room while my mother and I cleaned the dishes. My brother was relegated to his room to finish his homework and get ready for bed. My dad always offered to drive Chaver B home, but almost like a ritual, Chaver B would respond, "No, thank you. The air will do me good," even if it was twenty degrees below zero.

Typically, Chaver B was quite reticent, but as he got to know us, he gradually became more talkative and animated, especially during my violin lessons. And I couldn't help but notice his left arm as he did things. True, he was right-handed, but he seemed to eat without difficulty. He had no trouble tying his shoelaces or doing up the buttons on his coat.

On one particular evening, I specifically watched him as he reached into his trouser pocket with his left hand to take out some foreign coins that he wanted to show my brother. The coins emerged with ease, and he even grabbed them by their edges with his left hand and held them up to the light so Sammy could better appreciate them.

But that certain reserve about him remained. Like the man in the moon with his inscrutable face and his mouth forming an O, he sometimes seemed poised to speak, but then would stop, almost abruptly, as if something was preventing him from fully expressing his feelings. It was as though on a cold and windy winter's day, he had put on his long, warm coat, leather gloves, fur hat, and wool scarf. Ready to go outside, he had opened his front door, but before he could cross the threshold, he was confronted by a wall of frigid air, like an enemy whom he could not fight back and whom he was powerless to overcome.

CHAPTER IX

We have a secret, just we three,
The robin, and I, and the sweet cherry-tree;
The bird told the tree, and the tree told me,
And nobody knows it but just us three.

—Anonymous

Chaver B had a secret. What was it? I wondered if everyone had secrets that they kept hidden inside their hearts, secrets that belonged exclusively to their owner, like the heart that encased and protected them.

Although Annie and I were best friends and told each other many things, did we tell each other everything? What were *my* secrets? Well, I had a crush on Kenny, Annie's brother, but I hadn't told anyone about that, especially not Annie. I was over at her house so often; it would have been extremely embarrassing. And I sometimes imagined that one day I would become a famous actress, but I hadn't told anyone about that either. Neither had I shared with Annie my suspicions about Chaver B. And even though at times it seemed that Annie could effortlessly discern what I was thinking, she seemed oblivious to my preoccupation with Chaver B; he garnered no more interest for her than did any of our other teachers.

People began to look different to me and assumed strange auras. They all seemed to avert their gaze and walk furtively down the hall or down the street as I passed them, afraid that if I looked them straight on, I would uncover the secrets they were concealing. What about my parents? What were their secrets? And my grandparents? My mind was racing. No one was immune to my probing thoughts.

There were some secrets that I did know about. You could call these shared collective secrets—things that were talked about only within the confines of our family. My father's parents had come from Russia, just like Babbi Rachel and Zaidi Harry, and they still lived in their original home, a large, rambling house that had two staircases, one located just inside the front entryway that was not often used, and the other at the end of their long, roomy kitchen. Their house had, at varying periods of time, been home to four children and sometimes their spouses, and my Babbi Hannah's two unmarried sisters, Lillie and Bella. Auntie Lillie was a seamstress and made many of my clothes in her sewing room located off the main foyer. My mom and I would bring her a dress from Eaton's; she would copy the design, purchase the fabric, and make me an exact replica, following which we would return the dress to the store, unworn, of course. Whenever she saw me wearing a dress that was not of her creation, she'd inspect the hem and overall workmanship—while I was wearing it—and assert that her handiwork was far superior.

Aunt Bella was more of a recluse and somewhat frightening to me as a child. She generally stayed in her room upstairs and tended to sway back and forth when she walked, seemingly taking two steps forward and one step back until she reached her destination. Sometimes Sammy and I would sneak up one of the two staircases and spy on her in her room through the crack in the door, but as sleuths, we were dreadful. We never saw anything unusual.

When she did emerge, she preferred darkness, and if we turned on the lights, she would quickly bring her hand up to shield her eyes, stagger backwards, and exclaim, "*Oy*, lights!"

Auntie Lillie and Aunt Bella were so unlike any of my other relatives that at times their eccentricities seemed to take on Dickensian proportions. I always wondered why they had never married. I had difficulty imagining them being young, despite their still slim figures, but purportedly they had both been very pretty. My mother had said that Aunt Bella in particular, with her brilliant blue eyes and porcelain complexion, had had many admirers.

One rainy afternoon, I was sitting at the kitchen table, keeping my mother company while she was making *prakehs*, or cabbage rolls, when I decided to ask her for more details about my aunts' pasts.

"Well, Auntie Lillie was engaged," she began, "but her groom turned out to be a 'no-goodnik,' as Zaidi Max would say, and left her on her wedding day, alone and humiliated. After that, she adamantly proclaimed that she had no interest in men and would do just fine on her own, 'thank you very much!'"

I chuckled to myself; I had often heard Auntie Lillie use that phrase in a variety of different circumstances. I expected my mother to continue, but she seemed to be focused on rolling the meat into little balls and wrapping them in cabbage leaves. I sensed that she was stalling, but I didn't know why. "What about Aunt Bella?" I prodded.

"Well, I guess you're old enough to know," she sighed as she stirred the thick, pungent, tomato sauce cooking in the pot. "Aunt Bella's story is sadder. Before she left the Old Country, she fell in love with a Gentile—you know, someone who isn't Jewish, a *goy*. Worse yet, she became pregnant. And they weren't married."

"Her parents must have been furious!" I exclaimed dramatically. "What did she do?"

"Sometimes, when women become pregnant and don't want to have a baby, they try to get rid of it."

"Get rid of it?" I repeated questioningly and slightly alarmed. "What does that mean?"

My mother didn't say anything right away. She kept her eyes focused on gently placing each roll into the simmering sauce and wouldn't look at me. "They try to abort the baby. To end the pregnancy."

"How did she do that?" I asked in a puzzled voice.

"I don't know the details," my mom replied, although I was sure that she did, "but the baby didn't survive, and Aunt Bella almost didn't survive either. Just like you said, her parents were very upset and angry, for obvious reasons, the least of which was that her lover wasn't Jewish. They refused to let her see him again, and her father, your great-grandfather, Berel, *alev ha' sholem*, was ready to pull him apart limb from limb. His wrath knew no boundaries."

"Did they have a fight?" I asked, imagining my great-grandfather challenging Aunt Bella's lover to a duel over her honour, although I didn't truly believe that was how disagreements were settled in the *shtetl*.

"Fortunately, not," my mom said. "Aunt Bella's lover was no fool, and he moved away to save them both. But after that, she wasn't sure if she would ever be able to have children, and the question remained, with that past, who would take her? To lose a child and to have her lover so abruptly snatched away was shattering for her, and she never fully recovered."

The stories my mother recounted were much different than what I'd expected to hear. After learning of Auntie Lillie's and Aunt Bella's hardships, I developed a respect for them that was deeper than them being simply my older aunts. People were much more complicated than what we saw on the surface, I realized, a notion I'd been harbouring about Chaver B since he was first introduced to our class.

All this talk of romantic love and secrets filled with passion and longing was fascinating. But my obsession with secrets was exhausting, and fortunately, it gradually waned as I became involved in other activities. The holiday Purim was approaching, and I had to start thinking of a costume for the carnival. Our teachers were assigning a lot of homework, and of course, there was violin practice; I didn't want to disappoint Chaver B. By nighttime, I was worn out.

A few nights later as I was putting on my pajamas, I asked my mom, "Do you think Chaver B is starting to like us more?"

"I think he's always liked us," she said as she pulled back the quilt from my bed, "but he does seem more relaxed than when he first came here." Then, as she often did when it came to the subject of Chaver B, she shifted the focus of the conversation, this time to our bedtime ritual.

Even though I was soon to turn twelve, my mother and I had not yet given up this nighttime routine. I would lie under the covers, and she would stretch out on top of them beside me.

Sometimes she would choose the book we would read, and sometimes I would. I still liked her to read to me, and she enjoyed doing it. Once in a while, we would reverse roles, and I would be the mother. But tonight, it was her turn.

"Miraleh," she asked, "do you have any new library books?"

"Just one," I replied, "but I've already finished it. Do you want to pick something from the shelf?"

She walked over to my bookshelf, perused the titles, and came back to bed carrying a slim but large volume with a dark orange cover.

"*The Forgotten Secret!*" I exclaimed. "We haven't read that one in ages."

Mrs. Walker, my grade three English teacher—and now Sammy's teacher, too—had given it to me. At the end of the school year, she had given each student a book as a gift, and she had gone to the trouble to select a special one for each of us. *The Forgotten Secret* was a lovely story about an old man who lived in a small town. Each day he would walk down the road carrying his sack on his back. The children would follow him, peek into his sack, and skip away in sheer delight.

The adults in the town were mystified and concerned, wondering what hold the old man had on their children. What exactly was in his sack, they demanded to know! One night, the mayor snuck into the old man's house, and while he was asleep, opened the sack and peered inside. After gazing at the contents for a long time, the mayor, pale and shaken, slowly raised his head. What he had seen was his own true face when he was a boy. The sack was filled with childhood happiness.

As young as I was, I could still appreciate the poignancy of the story. I couldn't imagine ever forgetting my days as a child, probably because whenever I complained about doing homework or practicing violin, I was frequently reminded how lucky I was that those were my only responsibilities and that I should enjoy being a child while I was one.

"This is a beautiful tale," my mom said while yawning, strands of her usually neat hair falling loosely by her ears. She looked at the illustrations for a few minutes, then closed the book and placed it on my nightstand. "But now it's time for you to go to sleep."

She swung her legs over the side of the bed and stood up. After pulling the covers around me, she kissed me on the forehead and whispered, "Pleasant dreams, Miraleh."

"Good night, Mom. See you in the morning."

She left the room and partially closed the door behind her.

I wasn't too sleepy yet, so I lay in bed reciting what I could remember of the story. And then I thought again of Chaver B. He had a secret, but it was clearly not forgotten. It. seemed to be woven into every fibre of his being.

CHAPTER X

Haynt iz Purim, brieder,
Es iz der yontef groys,
Lomir zingen lieder
Un geyn fun hoyz tsu hoyz.

Today is Purim, brothers,
It is a great holiday,
Let us sing songs
And go from house to house.

—Yiddish folksong

March came in like a lion and went out like a lamb, and somewhere in that transition fell Purim. Although it only lasts for one day, it was one of our livelier holidays and was celebrated in a somewhat chaotic and often very noisy fashion. Purim seemed to have lifted even Chaver B's spirits.

Sammy had been home from school for a few days with a bad cold and was missing all the Purim preparations. He was becoming increasingly restless, so I offered to read to him in order to give my mother a break. She looked more worn out than Sammy did, from her frequent trips upstairs bringing him hot cocoa, checking his temperature, and refilling the kettle with water that she kept boiling in his room to humidify the air.

Sammy was a cute kid, for an eight-year-old. His ink-black straight hair was cut short with bangs, in the style of the day. He had big brown eyes like saucers, and cheeks that were just right for squeezing with a *knip*, a little pinch, or a *joolique*, which was something more substantial.

I decided to read him the Purim story, the *Megillah* or *Book of Esther*, a classic tale of good versus evil replete with kings and queens, ambition, intrigue, narcissism, bigotry, and of course, loyalty and heroism.

When I walked into Sammy's room, he was lying in his bed, surrounded by his stuffed animals. I was surprised to find him looking so pale and unkempt.

"How are you feeling?" I asked him.

"A little better," he croaked, "but my voice is really hoarse."

"You know, you're missing all the fun at school. Today they gave everyone baskets of delicious candy," I teased him. "Chocolate with creamy caramel filling. Your favourite. Everyone loved it!"

"What?" he cried out, tears welling up in his eyes and gathering along his eyelashes. "I hate being sick!" he wailed.

I took a lot of pleasure in teasing Sammy, but he was so upset about having missed this fictitious candy, that even *I* felt bad.

"Don't be silly!" I reassured him. "There was no candy. I made it up, just to bug you."

"You're mean," he whined between sniffles, while wiping his eyes with his pajama sleeve.

"Here, I'll read to you," I said. "That should make you feel better."

I sat down on the edge of his bed and shoved him with my

elbow so that he would move and make room for me. He scooted over, and then I lay down beside him and began the story. "When the Jewish people dwelled in the kingdom of Persia over two thousand years ago, they lived under the rule of King Achashverus, whose trusty advisor was a villain named Haman. At a seven-day drinking feast, the king ordered his wife, Queen Vashti, to dance before him and his guests wearing only her crown."

"Yuck!" exclaimed Sammy, wrinkling his nose and ducking underneath his blankets. "You mean they wanted her to dance naked?"

"I guess so. That's what grown-ups did back then, I imagine." I continued reading. "Vashti refused, but as a consequence, she could no longer be queen. In search of a new wife, the king had his officers present all the beautiful, young women of the kingdom before him for his review. The king's eyes cast upon Esther, an orphan who had been adopted by her cousin, Mordecai, the leader of the Jewish people of the city of Shushan. She became the new queen."

Sammy had stopped his sniffling by then, too engrossed in the story to think about his runny nose.

"In the meantime, Haman was appointed Prime Minister of Persia and ordered everyone to bow down before him when he passed. Mordecai refused to obey, angering Haman who decided to kill not just Mordecai, but all the Jews in the Empire. Seething over Mordecai's disobedience, Haman built a gallows to hang him."

Sammy's eyes widened as he stared at the illustrations, clearly not bothered by the words that were too difficult for him to understand.

"Mordecai begged Esther to speak with the king in order to stop him from performing such a horrible act. But Achashverus did not know that Esther was Jewish, and she was not sure how this news would be received. Fearful for her people, she emboldened herself; she told the king of Haman's scheme and informed him that she too was Jewish. Outraged, King Achashverus had Haman executed on the very gallows that was built for Mordecai. As the Bible says, 'He who digs a pit will fall into it,' and a new decree was issued, saving the Jews."

"I like that story," Sammy said in a ragged voice, and then looked up at me. "Do you think I'll be well enough for the Purim carnival?"

"I think so," I replied. "It's not 'til next week."

As we did every year, the school held a Purim carnival with games, singing, and of course, food. We all wore costumes, even our teachers. Annie and I both dressed up as Queen Esther, and we decided to make a crown out of construction paper and tinfoil for Chaver B, as we assumed that he would not take the initiative to make a costume for himself. We anticipated that he would feel awkward wearing it, but to our surprise, he smiled broadly as we handed it to him. He immediately inspected it while turning it from one side to the other and then placed it on his head while adjusting it with both hands.

We reviewed the *Megillah* in class and read parts of it in Hebrew. Each time evil Haman's name was mentioned, we would twirl our *graggers* or noisemakers, and shout, "Boo! Boo!" Chaver B joined in with the rest of us.

"But," said Chaver B as he stood at the front of the classroom, his fingers extended, their tips pressed together as if forming a tent, "you have read and heard this story many times before. Now that you are in grade six, it is time for you to delve more deeply into the story and discover its significance."

He emphatically raised his right index finger into the air, as a conductor would raise his baton to ready the orchestra, and began in Yiddish. "First, Esther's Hebrew name was Hadassah, but in the *Megillah* she is referred to as Esther. Some scholars believe the name Esther comes from the Aramaic word *sihara*, which means moon. According to the *Talmud*, the collection of Jewish law and tradition," said Chaver B, "all the nations referred to her as Esther because she was as beautiful as the moon."

We were all rapt with attention. Chaver B was right. Until that year, our teachers had been mainly concerned with facts. It was refreshing to learn what more lay behind these stories.

"There are many questions one can ask about Purim," he went on. "The *Talmud* also says that Purim is the only holiday that will be celebrated forever, even after the Messiah comes. I don't know why that is," he continued, "but for homework, I would like you to write me a paragraph, in Yiddish, discussing why you think this is so."

On our way home from school, Annie and I discussed his question. "Don't you find it curious that Purim is so special?" I asked her. "After all, there are so many other holidays that we celebrate for more than just one day and that seem more important, like *Chanukah* and Passover. We spend a lot more time in school studying those holidays."

"I know," she replied. "Purim isn't even considered a holy day. People are allowed to work and do whatever they like. Also, Chaver B told us that the *Book of Esther* is the only book of the Bible that doesn't even mention God. Why then would God choose it to be celebrated forever?"

Annie and I paused at the corner before we took our separate paths home, and we promised to call each other later that evening to discuss our conclusions.

My parents didn't seem to have a specific answer to Chaver B's question either, although my father provided me with some historical information. "Purim is probably more well-known and important than you think, Miraleh," he offered. "Surprisingly, even Hitler knew about it. Did you know that Hitler banned Jewish people from celebrating Purim, and in a speech, even compared the Nazis to Haman?"

When I thought about all these interesting pieces of information, the answer to Chaver B's question became obvious. Purim was not a story of clashing armies or of might and physical strength; it was not a story of miracles. It was a story depicting the power of the individual, where all change begins, and that is why it will be celebrated forever.

How brave Esther had been. Could I ever have that much courage? We learned that six million Jewish people and millions of others died at the hands of the Nazis. Would I have had the courage to confront the enemy? Would I ever be able to stand up and fight for what I believed in?

And then I thought of my project on the moon and the moon's role in reflecting all the light of the sun. The relationship of Esther's name to the moon was no accident. She was clearly an embodiment of light and renewal, and the moon could not have a more worthy representative.

CHAPTER XI

To see a world in a grain of sand
And a heaven in a wild flower,
Hold infinity in the palm of your hand
And eternity in an hour.

—William Blake, "Auguries of Innocence"

Springs were short. In the twilight of winter at the end of March, the snow began to melt and transformed itself into a grey slush. Passover, or *Pesach*—the story of Moses, Pharaoh, the Ten Plagues, and the release of the Jewish people from bondage in Egypt to freedom in the Promised Land—came and went.

By May, the sweet, intoxicating scent of lilac blossoms suffused the air and heralded warmer weather. Israel had just become a state the year before, so now we had a new holiday to celebrate, *Yom Ha'atzmaut*, Israeli Independence Day. We were fascinated by stories of how the *chalutzim*—the pioneers—had battled swamps and malaria and made the desert bloom, but while all this sounded very romantic to me, it was extremely arduous and sometimes dangerous work for them. Before you knew it, the days were getting longer, the temperature was approaching ninety, and school was out!

Summers were glorious. On weekends, we would go to the beach. We usually went to Winnipeg Beach on Lake Winnipeg, although it might just as well have been an ocean. The lake was so large that I could never see the other side, and the sand was soft and fine.

My parents had met while they were both studying in Winnipeg, my father in medical college and my mother in secretarial school. They would recount stories of their courting days, when on Saturday evenings, they and their friends would ride the Moonlight Train from Winnipeg to the beach and back. It all sounded lovely.

Sometimes, for a change, we'd drive to some of the other beach communities on the lake, like Gimli, a town founded by Icelandic immigrants. But not all the communities were open to Jews. Some of the beach towns had laws restricting Jewish people from owning property there. And so, through this summer haven, I encountered my first taste of anti-Semitism. But we rarely talked about this imperfection in our otherwise seemingly perfect world. The lake was huge, and there was certainly enough room for anyone who wanted to enjoy it.

Going to the beach was always an adventure, especially when Babbi Rachel came along. No more than four foot nine, she was round like a roly-poly and waddled when she walked. She spoke an interesting mix of Yiddish and English, but primarily the former.

On our trips to the beach, Babbi would sit in the back seat between Sammy and me. She always wore her white cotton sun-dress with pink polka dots and short sleeves, her fine white hair tied into a chignon at the top of her head and concealed under a matching pink cotton sunhat with a wide brim. We usually kept the windows open to circulate the air and keep the car cool, which caused Babbi to be engaged in a perpetual battle with her hat to keep it affixed to the top of her head.

The Babbi Rachel I knew was afraid of everything. One summer, we had a lot of car trouble. The radiator had a leak, and while travelling the seventy-five miles to the beach, the car would inevitably overheat. On one such Sunday afternoon trip, Sammy and I were playing I Spy in the back seat, when suddenly, black smoke billowed out from under the hood of the car.

"*Reuven, Reuven, vos iz dos?*" Babbi said nervously. "*Vos iz der mer?*" What's this? What's the matter?

"Don't worry, Ma," replied my dad nonchalantly. "The car's overheating a little. I'll just pull over and add some water to the radiator."

"Vhere is *dos vaser?*" she asked. "*Mir zaynen in yehupets,*" she added, raising her hand and pointing outside the windows to the golden fields surrounding us in all directions. "We're in the middle of nowhere."

I had to admit; Babbi had a point. There didn't seem to be anyone else around except for the occasional car going in the opposite direction, and I didn't see any farmhouses.

"I brought some water along in these bottles," he said, while leaning over and lifting up one of several containers sitting on the floor in front of my mother's seat.

"Watch where you're driving!" screamed Babbi. My dad slowed the car and after several seconds, Babbi calmed down. "You mean you knew the car was broken before we went?" she scolded him, as if he were a schoolboy.

"Ma, don't worry. We'll be fine," my dad responded placatingly as he pulled the car over to the shoulder of the road.

"Careful, careful!" she cried out, her typically soft voice

becoming shrill as my dad opened the door to step out of the car, even though there were no other cars in sight.

He walked around to the front and lifted up the hood. The smoke was thicker than before and smelled awful.

"*Oy vey,*" wailed Babbi, cupping her face in both hands and tilting her head from side to side. Sammy and I started to laugh, but my mom turned around and flashed us a reprimanding look.

Sammy and I tried to mollify her. "Babbi, it's okay," we said almost in unison. "Daddy knows what he's doing. Why don't you play I Spy with us?" I suggested.

"Ma," my mom interjected calmly, clearly used to Babbi's histrionics. "The radiator just needs more water, and then we'll be on our way again."

But Babbi's anxiety only increased. She leaned forward as she called out from the backseat, "*Reuven, Reuven, mir darfn aheym geyn!*" We need to go home!

My dad behaved as though he hadn't heard her and continued to replenish the parched radiator. The car eventually cooled off, and after sitting for several minutes, Babbi finally cooled off, too, and we resumed our trip to the beach.

I found it peculiar to see my grandmother in such a panicked state. After all, here was a woman who as a young girl from the shtetl had travelled by herself on a ship across the Atlantic to marry a man whom she had never met and to live in a strange country where she had no family or friends. She had maneuvered her way through Ellis Island without being able to speak English and had then taken a train halfway across the continent to Manitoba. Her ship had become mired in the ice for a week, and I envisioned her barging into the captain's cabin and advising him how to navigate through the frozen blocks. "*Geyt azoy. Neyn, dreyt zich arum, dreyt zich arum!"* Go like this. No, turn around, turn around!

Then there was the incident that made Babbi a town legend. She and Zaidi Harry had hired a man to do some repairs at their house, but when she walked into the kitchen—the worker's back turned towards her—she saw him rummaging through one of the drawers and pocketing the money that he found there. Without saying a word, she grabbed the nearby broom, and with all the force that every pound per square inch of her small frame could muster, she wacked him across the back of his head with the wooden handle. Dazed and stunned, he dropped the money and ran from the house as she chased after him screaming, "*Ganev! Ganev!*" Thief! Thief! News travelled quickly, and the whole town was buzzing. "Did you hear about little Rocheleh? Good for her!" was the refrain.

I wondered what had transformed this once brave woman into someone who now viewed everything around her as being dangerous and foreboding. Was it one specific incident? Was it the weight of all those years? I never figured it out, but it made me wonder if I would always be me, or, if as I grew older, I would turn into someone else, too.

One night in early July, shortly after the end of grade six, I was awoken abruptly from my sleep by the sound of sirens wailing. Startled and frightened, I ran to my parents' bedroom. It was two in the morning; my father had just turned on the lights and was standing by the open window trying to determine what was happening.

He quickly changed into his trousers and a shirt, found his shoes by the bedroom door, and grabbed his car keys. "I'm going to see what's happened," he said. "I'll let you know."

He raced downstairs, and I heard the screen door slam shut.

By this time, Sammy had also woken up and stumbled into the bedroom, bleary eyed and mumbling, "What's going on?"

"We don't know yet," replied my mom. "Daddy has gone to find out and to see if anyone is hurt." Just then, she saw flames leaping up in the distance, and there was the sharp smell of smoke in the air. "Something's on fire!"

"Didn't a shoe store burn down in Morton last week?" I asked. I had heard my mother and father talking about it.

"Yes," she answered, "but they still don't know the cause. Two fires so close together in time and distance," she continued. "Morton's just fifteen miles away. That's an odd coincidence."

As the orange flames leaped higher, setting the night sky aglow, my mother could tell that the fire was only several blocks away in the direction of downtown. "I'm going to go, too," she said. "Maybe I can help. Mira, you can watch Sammy."

"Can't we come, too?" I pleaded. "We'll stay out of trouble. I'll look after Sammy. I promise."

After hesitating for several seconds, she said, "Fine. But if I tell you to stay put, I want you to listen to me."

Sammy and I didn't even bother to change out of our pajamas, but put on our shoes that were lying by the front door, where we always left them when we came into the house. It was a warm summer night, clear and cloudless, and we didn't even need sweaters.

I squeezed Sammy's hand tightly in mine as we walked at a fast clip towards the fire—two blocks towards Salter Street, then turned right at the corner and walked an additional six blocks towards downtown. One of the buildings just on the outside edge of the central area was burning. There were three different stores on that block: a dress shop, a restaurant, and a bookstore at the far corner. The fire had broken out in the bookstore. The store was owned by a Jewish couple, Mr. and Mrs. Rosenzweig, and was where we bought our Yiddish textbooks at the beginning of the school year. The Rosenzweigs lived in an apartment in the rear of the building.

The firemen had barricaded the street. I could see them in their shiny black coats and red fire hats wielding heavy hoses as they tried to douse the flames, preventing them from spreading to adjacent structures. Two people lay on the ground, and there was my father, kneeling beside them and tending to them. I could see his mouth form words, but he was at least half a block away from me, and with all the noise and commotion, I couldn't make out what he was saying. But he's talking to them, I reasoned to myself, so they must be alive. An ambulance with its white exterior and bright red cross painted on its side had already arrived, a beacon of hope, waiting to take away the injured.

I glanced around at the rather large crowd that had gathered, probably twenty or thirty people. We weren't the only ones crazy enough to come out in the middle of the night. I could hear snatches of their conversations. Everyone was worried, it seemed. Words like *arson* and *faulty wiring* drifted over to me above the brouhaha.

As I perused the scene, my eyes rested on a man standing near one of the fire trucks. He was talking to a police officer. His face was streaked with black, and his clothes were coated with a dark, sooty film. He was talking in an animated fashion, pointing towards the bookstore on his right and then turning his head one-hundred-eighty degrees and raising his arms towards a building across the street to his left, almost directly across from the bookstore.

"That must be Mr. and Mrs. Rosenzweig lying on the ground," said my mom. "They live behind the store. The firemen must have rescued them from the building."

"Who's that man standing and talking to the policeman?" I

asked. "He looks like he was in the house also. Did they have a relative staying with them?"

My mother squinted as she looked across the crowd. "It looks like Chaver B," she said, surprised. "But why does he look like he was also in the fire?"

As soon as my mother said that, I caught my bearings. The building across the street from the bookstore that Chaver B had been pointing to was the drugstore. With the fire engines and crowds of people milling around, I hadn't recognized it in the dark. And Chaver B lived in an apartment above the drugstore.

Just then, I saw the ambulance attendants load Mr. and Mrs. Rosenzweig onto stretchers, carry them to the waiting ambulance, and place them into the rear section. One of the attendants climbed into the back with them, and the other shut and secured the two doors to the rear, climbed into the driver's seat, and drove off.

My father walked over to us and didn't seem surprised that we had come. "What happened?" the three of us asked simultaneously, sounding like a Greek chorus. "What happened to Chaver B?"

"Chaver B wasn't able to sleep," said my dad. Apparently this was a regular affliction of his that I'd only just discovered. "He was sitting by his living room window when he saw a glow coming from the back of the bookstore and then smoke rising upwards. He quickly called the fire department and then ran downstairs and across the street to the back of the store. Fortunately, the fire had started in the corner of the building farthest away from the Rosenzweigs' residence, but it was fast moving. Chaver B found a rock on the ground and threw it through the window of the back door, reached his hand through the opening, and was able to unlock the door from the inside. By then, the home had filled with smoke. He was able to find Mr. and Mrs. Rosenzweig sleeping in their bed, but they were barely responsive from all the smoke that had filled the bedroom. He quickly lifted up Mrs. Rosenzweig and carried her outside, laying her down on the grass behind the building. Afterward, he ran in for Mr. Rosenzweig. By then, flames were licking through the wall that the bedroom shared with the storage area, where the fire had started, and while Chaver B was carrying him to safety, the firemen arrived.

"Shouldn't Ari go to the hospital, too?" asked my mom.

"I told him to go," said my father, "but he was adamant that he was fine and didn't need help."

Two nights later, there was a town meeting in the high school auditorium that was filled to capacity. My parents and I went, but Sammy stayed at Babbi's house. Everyone we knew seemed to be there, including Chaver B. The police chief, a broad man with heavy black eyebrows, deep-set eyes and a ruddy, weathered complexion, led the meeting.

"We initially thought that the fire in Morton last week was due to faulty wiring," he informed us in an even tone. "We have no information to the contrary. However, so much of that building burned down that it's made the investigation difficult. Unfortunately, it appears that the fire here in Ambrosia was purposely set by an arsonist." Waves of "ohs" and "ahs" rolled over the crowd. "We found evidence of rags soaked in kerosene. As of yet, we have no clues as to the identity of the perpetrator," he paused, "or perpetrators."

Chaver B raised his hand and was acknowledged by the police chief. "Thank you for holding this meeting," he began tentatively while standing up. "As you know, the owners of both stores are

Jewish, that is, the shoe store in Morton and the bookstore here in Ambrosia, and we in the Jewish community are concerned that these fires are aimed at us." People murmured their agreement, which seemed to bolster Chaver B's confidence. "I think I can speak for everyone," he continued more emphatically, "by asking that the police increase their nighttime patrols and pay particular attention to those establishments owned by members of the Jewish community." Several people began to clap.

"Thank you," responded the police chief. "No one individual or group in our town should be unjustly targeted. And I would also like to add that although the fire did a significant amount of damage to the back of the building, the front part of the structure was spared. Unfortunately, a good number of books were damaged by water. But fortunately, Mr. and Mrs. Rosenzweig have recovered without significant injury and will be discharged from the hospital tomorrow. I would like to thank Chaver B for his presence of mind in calling us at the first sign of danger and for his courage in saving the Rosenzweigs." Everyone applauded.

"I would just like to suggest one more thing, if you don't mind," added Mr. Clark, the owner of the drugstore. Mr. Clark was an amiable looking man, middle-aged, short and stocky, with a full face and thinning hair and a rather high-pitched voice. "It would be nice if we could each contribute something, however small, for the Rosenzweigs until their home is repaired and they are back on their feet," he said. Upon spying an empty box in the corner of the auditorium, he walked over to it and picked it up. He searched in his pockets for some coins and a dollar bill that he placed into the box, and then passed it around the room.

"Didn't Zaidi Harry's store burn down, too?" I asked my mom while we were driving back home. "Do you think someone intentionally started that fire also?"

"Who knows?" she replied. "It was a long time ago. I don't know if anyone even tried to find out the cause."

A couple of weeks later, the arsonist was apprehended, a six-teen-year-old boy, not from Ambrosia or Morton but from another neighbouring town ten miles from us. His father had suspected his son of foul play. As the story went, the boy had targeted our Jewish community simply because we were different. When his father coerced the truth from him, he was so outraged and disgraced by his son's behaviour that he gave him up to the police. There were no more fires after that.

Chaver B had always been so quiet when I saw him with others, diffident, almost meek at times, that I especially marvelled at the courage he had demonstrated the night of the fire and at his fear-lessness when speaking out at the meeting. And it reminded me of how courageous Babbi Rachel had been at one point in *her* life, too. I wondered, if like Babbi Rachel, Chaver B had also turned into someone else over the years. Who *was* Chaver B before he came here? Was he the sad, sensitive, vulnerable teacher I first met at the beginning of the school year, and if so, what had transformed him into the confident man with a conscience and a voice, willing to speak out and willing to risk his life to save others? Or perhaps it had been the other way around. Perhaps his vulnerability was only an interlude. And, where *was* the real Chaver B? Was he here with us on the Manitoba prairies, or was he in some other world far, far away, as he often seemed to be?

Who *is* Chaver B? I asked myself again and again. Will the real Chaver B please stand up?

CHAPTER XII

Is man merely a mistake of God?
Or God merely a mistake of man?

—Friedrich Nietzsche

L ife is full of paradoxes. Things from our past, from our childhood, can seem like they happened so long ago, and at the
same time like they happened only yesterday. We quickly learn that
the only constant is change. Or does nothing ever change? Are
things immutable? The mystery of time and change.

The fire had been exciting, like watching a scene from a movie.
It had lit up the night sky and awoken the town from its blissful
nighttime slumber. At first, this unexpected event had been invigo-
rating, but then, as the seriousness of what had transpired sank in,
it became heavy and depressing. Knowing that someone living in
our midst would perpetrate such an evil act was frightening. My
emotions fluctuated like the waves on the lake on a windy day as
I tried to make sense of it all. Things no longer seemed simple or
straightforward. I saw contradictions everywhere.

Even the library, my refuge of infinite delights, was a paradox.
Many of the older people in town would often come there in

the afternoons. Some read the newspapers and magazines, but many just sat, coming for human companionship and a change of scene. Old men with grey full beards, never removing their caps, dreaming of days past, days that could have been but never were, and of the fewer and fewer days remaining, still to be. The library served as a communal gathering place, people coming so as not to be alone yet not being allowed to speak to one another; comforted by the nearness of others, yet each wrapped, enveloped, in his or her own thoughts. All of us together, I thought. Each of us alone.

Chaver B was a paradox. One moment he was timid, and the next he was a hero. But he wasn't the only one of my teachers whose behaviour was perplexing. Lererine Malka, my Yiddish teacher in grade four, was also a puzzle.

There are three things that I especially remember about Lererine Malka. The first was her having us make three columns in our notebooks, one headed by *Der*, the second by *Di*, and the third by *Dos,* the three articles used to define masculine, feminine, and neuter nouns, respectively. We would then, of course, put the corresponding nouns in their correct columns. This exercise proved to be a valuable organizational and learning tool that served me well over the years, and I thank her for that.

The second recollection was of her telling us that we were all *eireh kinder,* her children. At the time, I thought it strange that she would have said that, but I knew that she didn't have children of her own. She had mentioned that to us before.

And this leads me to the third thing. It was a grey November day, and we were sitting in class reading a Yiddish story about a mischievous boy named Motl. Lererine Malka stood at the front of the room facing us and directed each student in turn to read a paragraph. When the last student had read, she lowered her book and raised her head to look at us.

"I had a daughter," she said, almost as if in a trance. "She would have been about your age, a little younger. It was 1942, and we had just celebrated her third birthday. We had a party for her, but in Warsaw in those days, parties were quiet affairs. A week later, the Nazis rounded up my entire family in the middle of the night.

"They loaded us onto trains, along with thousands of other Jewish people, and sent us all to a concentration camp." And then she rolled up the sleeve of her brown wool dress and showed us six dark-blue digits tattooed on her left forearm. "We had heard stories about these camps. Those few people who had miraculously managed to escape and return to Warsaw had provided us with tales of unthinkable things that went on there."

But Lererine Malka did not elaborate.

"People listened to the rumours and tried not to believe them, but deep down inside, all of us on that train knew that we were likely going to our deaths. After all, my husband had been arrested six months earlier, and I had not heard from him since."

We sat in our seats staring at her, transfixed by her story. No one fidgeted. Even the most restless among us was quiet. The stillness in the room engulfed us as she continued. "Our train slowed down while passing through a Polish town; I knew that the villagers would be lining the tracks and watching us, like watching a circus train with its caged creatures. As the train crawled almost to a stop, I pushed my way to the one small window and threw my daughter out of the train car. Whether she landed uninjured in a bed of soft, tall grass, whether a young boy with quick, strong arms and agile feet was able to catch her, I don't know. But I never saw her again."

As a nine-year-old, this information was interesting but hard to sort out, and Lererine Malka gave us only sparse details. We were all too shocked by her story to ask any questions. When the bell rang for recess, we remained riveted to our seats. Typically, we would have jumped up and raced to the closet to put on our coats, but not this day. Lererine Malka fell silent for a minute after the bell sounded, as if waiting for the commotion of children in the hallway to dissipate, and then she instructed us to go outside.

Annie and I went to the playground and stood on the paved area by the back doors. We were still too stunned to say anything and for several minutes simply watched some of the girls playing hopscotch or skipping rope. The rhythmic tapping of the rope hitting the ground and the regular metre of the girls' chants lulled us into a more comfortable frame of mind and almost seemed to numb our senses.

"What do you think?" Annie finally asked me. "Do you think what she said really happened?"

"I don't think she would make up something like that," I replied, "but it almost sounds like a story from our reader."

Admittedly, I don't recall spending much time talking about it with my friends after that. But over the years, I sometimes pondered the enormity of Lererine Malka's decision. As she rode to an unknown destination but to an almost certain destiny, her decision must have gradually declared itself amidst the crush of desperate humanity. And once it did, it must have been as though there had never been any decision to make. The uncertainty of life versus the inevitability of death. There was no choice after all. It seemed so incontrovertible.

I often wondered. Was her daughter raised by a strange family, and did she survive the war? Was she ever told the truth or just treated as one of their own? Would she ever have been able to understand why her mother did what she did?

When I was much older, my mother told me that immediately after the war ended, Lererine Malka had traced her train route from Warsaw to the concentration camp, Majdanek, where she had been interned, and stopped at every Polish town along the way. She knocked on doors. She went to schools. She visited the town municipal offices looking at lists of all the children in the area who would have been about her daughter's age. With no vestiges of her past and no photographs, all she had was the memory of what her three-year-old daughter looked like before and her impression of what she might look like then. How much would she have changed in those few years? Would she look like one of her relatives? Everyone had said that she'd reminded them of Lererine Malka's younger sister, Leah, whose hair and complexion had also been fair. Had her features fit in with those of her adoptive family? That could have been a clue. But alas, no one came forth. No family was willing to give her up. Or had she already been given up?

Over the years, Lererine Malka routinely checked with the registries of displaced and missing persons. But her daughter had been so young—too young to have formed firm memories of her past life and too young to assist in her own rescue. Would she have remembered her real name or her mother's name? All Lererine Malka had to go on was an image in her mind's eye, as though from a dream, and a mother's intuition. Had her daughter been rescued by the partisans? Or did she endure the fate that Lererine Malka had hoped she would shield her from?

Lererine Malka was presumably the only one of her family to have survived the war. Would she have made the same decision if she had to do it all over again? Would I ever be faced with a decision so monumental and unimaginable? It makes the decisions that I toil over regularly seem so frivolous and almost ridiculous.

So, it seemed that Chaver B wasn't the only one of my teachers who was a paradox. Lererine Malka was a paradox, too. Even though she had endured such horrible things, one would not have suspected that when talking to her. She always had a smile on her face when she greeted you, and she treated her students warmly and lovingly.

I suppose that's yet a fourth thing I remember about her. Feisty and forthright, she faced each new day with joy and humour. I wonder where her strength had come from. Perhaps she could have shared her secret with Chaver B.

CHAPTER XIII

Summer afternoon—summer afternoon;
to me those have always been the two most beautiful words
in the English language.

—Henry James

Summer days were lazy, exciting, thoughtful, and busy. But they were never wasted. After enduring the long prairie winter, every day of summer sun was a dazzling treasure to be cherished.

On summer evenings, we'd sit on the front steps eating sunflower seeds that we had picked from the sunflower heads and roasted and salted ourselves. Putting up with mosquitoes, especially in the evenings, was just part of the territory. Once I counted; I had ninety-six mosquito bites! Annie and I spent much of our time riding around the streets on our bicycles, stopping for a milkshake at the local drugstore soda fountain or a popsicle at the corner store, passing houses and wondering what was going on inside them, imagining what dramas were unfolding.

We rode our bikes along the curving, tree-lined roads of the park near the library, our long hair dancing in the wind. We rode through the neatly groomed gardens and around the bean-shaped pond with the Grecian fountain, where we'd stop and dip our toes to cool off and refresh ourselves on a hot, sunny afternoon before continuing on our journey.

Occasionally we'd venture downtown and stop at the ice cream store, which unfortunately, was no match for the Dairy Dell, the ice cream store near my grandparents' home in Winnipeg that had the most wonderful ice cream I'd ever tasted. Whenever we visited Zaidi Max and Babbi Hannah, my father would take me there for my usual, a cone with two scoops—chocolate and vanilla, with the chocolate on top. I remember the first time I ordered this specialty; I was five years old, standing beside my father in the brightly lit store, my hand lightly resting in his, his fingers gently folded around mine as I surveyed the array of colourful choices behind the glass. I must have made my request with a great sense of authority and decisiveness, because after I placed my order, the woman standing high above me behind the counter called out, "Good for you! You should get what you want!" Later in life, I would think back at how prescient those words were. At times they would echo in my head, jogging me out of my self-imposed complacency and smug sense of self-satisfaction.

But summer days in Manitoba were so perfect, I had no desire to change anything, and my memory of the woman's words to me would melt away even faster than did my ice cream.

On some afternoons, I would simply lie on the grass in front of our house, stare up at the sky, and listen to the soft summer breeze sing its song. The air seemed to be hanging there, just waiting to be filled with music. Sometimes a song would start with the faint, low sound of the rapid beating of a hummingbird's diaphanous wings, one thousand beats per minute, as it hovered in mid-air, drawing nectar from my mother's daylilies that grew in the flowerbed in front of our white brick house or from the impatiens that lined the sidewalk leading up to our covered porch and front door. The hum would begin like the soft roll of drums. The grass would rustle as the wind passed over it; the leaves of the trees would murmur and whisper among themselves. The birds would sing, more and more joining in, their voices like a round, a fugue, never sounding dissonant, sometimes one calling to the other, answering each other's questions. Short staccato chirps, trills, the rising and falling of their sweet cadences. Towards evening, I could hear the delicate sparrows' clear whistles followed by their melancholy "Oh dear me, I'm so weary," their voices crescendoing as the sun grew lower and the sky decided what colour to paint itself that evening—flaming red, glowing orange, deep magenta. Finally, as dusk filled the pale blue sky and night fell, crickets would lend their voices in a rousing finale. They all seemed to be inviting me to join in their choruses and sing their melodies. But who was conducting these musical geniuses? Surely it was not I, I thought.

Sometimes the sky would be crystal clear and the air still, and the sun would glitter down unimpeded, its rays warming the earth. Other times I was transported to different worlds, there for the taking; the clouds were like whimsical drifters lost in a reverie of blue. They could be anything I wanted them to be.

Some days the clouds would be fast moving, hurtling along as if being propelled from behind by a giant wind, a never-ending, relentless stream of billowing white forms. Like teams of galloping horses, they seemed to be racing to an unknown destination, as if every minute counted, and I would be afraid to take my eyes off them for fear of missing something.

That summer—the summer before grade seven—I volunteered at the hospital, as I had the previous year. There were anywhere from five to ten girls volunteering on a given day. Mrs. Jones was in charge and made the assignments.

Mrs. Jones had a narrow face, long nose, and thin, arching eyebrows. She also had a head tremor, and her head would shake from side to side as if she were saying "no, no," giving the impression that she was always disagreeing with you no matter what you said, or even before you said it. Her tremor fluctuated with her emotions, so one had an instant gauge of the intensity of her feelings.

She kept tabs of our hours and offered us a red ribbon if we worked a total of one hundred hours. Jobs included welcoming visitors at the reception desk, delivering flowers to patients, and taking the snack cart and the library cart to the wards and patient rooms.

My favourite job was working in the gift shop. We stocked the shelves, helped customers select gifts, and rang up sales on the cash register. Unfortunately, I had been banished from the gift shop for the foreseeable future. I was surprised at my carelessness, but one afternoon, I sold a ten dollar necklace for one dollar. One of the zeros had been poorly written on the price tag, so I thought the mistake was honest, but Mrs. Jones was not convinced. When she discovered the error, her head shook violently, and thereafter she made every attempt to assign me to jobs that did not involve handling money, although I tried to assure her that I was very good at math and would be much more careful in the future.

My next favourite job was wheeling the snack and library carts around the wards. Some of the patients were too sick to want anything. They were in no position to either eat or read. I was instructed by the nurses that if there was an NPO sign over the head of the bed, it meant *Nil Par Oris* in Latin—nothing by mouth—so I should be sure not to give those patients any chocolate bars or snacks. The library cart offered a selection of books and magazines. There were the typical Canadian magazines—*Maclean's*, and for the ladies, *Chatelaine*. Books ranged from the popular to the classic.

Only once in a while would I come across a patient who was a friend of the family. More often, there would be patients who just kept coming back over and over again, and as a result, I got to know them. One of these was Mrs. Singer, the same Mrs. Singer with her very ample figure and signature frown who I had encountered in my dad's office, a woman in her seventies who was always happy to see me. She was actually very congenial but was what we would call a *kvetsh*. Either everything hurt her or everything cost her "an arm and a leg." She, like my grandparents, had also come from the Old Country, so I forgave her imperfections.

Apart from her various aches and pains, Mrs. Singer had emphysema; that's what accounted for her repeated hospital admissions. The tiny air sacs in her lungs had lost their elasticity, making it harder for her to breathe in and out. At her best, she could walk no farther than one block, but when she developed a cold or bronchitis, she could barely talk without becoming short of breath.

One splendid, clear, Wednesday afternoon, Mrs. Jones assigned me the library cart. By that time, Mrs. Singer had already been in hospital for a week receiving antibiotics and physiotherapy and had regained some of her strength. Her acute bronchitis seemed to have resolved except for the harsh, jarring, recurrent cough that stayed with her. She was always looking for a good partner for a quick game of cards, and although I was probably not supposed to, I usually obliged. No one seemed to mind.

On this particular day, we became engrossed in a very competitive game of gin rummy.

"Miraleh," she said in her thickly accented English, "please hand me that piece of paper on my nightstand. And there's a pen in the drawer to keep score." I gingerly walked over to the nightstand, trying to avoid the wires, tubing, and other paraphernalia, but when I opened the drawer, there lay an open box of cigarettes.

"Mrs. Singer!" I exclaimed. "You're not supposed to smoke! You're not smoking in the hospital, are you? How will you get better?"

"Shh…" she whispered, furrowing her forehead even more intensely than usual and placing her right index finger on her lips. "Don't tell anyone. I can't help it," she said almost apologetically. "After more than thirty years of smoking, it's hard to stop."

"You need to keep trying," I suggested.

"It's not as easy as you think, Miraleh. Sometimes things are not as easy as they seem."

"Can't the nurses tell you've been smoking?" I asked somewhat perplexed.

"I stand by the open window after they've given me my medication, so I know they won't be back for a while. By the time they return, they don't notice a thing. Come on," she said. "Forget about me. Let's play cards!"

We each sat on the edge of the bed and placed the cards between us. Our game, or I should say match, proceeded methodically and deliberately. Only three draws into our first game, I put down the jack of spades. With raised eyebrows and a twinkle in her eye, she quickly snatched it up and with great bravado announced, "Gin!"

"That's an easy win, Mrs. Singer," I said rather accusingly.

"Sometimes we are lucky," she replied impishly, shrugging her shoulders. "Come on, deal the cards," she ordered. "Let's play. *Shpiel!*"

The next game dragged on almost to the bottom of the deck. I had three possible ways to win, either with a set of twos or fours, or a run with either a six or a ten of diamonds to complete it. I waited for Mrs. Singer to throw a card, but her indecision was apparent. First, she placed her thumb and index finger on the card she was holding on the far left, was about to remove it, and then decided otherwise as she studied her hand intently. Her forehead would frown and relax, frown and relax, like a bellows contracting and expanding, as she considered her strategy and then changed her mind, decided on her next move and then changed her mind again.

Finally she came to a decision, grasped the card in question, and placed it on the table. It was the ten of diamonds.

"Aha!" I said while scooping it up and then laying down my winning hand. "Now it's my turn!"

With each of us alternating victories, the match became very intense. Mrs. Singer clearly liked to win, and even though she was the adult, she proffered me no handicap. We were virtually tied by the time four o'clock rolled around, although she was slightly ahead.

"I have to go," I said urgently, feeling like Cinderella at the ball when the clock struck midnight. "The volunteer office will be closing, and I have to return my cart. Mrs. Jones will be upset if I'm late."

"Alright, dear," she sighed breathlessly as she lay down on the bed. "You've worn me out, anyway. We'll continue next time. Thank you for stopping by."

I felt somewhat guilty having neglected the other patients. I hadn't even made it through more than half the ward. I rolled the cart down the hall to the volunteer office and took off my smock. After I hung it up on a hook, I said goodbye to Mrs. Jones, rode the elevator down to the main floor, and walked outside. There was my bicycle in the bike rack on the sidewalk, just where I had left it.

The day was warm and the sun still high in the sky, so I decided to take the long way home, down the lane behind the last row of houses on the outskirts of town that bordered the sunflower fields. I loved that road because there were rarely any cars, and I could bike as fast as my legs could turn the pedals and feel the warm wind blowing in my face, the sunlight highlighting red glints in my brown hair, as the wind pushed it upwards and behind me, like a sail fluttering in the breeze.

I was singing to myself while blissfully riding along, when off in the distance I could see a figure standing alone in the lane. As I approached closer, I began to make out his features. It was Chaver B.

"Chaver B!" I shouted while holding the handlebars with one hand and waving with the other. "Chaver B!"

He didn't answer. As I drew nearer, I called his name again, but still he didn't respond. Except for the breeze rustling his wavy hair and the blinking of his eyelids, he was motionless.

Chaver B stood there, a solitary figure silhouetted against the blue sky. I had never seen anyone look so alone and so lonely. He reminded me of the sunflowers standing tall and straight. And like a sunflower when it reaches maturity, his head was bent forward, as though the weight he was bearing was too great and if he leaned over any farther, he would break. He just stood there, silent and secretive, overcome by an inexplicable sadness.

I dropped my bike, walked over to him, and shook his arm, but he neither looked at me nor spoke. I suddenly became frightened.

I got back on my bicycle and raced home, hoping that my father had already returned from work. I reached my house just as his maroon Dodge sedan was pulling into the driveway. As I rode up alongside his car, he lowered his half-open window, and I began to tell him what I'd seen, my discovery pouring out faster than I ever imagined I could speak.

"Show me where he is," my father commanded in an authoritative voice. I quickly leaned my bike against the garage door, sat down in the car beside him, and directed him to where I had left my teacher.

We were silent as we anxiously drove down the road by the fields, my father tightly gripping the steering wheel as we searched in the distance for Chaver B. "There he is!" I shouted eagerly as I caught sight of him. He was still standing where I had left him.

My father slowed the car down as we approached. He stopped on the side of the road opposite Chaver B and quickly got out. But upon seeing Chaver B standing there, looking so desolate, he slowed his pace and gently walked over.

"Ari," my father called softly as he held him by his shoulders and searched his eyes for an explanation or a sign. But his entreaties were no more successful than mine had been.

"Mira, help me get him into the car, the back seat," he said with urgency. Somehow we were able to maneuver Chaver B into the back of the car, although my contribution to that task was negligible. "Sit beside him," my father ordered. I got in, and my father drove off, but when we passed our house, he stopped and told me to go inside.

"Where are you taking him?" I asked incredulously.

"To the hospital," he replied tersely. "Tell your mother what's happened and that I'll call her from there."

CHAPTER XIV

Feygl, feygl, feygeleh,
Kum aher tsu mir.
Zog mir tayer fegeleh
Ver es lernt dir.

Bird, bird, little bird,
Come here to me.
Tell me little bird,
Who teaches you.

-Yiddish Folksong

That night, my father came home very late. Through my frag-
mented sleep, I heard snatches of his conversation with my
mother. "He was catatonic. . . sedated him. . . left orders to call me
should he wake up."

Although I was up by seven the next morning, my father had
already left for work. From what I gathered from my mother,
Chaver B had a nervous breakdown, as they called it in those days.

"What caused it?" I asked.

"Bad things happened during the war," she said. "A lot of Jewish people were put in concentration camps, and a lot of them died." I remembered what Lererine Malka had briefly told us about the concentration camps and recalled seeing the number that had been tattooed on her left forearm —— six dark-blue digits. Did Chaver B have a tattoo? I wondered. I had never seen one.

I wasn't scheduled to work at the hospital until the following week, but I planned to visit Chaver B regardless, to see how he was feeling. I went downstairs to our basement and found my dad's old sky blue work shirt sitting in a pile of clothes that my mom was planning to give away. I put it on over my blouse and skirt; it was perfect. The sleeves extended well below my fingertips but could be easily rolled up, and the bottom hem reached to a few inches above my knees. Because it so closely resembled the smocks the volunteers wore, I was sure that no one at the hospital would question my presence and that I would be allowed to enter the wards. I asked the clerk at the welcome desk, and as predicted, after checking the list of names on her clipboard, she gave me Chaver B's room number. He was on the fourth floor.

I stood at the doorway to his room. There were four beds altogether, and his was by the window. He was looking outside, and I don't think he saw me, or if he did, he probably didn't recognize me with my long blue shirt and hair pulled back. He looked so delicate, so defenseless, like a wounded bird. I wanted to heal him and make him fly, make him fly and sing again.

I was about to enter his room, but then hesitated. I felt so awkward. Would he want to speak with me? I felt embarrassed, as though I was prying into his personal thoughts. Maybe he would be embarrassed, too. I couldn't bring myself to cross the threshold, and when a nurse walked into the room carrying a tray of medication, I turned around and left.

CHAPTER XV

Alleh mentshn zaynen brieder, fun eyn tatn, fun eyn mamen.

All people are brothers (and sisters),
from one father and one mother.

—I. L. Peretz, sung
to Beethoven's "Ode to Joy"

Chaver B recovered, and when school resumed in the fall, there he was, seemingly looking like his old self. I was now twelve years old and in grade seven, my final year at Peretz School. After this, I would be attending the public high school. My English teacher was Mrs. Brooks, and at this pinnacle of our education, commensurate with our revered status as the graduating class, exciting things awaited us, like chemistry experiments using Bunsen burners and glistening beakers, and learning yet another language, French.

The year was passing along quickly, with all the gifts the moon brought. By the time school began, the leaves were already turning, and as usual, there was the whirlwind of holidays: *Rosh Hashanah* (the Jewish New Year), *Yom Kippur* (the Day of Atonement), *Sukkot* (the harvest celebration), and *Simchat Torah*. My father, brother, and I built a wooden hut or *sukkah* in our backyard and made the roof with *schach*, leaves and branches, so that we could still see the stars and sky above. Although nights were chilly, we ate our meals in the sukkah, which we decorated with colourful paper streamers and hanging gourds. And of course, we invited Chaver B to join us. Immediately thereafter came Simchat Torah, another joyous celebration like Purim. It recognized the completion of reading the *Torah* for the year and the start of a new cycle. The *Torah* scrolls were held aloft, and people marched, sang, and danced throughout the shul, as fervently as they had at Purim.

I was making significant progress on the violin. My technical work now included scales, double stops, arpeggios, and first, second, and third position exercises. Over the summer, before Chaver B became sick, he had started to teach me vibrato, the tremulous sound that the violinist makes by slightly moving his finger on the fingerboard. This was particularly difficult to master. Much of the time the whole violin would shake, not just my hand. But Chaver B was patient, and seeing how trying it was for me, he let it go for a while.

He continued to come to our house every Tuesday at five o'clock and stayed for dinner. Although outwardly he appeared the same, he seemed to have lost that glimmer of light that had started to emerge during the previous Purim, that sparkle in his eyes that although evanescent, had begun to appear with more and more regularity.

One warm Indian summer day in early October, Chaver B assigned me a new piece to work on. I remember that day vividly because "Salut d'Amour" was the most beautiful song I had ever heard, and I remember everything associated with it. Sir Edward

Elgar, a British composer, had written it as an engagement gift for his future bride. To my mind, it expressed all the lightness and joy that came with being in love and all the deep passion that I supposed lovers felt. After studying for a year with Chaver B, I had developed some of my own interpretive skills. In fact, for the first time, Chaver B didn't express any of his own ideas about the piece. Instead, he brought me a recording of the song by a famous concert violinist and told me to listen to it, saying it would offer me far more than anything he could teach me.

I played the record over and over, committing every note, every rest, every phrase to memory. My mother, who had a keen eye for bargains, had bought a used gramophone at a thrift shop and had given it to me for my twelfth birthday. I would lower its arm, place the needle on the outermost grooves of the shiny disc, lie on my bed, and listen to the song, feeling as though with each revolution the music was flowing out of the record like a spool of thread unravelling, floating out my window beyond the curtains, across the fields and through the trees, to towns, cities, and beyond, the violin strings magically and invisibly extending for miles and miles across the countryside, carrying the music to unknown destinations, allowing it to seep into every crevice, fill the atmosphere, and take up residence in every soul.

I revelled in every moment I spent practicing "Salut d'Amour" and in all the images it conjured up in my mind. I was so involved with practicing violin and with what we were learning at school, that I barely noticed the warm autumn days quickly drifting away, and during my violin lesson at the beginning of November, we were greeted by our first snowfall of the season.

As the snowflakes silently dusted the earth, Chaver B gave me some suggestions for playing the piece, so I knew that he must have been feeling better. "The phrases of the music are like sentences," he said. "The composer is speaking to his beloved, telling her how much she means to him. The volume of his voice rises and falls as he expresses his feelings to her. Make the passages smooth, legato, lyrical." He was very encouraging, telling me how much progress I'd made in such a short time, and concluded the lesson with his usual "*Zeyer gut.*"

Chaver B was sitting on the sofa, and I was putting my violin and bow back in the case, when we heard a heavy knocking at the front door.

"I wonder who that could be?" my mom called out in a concerned voice as she left the kitchen, wiped her hands on her apron, and walked towards the front entryway. She opened the door to find two officers from the Royal Canadian Mounted Police, the RCMP, in full regalia, standing on our front porch.

"May I help you?" she asked them quizzically.

"Thank you, ma'am," they replied respectfully. "We're looking for Dr. Reuven Adler. Is this his residence?"

"Yes, it is, but he's not home at the moment. I'm expecting him shortly. Is there something I can help you with?"

"We'd like to ask him a few questions about an acquaintance of his. May we wait for him?"

"Certainly, please come in," she replied without hesitation while holding the door open for them. The officers were fantastically tall, and their presence filled the foyer, their hats seemingly touching the ceiling. They brushed the freshly fallen snow off their sleeves and wiped their boots on the rug by the door.

As my mother ushered them into the living room, Chaver B immediately stood up. The strapping officers were quite intimidating in their scarlet jackets, navy trousers, and high brown leather boots, and I almost had to catch my hand before it involuntarily rose upwards to my forehead in a salute. The officers exuded self-assurance and confidence, but their bearing divulged no inkling of why they had come to visit us. Their faces were inscrutable, almost as though they were chiselled out of stone.

But these feelings were tempered by thoughts of a movie I'd seen two weeks earlier in which Nelson Eddy played an RCMP officer and serenaded Jeanette MacDonald with "Rose Marie," and I started to smile. I glanced over at Chaver B, half-expecting him to be chuckling at the same thought, but instead, his face had become ashen, and he was squeezing his hands together to hide their trembling. My mother, who was nervous herself, was too overwhelmed with the situation to notice. I was surprised by his reaction and was about to walk over to him when my mother said, "Mira, why don't you take Sammy upstairs. Chaver Bergman, would you like to wait in the kitchen?" she asked very formally.

"Thank you, but perhaps I should leave," he said motioning towards the front door.

"Oh, no, no," she insisted. "Reuven will be home any minute. He already called me to say that he was about to leave the office, and I'm sure the officers won't be here very long."

Chaver B seemed very anxious to go home, but he must have felt uncomfortable leaving us alone with two burly strangers, for he assented and made his way to the kitchen.

The snow continued to fall lightly outside. Sammy and I obediently climbed upstairs. Sammy immediately rushed to his bedroom window that overlooked the street to see if the Mounties had indeed arrived on their signature horses but was disappointed when all he saw was a black car with the RCMP logo emblazoned on its side. Several minutes later, we heard my dad's car pull into the driveway and then into the garage, and my mother rushed to greet him at the back door as he came into the house.

I was very curious to know what had prompted this visit from the RCMP, so I assumed my usual position at the top of the stairs. I wondered if their visit had something to do with Chaver B. He had seemed so pale and shaken upon seeing the officers, but I couldn't imagine what interest they would have in him. He'd only been in Canada such a short time, barely over a year.

The officers stood up as my dad entered the living room, and the three men shook hands cordially. "Dr. Adler," one of them began as they all sat down, "we are here to ask you about an acquaintance of yours, Dr. Jacob Greenberg."

"Jacob!" my father exclaimed, taken aback. "He's a good friend of mine and a fine fellow. We went to medical school together. But he no longer lives in Manitoba. He moved to Edmonton a few years ago."

"Yes, we know," they responded. "He has reapplied for his Alberta medical license, and during the process, his application was flagged because of concerns regarding affiliations with the Communist Party. Do you know anything about that?"

"Well, as university students we had attended one or two meetings of the Socialist Party, purely out of curiosity. Many of the students took a passing interest in it, but most of us weren't serious."

"Do you know if he has any ongoing affiliation with the Socialist or Communist Parties in Alberta?"

"None that I know of. We write to each other fairly regularly, and he's never mentioned it."

"May we see the letters he sent you?" one of the officers asked straightforwardly.

"I don't have them," replied my father unflinchingly and without delay. "I discarded them after I read them."

I thought this out of character for my father. He was extremely organized and rarely parted with anything. In our basement lay stacks of old *National Geographic* and *LIFE* magazines, just in case he wanted to look up an article he'd previously read or if Sammy and I needed pictures for a school project. There were tall, cylindrical, cardboard containers filled with used tin cans that he collected for unclear purposes, an old habit from his days of working in Zaidi Max's ironworks business. I thought of his two large wooden filing cabinets amidst all this organized clutter and was certain that if I looked under *J* for Jacob or *G* for Greenberg or even *L* for letters, I would find all the correspondence my dad had received from his friend, each letter chronologically and neatly filed, one after the other.

"Is there any particular concern, other than him attending a few meetings?" my father continued.

"We're not at liberty to say, but is there anything else you can tell us about Dr. Greenberg?"

My father launched into a glowing description of his friend, both as a decent, caring human being and as an outstanding physician who was constantly thinking of the well-being of his patients, even long after they had left his office.

The conversation continued for about fifteen minutes more, and then the officers left. Needless to say, we were all excited and somewhat agitated about what had transpired.

"What's the Socialist Party?" I asked my dad as soon as the front door closed behind them. I'd heard my parents discussing communism before, but socialism was a term I'd never previously heard.

"Socialism is a system where most institutions are owned and run by an elected government, rather than by individuals," he explained. "Socialists believe that this leads to more equal wealth among people. Some view it as a stepping stone to communism."

"Has it been around for a long time?"

"Socialism began in the middle of the nineteenth century with Karl Marx, a German philosopher, and many of the Jewish immigrants who came here from Eastern Europe were socialists and belonged to the Labour Movement. In fact, Peretz School was founded by people who were not just passionate about socialism, but who believed in social justice, too. Most of them spoke Yiddish and believed in a non-religious rather than religious form of Judaism. But not everyone who spoke Yiddish was a socialist. Although social justice remains an important part of Judaism, those socialist ideas have waned over the years. I don't know anyone today who would call themselves a pure socialist, and I definitely don't know any communists."

"But why are the RCMP so concerned?" I asked.

"Since the Second World War ended, many people believe that communists around the world are trying to stand in the way of democracy. The Canadian government is trying to find those people who they believe have communist leanings. As far as I'm concerned, it's all a witch hunt."

I hadn't known that Peretz School had been founded by social-ists and that Yiddish had been so intimately intertwined with their political philosophy. Then I recalled some of the songs we sang in choir expressing hope for a freer life and emphasizing that we are all brothers and sisters. I also remembered the spring of grade two when the entire school celebrated May Day, the workers' holiday, with a picnic and games in the schoolyard. At the time, it seemed odd even to me, because no one else in town was talking about the holiday. But daily life had been difficult in the Pale of Settlement, and there was so much disparity between rich and poor that I could easily understand how socialist and even communist ideals could have flourished there. But this is Canada. Things are different here, I reassured myself.

Chaver B had been so unnerved by the appearance of these representatives of the Canadian government that I wondered if that was his secret. Was he a covert communist, and did he attend clandestine meetings in the cellars and attics of people's homes, or perhaps even in remote farm buildings in out-of-the-way places? Is that how he spent his time? Is that why he came to Ambrosia, because of Peretz School's socialist founding principles? We called him Chaver B, the same way we greeted all our other male teachers. I always assumed that *Chaver* was just a warm salutation, indicating that he was more than just a teacher, but also a friend. But didn't Russians call each other *comrade*? Is that what *Chaver* referred to?

The arrival of the RCMP had been so unexpected and unsettling that we couldn't stop talking about it during dinner. My mother was quite frazzled in the kitchen, going through one drawer after another while searching for a specific platter and even forgetting to serve one of the dishes she'd prepared. Chaver B remained very quiet during the meal and didn't offer any of his political views or comment on the event at all. Clearly upset, almost dazed, he excused himself after dinner and didn't even stay for dessert. My parents apologized profusely for the disruption to our usually relaxed meal, and my mother gave him a package of food to take home.

"You can eat it tomorrow," she said.

The following Saturday, I spent the afternoon with Annie at her house. I wondered if Kenny would be there, and if he even noticed me when I was around. When I arrived, Annie's mom had gone out shopping, and Kenny was downstairs in their basement working on a school science project. Annie and I went up to her bedroom, and while I sat down on her pink bedspread, she went over to her white dresser and removed a polished walnut wooden box from the top drawer. She lifted the lid and proudly showed me the sea shells she'd collected from the beach over the summer. We chatted about the boys in our class and then looked through her selection of Nancy Drew mysteries. I was about to tell her about our unexpected visitors and Chaver B's strange reaction, but then I thought otherwise. Annie was a caring and sympathetic friend, but not always discreet. Plus, I wasn't sure exactly what I would say. Best not to tell her, I thought. At least, not yet.

"Want to play a game of Monopoly?" she asked me. "Maybe Kenny will play with us."

We walked downstairs and found Kenny lying on the living room sofa, reading one of the books assigned for his English class.

"*Animal Farm*," I said reading the title, as if I was parsing out each word. "By George Orwell. What kind of book is that for grade nine?" I asked. "Sounds kind of childish."

"It's an allegory," he said. "Do you know what an allegory is?"

"No, I don't," I confessed sheepishly. "What's it about?"

"It's about animals on a farm who overthrow their human masters and try to create a more just society where everyone is treated equally, like in the Communist Revolution of 1917. Only the system becomes corrupt. 'All animals are created equal, only some animals are more equal than others' eventually becomes their slogan. Although the intentions are honourable, in the end, it's hard to have a society where everything is divided equally. There will always be those people to whom greed and ambition are more important than altruism. It's human nature."

Kenny's account of *Animal Farm* gave me much to think about. For a brief period during the summer when Chaver B had rescued the Rosenzweigs from the burning bookstore and had spoken out at the town meeting afterwards, I could envision him as an activist who would struggle to improve the lot of the downtrodden, even at risk to his own life. But it still didn't all make sense to me. Chaver B would never devote his efforts to a system that was destined to be corrupt. And now that he was living in Canada, a country with so many riches and one that took care of its citizens, I was sure that he would no longer find communism a noble cause and would likely abandon it. Nevertheless, Chaver B *was* an enigma, and I wondered if with the arrival of the RCMP, I had inadvertently stumbled upon his secret, or if this unexpected encounter had only served to make things more complicated.

Part II

CHAPTER XVI

For man does not know his time. Like fish that are taken
in an evil net, and like birds that are caught in a snare,
so the children of man are snared at an evil time,
when it suddenly falls upon them.

—Ecclesiastes 9:11

The following week, I visited the library on my way home
from school and thumbed through the card catalogue to look
for books on communism. I found a biography of Karl Marx and
a thick volume on the history of the Bolshevik Revolution. The
librarian raised an eyebrow as she opened each book's cover and
stamped the due date on the blue card affixed to the first page. She
then gazed at me questioningly, I suppose wondering what they
were teaching us at Peretz School.

I studiously observed Chaver B in class, searching for any man-
nerisms or speech patterns that might link him to the communists. I wasn't sure exactly what I expected to find. An erect and
stiff posture I had not previously noticed? A tendency to use the
pronoun *we* rather than *I*? My observations, unfortunately, were
prematurely halted when Chaver B developed a bad cold. He

missed school on Thursday and Friday, and was too ill to join us for Friday night Shabbos dinner. Our principal, Chaver Lieberman, substituted for him in class, which was rather auspicious because he was directing us in the annual grade seven play, *Bontsha Shvayg*, or *Bontsha the Silent*, and he took unmitigated advantage of this opportunity to focus on the production.

Early Saturday afternoon, the smell of my mother's noodle *lockshn kugl* filled with apples and raisins drifted through the house. As if hypnotized by this wonderful aroma, I made my way to the kitchen hoping to taste some. When I walked in, my mother had just finished putting on her blue floral oven mitts, and was leaning over the oven and removing a large rectangular pan.

"Smells wonderful," I said. "Can I have some?"

"Of course," she replied as she placed the hot glass pan on the cake rack on the counter, took out a knife and metal spatula, and sliced me a piece. "When you're done eating, please take some over to Chaver B. He's not doing well. I brought him vegetable soup yesterday, but he barely touched it while I was there." She generously removed one-third of the warm kugl from the pan, much more than I'm sure he could eat, wrapped it in foil, and placed it in a covered tin.

"Bring him this, and try to get him to eat it for lunch," she said as she handed the tin to me. "His fever has broken, so Daddy says he's no longer contagious. He just needs to build up his strength. I'll telephone him to let him know you'll be coming."

I had no other plans for the afternoon, and I was happy to help out both my mom and Chaver B. I was also curious to see Chaver B's apartment, and viewed this as a marvellous opportunity. What secrets might I uncover there? Would I find pamphlets and literature about the Communist Party strewn about? Would a picture of Karl Marx or Lenin, whom I'd just read about, grace his walls? Feeling like Nancy Drew about to solve her next mystery, I put on my red coat, black boots, and maroon knit hat, and with my mother's kugl in hand, set out to visit him.

I climbed the stairs to Chaver B's small apartment over the drugstore downtown. I knocked softly on his door, then a little louder, but he did not come to open it, and I didn't hear any movement from inside. I gently turned the doorknob and was surprised to find the door unlocked. I slowly opened it and tentatively walked into his foyer. Within short order, I made a quick assessment of the surroundings.

His living room was neat and uncluttered but looked comfortable. My mother had previously informed me that most of his furnishings had been provided by the Hebrew Aid Society, collected from donations and garage sales. A brown velveteen sofa, a large, soft, black leather arm chair, and an oval coffee table rested on an oriental fringed rug. A wooden writing desk lay nestled in an alcove in the corner with a Venetian lamp sitting on its smooth, dark surface. The pale green walls were unadorned except for a single framed oil painting of Paris streets as seen through a drizzle: somber, muted, grey.

"Chaver B. It's Mira. Are you there?" I finally called out.

"Yes, yes, I'm here," he said weakly, "in the bedroom."

I walked towards the sound of his voice. His room smelled of menthol. A box of tissues and a glass of water sat on the nightstand. He was lying on top of his bedspread, wearing a loose brown sweater and a pair of dark grey trousers. He looked pale and drawn. His hair was disheveled, and his beard had started to grow out, which gave him a rough look, like Humphrey Bogart in *The Treasure of Sierra Madre*. How bizarre, I thought, to imagine him as a movie character, and a communist to top it off! He began to swing his legs over the side of the bed, as if to stand up, but I protested.

"Oh, no! Don't get up for me," I insisted. "I have strict orders from my mother to help you save your energy and get stronger. Would you like some of her delicious kugl?"

"Thank you, Miraleh. Under other circumstances I would, but I have no appetite."

"Well, then I'll make you a cup of tea."

"That would be lovely. With some honey, please. Let me show you where everything is."

"I don't do much in the kitchen," I admitted, "but one thing my mother taught me how to do was to make a cup of tea. I'm sure I can find what I need. I'll be right back."

The kitchen was small, so I didn't anticipate having trouble finding what I wanted. Everything was situated against one wall, and a kitchen table with four chairs stood under a window overlooking the back lane. It had never occurred to me before that Chaver B must have eaten most of his meals alone, and at times he was so taciturn that I couldn't imagine him entertaining guests.

I spied a copper kettle sitting on the stove. I filled it with water and lit one of the burners with a match I found in a box on the counter. While waiting for the water to boil, I walked towards the living room window overlooking the street to see who was walking around downtown, when I noticed some framed black-and-white photographs sitting on Chaver B's desk. There were three, to be exact. One was a portrait of a couple, a young man and woman who looked to be about nineteen or twenty years old. The woman was beautiful with large, dark, expressive eyes and with gently flowing dark waves cascading to her shoulders and framing her oval face. She wore an elegant light-coloured dress with a rounded neckline, long sleeves, and a lace bodice, and she held a bouquet of orchids in both hands. The man wore a suit and was also dark with a glint in his eye and the beginning of a smile on his face. They were standing next to each other, cheek to cheek, both gazing off into the distance, hopeful for what the future would bring them.

The second photo was of a young boy, about ten, fixing the chain on his bicycle that was turned upside down and was resting on its handlebars. The third photo was of a mother and father— about the same age as my parents—and of two young boys, ages three and nine, I guessed, lighting the nine-branched Chanukah menorah. The younger boy was standing on a chair so that he could reach the candelabrum. The *shamash*, the helper candle that stood above the rest, was clutched in his little fingers. His older brother's hand was clasped around his as together with the shamash, they lit the last of the eight candles, marking the final night of the holiday.

I was totally engrossed in these unexpected photos and hadn't heard Chaver B get out of bed, put on his slippers, and walk into the living room, until I felt his presence beside me. I quickly turned to look at him and unhesitatingly asked, "These are photos of you and your family, aren't they?"

"Yes," he replied in a voice barely louder than a whisper.

Where are they? I wanted to ask. Why do you never mention them? I screamed in my head. But I couldn't hold back. "My mother told me you didn't have any family. You said you didn't have a brother. What happened to them?" I finally blurted out.

He'd told me, more than once, that he had no photos of himself, that he had left them all behind in Europe. But the portrait on his desk was of him and his wife on their wedding day, I realized.

I glanced at the photo and then at him; I could see that he was a thread of what he once was. His physical features were the same—the same hair, the same eyes, the same nose and mouth—but now they created a different effect.

We stood facing each other, a silent struggle of the wills. I could be stubborn if I wanted to, although I don't recall Chaver B ever having seen that side of me before. As unforthcoming as he was, he must have had a defiant streak as well. If he wanted me to know about his past, surely he would have told me by now. I felt fire blazing in my eyes, but I didn't see any in his. Would he let me glimpse into his past life?

He stared at me intently; in retrospect, I realized that he was deliberating whether or not I had the fortitude to shoulder the weight of his confession. Or perhaps he was wondering if he should spare my waning childhood any burden it did not need to bear.

He stood in front of me, about three feet away, never averting his gaze. "I will tell you what happened," he finally relented. And therein began my journey through a doorway I wished I had never crossed.

Chaver B motioned me towards the sofa, and we sat down beside each other. I had longed to know his secret ever since I'd first met him, but despite my desire to learn more, I felt uneasy and apprehensive as I wondered what he would tell me.

I relived moments from the short time I'd known him. The shy teacher who was introduced to my class. The forlorn patient leaving my father's office. The solitary figure standing at the edge of the sunflower fields. The visit from the RCMP that had so unnerved him and almost sent him fleeing from our safe, comfortable home.

It was becoming clear to me that Chaver B was a wounded creature, but how deep were those wounds? I wondered.

"I was born in Prague in Czechoslovakia, to loving parents, much like yours," he began while turning towards me, his voice lighter than I had expected. "I had a brother, six years younger than myself. His name was Yosseleh, but we called him Yossi when he got older."

"What was Prague like?" I asked him, but then wondered if I should say anything at all or just let him tell me what he wanted to, at his own pace. It was obvious from his statement that Yossi was no longer alive. But Chaver B politely answered my question and resumed.

"Prague was a majestic city, a cultural center of Europe," he said wistfully, closing his eyes momentarily as if realizing a grander and happier time. "The famous Jewish writer, Franz Kafka, and the great composers, Dvorak and Smetana, all came from there. It was an architectural gem with splendid buildings, the Vltava River, and the Haradny castle looming above its banks." I, too, shut my eyes and imagined an elegant city teeming with intellectuals and aristocrats, ladies and gentleman dressed in finery and furs. "Prague had one of the largest Jewish communities in Europe," he went on. "It had six synagogues and even its own Jewish hospital. It was a wonderful place to grow up."

"What did your parents do?" I asked.

"My father taught mathematics at the university, and my mother, like most women, stayed home and raised my younger brother and me. We spoke Czech at home; we knew German, but we didn't converse in it. Unlike most Czech Jews, we even spoke some Yiddish in the confines of our own house. My father had learned it from his own father who had moved to Prague from

Poland, and he insisted that we carry on this tradition - even my mother. We celebrated the Jewish holidays, attended Jewish schools, *davened* in shul on the High Holidays, and ate only kosher food. But we were not religious."

"Just like my family," I interjected, finding comfort in the fact that despite growing up in different countries, our religious upbringings had been so similar.

"I started playing violin when I was four years old," he continued. "We had a violin at home; my grandfather had played, and after he died, my mother kept his violin in our glass bookcase in the front hall. One day, I took it out and began to explore it. Violin was a common instrument in Prague, and music was an important part of life among Jewish families, almost a way of life. I had watched enough people play violin at various family gatherings, so I was able to teach myself to play simple songs. After that, my parents arranged for me to have formal lessons. By the age of fifteen, I was playing with the Prague Philharmonic as a soloist, and my future as a violin virtuoso was almost certain."

I was not surprised by this admission. I had always believed that Chaver B must have been a wonderful violinist. Even at my lessons, despite his reserved manner, it was almost as though I could feel the music resonate in his soul, and I often wondered if at some point, it would burst forth from him. How frustrating it must be to teach me, I thought, and for him not to be able to play anymore.

"My family insisted that I complete my general education," he continued, "which I did, but as soon as I graduated from the gymnasium, what you call high school, I enrolled in the Prague Conservatory. My plan was to spend two years there and then study in Paris or Vienna."

He paused, then asked me, "Have you learned much about the Second World War in school?"

"Only a little here and there. You know, from the newsreels they show at the movie theatre. On Poppy Day we talk about the soldiers who fought for us. And Lererine Malka told us a little bit, also."

"Did she?" he sounded surprised. He hesitated and shifted in his seat. He looked downward, seemingly studying his hands that lay quietly in his lap, and then turned and looked towards the single painting hanging on his wall of a misty and gloomy Paris. "Well, let me teach you a little," he said after a minute as he returned his gaze to me, a gaze that was at once serious, sad, and deep.

"In October 1938, Nazi Germany took over the Sudetenland, the mountainous region of Czechoslovakia bordering Germany. We were all shocked. England, France, and Italy had betrayed us, giving Hitler the territory as part of the Munich Agreement that had been signed just a month earlier; they believed that it would halt Hitler's aggression, but it didn't. Five months later, the Nazis marched into the remainder of the Czech provinces and into Prague, and we became part of the German Reich. I remember standing on our balcony with Yossi and my parents, watching with trepidation as the Nazis with their shiny black helmets and dark grey uniforms marched in perfect step and rhythm down our street, their boots thumping as they hit the ground, my fellow citizens lining the roads, some shockingly raising their arms in the Nazi salute, 'Heil Hitler.'

"I can still hear my mother trying to reassure us. 'This can't last long,' she said, but I could tell from the sweat on her brow and the pallor of her complexion that she didn't necessarily believe this."

"How frightening!" I interrupted. I tried to imagine soldiers invading Ambrosia, marching along the street below us, as Chaver B and I watched from his window. "What did you do?"

"We carried on as normally as we could, trying to believe that this was just an aberration that would pass as quickly as it had been thrust upon us. By that time, I had met Dvorah, my future wife. We met at a party in my parents' home that my father gave annually to introduce the new university mathematics students."

Chaver B stood up and walked towards his desk. "She came from a small town in the countryside and was stunningly beautiful," he continued. He picked up the photograph of them on their wedding day and touched his hand to her face, his fingers outlining the contours of her eyes and lips. "These annual parties were gala events," he continued in a brighter voice, still looking at the photo that he held in his left hand, and at that instant I had the sense that he had just been transported to another world and had forgotten I was even there. "All the faculty were invited, and all the mathematics students. I noticed Dvorah as soon as she walked into our home. Her black hair was swept back and upwards revealing two ruby earrings outlined with pearls. I watched as she gracefully removed her burgundy coat and handed it to an attendant."

"She sounds lovely," I remarked dreamily.

"From the time I was thirteen, old enough to attend these parties, I eagerly anticipated them. A string quartet would play in the background. A fire would blaze in the marble fireplace, and waiters in black trousers, white shirts, and black bowties would pass around caviar on toast, vegetable dumplings, and mushroom canapés neatly laid out on silver trays.

"That evening I watched as Dvorah stood under the elaborate hanging chandelier in the foyer, seemingly bewildered by the elegant scene in front of her, the light highlighting her pale-blue satin dress, slender arms, and small waist, and glinting off the crystals in her necklace, as if it were a sign. Who is she? I must swoop in before someone else does, I remember thinking, and I quickly bounded up the two steps from the living room to where she stood and introduced myself.

'I'm Ari Bergman,' I said. 'Professor Bergman's son.'

'Oh, thank you for introducing yourself,' she said in a soft voice, while smiling nervously. 'I don't know many people here, and this is so much more extravagant than anything I've ever experienced before.'

'You're not from Prague then?' I asked her.

'No, I grew up in the town of Rokycany. My family still lives there. They wanted me to attend university, and when I was given a scholarship, they... well, we all thought I should go.'

'A scholarship to study mathematics! That is an achievement. How did you become so interested in this discipline?' I asked her.

'It just seemed to come naturally,' she answered shyly. 'Even though I lived in a small town, one of my teachers had a strong interest in math, and she encouraged me.'

'So, you will become a mathematician,' I recall nodding admiringly. 'Here, let us toast to that,' I suggested as I deftly lifted two glasses of wine off a silver tray from a passing waiter and handed her one. 'I can attest that it is a very honourable profession. *L'chaim,*' I said as I gently touched my glass to hers. 'And what do you say on such occasions? Cheers?'

'*L'chaim,*' she replied, head slightly bent forward to sip from her glass, but eyes lifted upwards to mine. 'Just as you do.' Our eyes locked for a moment, and we each smiled knowingly. 'I believe I've been rude,' she said while extending her hand towards me. 'My name is Dvorah. It's very nice to meet you.' I held her gloved hand in mine for a few moments and felt her delicate fingers beneath the soft cotton.

'And will I be seeing you in class?' she asked.

'No, actually I attend the Conservatory. I'm a violinist.'

'A violinist! Well, I guess then neither of us will become rich,' she pondered aloud as though she had just mapped out the rest of her life in front of her. And then we both laughed."

A nascent smile appeared on Chaver B's face. "I wish we had parties like that in Ambrosia," I interrupted. And then he started and suddenly turned and looked at me.

"Yes, yes," he muttered, sounding flustered, the incipient smile waning and his eyes blinking as if coming out of a dream.

"A year and a half later we were married," he continued in a more realistic tone. "During the wedding reception, I gave a speech and then played 'Salut d'Amour' for her. I couldn't think of a more fitting way to express my feelings. If my words had not been enough to articulate all my love for her, surely this song had."

At that moment I realized why it had been so difficult for him to teach me "Salut d'Amour" when he first gave me the piece. Why had he? I wondered. Had it been an attempt to conquer whatever demons were keeping him captive?

Chaver B paused for several seconds, again lost in his reverie, and I could see how much he missed her. He placed the photograph back down on his desk and continued in a matter-of-fact tone. "Since travel across Europe was no longer possible, I planned to pursue my studies in Czechoslovakia and considered myself fortunate to be surrounded by so many wonderful musicians who could elevate my playing."

Just then, the kettle whistled in the kitchen, a shrill high-pitched sound. "Oh, no! I forgot about your tea. Let me get it for you." As I jumped up from the sofa and rushed to the kitchen, I sensed that Chaver B was relieved to have this pause in our conversation. I opened the cupboard over the sink and found a white mug and a box of Red Rose tea. I placed the tea bag in the cup and poured in the steaming water. While letting it steep, I searched for the honey, which was harder to find.

I looked around the corner to the living room. Chaver B had sat down in his black leather chair. His head was resting against its back, and his eyes were closed. "Chaver B," I said gently. "I can't find the honey."

"It's on the counter on the left, by the wall," he quietly replied.

"I see it," I said. I opened the jar and took the teabag out of the mug. I poured a teaspoonful of the golden-brown viscous liquid into the tea, stirred it, and set it down on the coffee table in front of him.

"Thank you," he said and then took a few sips.

I sat back down on the sofa, anxious to know more about him and Dvorah, and to hear about his illustrious musical career. "And?" I asked.

He turned towards me and spoke softly, but his story was beginning to take on a darker and more sinister tone than I had expected. "After the Nazi occupation, things changed. All Jews had to register with the Reich. Even though all Czechs were given identification cards, Jews were given ID cards stamped with J for *Jude*. Big, bright yellow Stars of David were issued and had to be sewn on to every piece of our clothing, perfectly, without any loose edges. My mother made us always carry a needle and some thread in our pockets so that at any time we would be prepared to comply with the regulation. The stars were large and easily visible, and we knew that receiving and wearing them augured only worse things to come. We were no longer Czech," Chaver B declared. "We were different, and we were targeted for something, something incredibly evil."

I remembered seeing a photo of a *Chassid* with his long *payos* or sidecurls, dressed in his black *kapota* or coat, and fur hat, wearing a band on his upper arm with the Star of David clearly prominent. I remembered feeling terrified for the man in the photo. And now I felt terrified for Chaver B, and I felt terrified for myself, too.

"Soon after that, every Jewish proprietor had to give up his business to a German. Even our bank accounts had to be surrendered.

"Pets were consigned to collecting centres. We had a beautiful golden retriever, Moishie. My parents had given him to me for my fourteenth birthday. He was a bona fide member of the family, who loved us unconditionally, and hardly a family photograph was taken without him being in it. But it was hard to keep a pet hidden, and penalties for disobeying were severe."

"Did you have to give him away?" I asked. I'd never had a pet, but I knew how much Annie's family doted on Fido.

"Yes," he said sadly. "Notices to bring in all animals were posted on buildings, and word spread quickly. My father and I put Moishie's leash around him and walked with him towards the collecting centre. I'm sure Moishie thought he was just going for his daily stroll. We entered the building, filled out a form listing our names and addresses and Moishie's name, and were given a receipt. 'We'll let you know when you can pick him up,' the officer said dispassionately. 'Bring this receipt with you.' A collar with a number was fastened around Moishie's neck. 'Take him to cage one-seven-four,' the officer ordered, pointing towards the corner of the room on the left.

"We walked down the rows of cages already filled with dogs, cats, and birds of various breeds, sizes, and colours. Moishie's cage rested on a table and looked much too small for him, but he was so obedient and so trusting that when we put him inside, there were no whimpers of protest. I'm sure he could never have fathomed that we would ever abandon him or do anything to harm him.

"I felt as though I was giving up my best friend. I put my arms around his thick body and buried my head in his lustrous, golden brown fur, but he only panted and searched my face with his large, moist tongue. As I hugged him, tears cascaded down my cheeks and mixed with the wetness of his nose, until a guard walked by, yanked me away, and abruptly slammed the cage door shut."

"How awful!" I exclaimed.

"Up until that point, I had never experienced so much pain. The guards virtually pushed my father and me out of the building. We knew we would never see Moishie again, that the receipt was a ruse to keep the truth from us. Once outside, I leaned my back against the building, doubled over in grief, and slid down to the cold ground. I felt as though I was being pulled into a vortex, that I was spinning and spinning, around and around, and there was no getting out. My tears would not stop.

'*Vos ken men ton?*' I remember my father repeating over and over again. What can we do? At last, he placed his arms around my shoulders and hoisted me to my feet. '*Kum, lomir aheym geyn,*' he said. We staggered down the street towards home, each supporting the other, his arm around my shoulders and mine around his waist."

Chaver B stood up and began circling his living room, his pace gradually quickening as he recounted one injustice after another. He had seemed calm when he initially started recounting his story, but I detected an ever-growing anxiety in his voice as he provided me with more and more details. "The restrictions continued to come. We were ordered to bring all radios to a centralized location. Not having a radio was a great loss, for then it became difficult to get the news. We'd been able to gain some information from listening to the radio, and our friends had gotten access to the BBC on short wave and relayed to us what they had heard.

"People, that is, Gentiles—non-Jews—were not allowed to speak to us. Some of my old teachers from the gymnasium would pass me on the street, their faces tense and guarded; they would avert their gaze and not even give me a glimmer of recognition rather than risk imprisonment or other retributions. It felt so horrible, and I felt dirty."

Chaver B's voice rose and fell as he continued, and my eyes fixated on his every movement. He seemed to be consumed by a nervous energy, and given his illness, I wondered if I should order him to sit down and rest, but I was too drawn to his story to interrupt, as lurid a tale as it was becoming. "Ration cards were distributed, and we were only allowed to go into certain shops at certain times, usually at the end of the day, when most of the shelves were empty. Curfew was eight in the evening. We couldn't attend concerts or go to cinemas or cafés, either. Shops and restaurants posted signs that read, 'Jews not wanted,' or worse yet, 'Dogs and Jews not welcome.'"

"How terrible!" I volunteered empathetically. As he spoke, I tried to picture Prague in my mind, and at the same time, I imagined similar events going on in Ambrosia, like being barred from the library or the movie theatre.

Chaver B walked over to the coffee table and picked up his mug. He looked thoughtful as he drank the healing liquid, but I wondered if at that moment he was deciding how much more he should impart to me. Finally, he resumed at a more measured pace. "Our friends and acquaintances were being randomly arrested on the street without explanation. We couldn't stop and talk to anyone. Mr. and Mrs. Karos, our Gentile neighbours in the apartment next to us, were kind enough and brave enough to help us get food after hours. One evening, Mrs. Karos knocked on the door. She whispered to my mother, 'Take these quickly. Don't ask questions,' as she handed us a basket of cakes from the bakery, milk, and some apples.

"But others spied on us and reported illegal activities. As more and more Germans entered Prague, Jewish people were ordered to move to a special section of the city, a ghetto, but without fences. Dvorah and I moved with my parents and Yossi. Our new apartment was much smaller than what we were used to and had only one bedroom, a small kitchen, and a living room, but we were grateful that we were still allowed to travel outside the district, albeit only on certain streets."

Chaver B turned in my direction, but he seemed to look right through me, to some point beyond me; his forehead furrowed and his eyes narrowed, as if he were trying to solve a puzzle.

"They chipped away at our lives, dismantling them bit by bit. Soon we couldn't own or use cameras, typewriters, phonographs, or musical instruments. Later, telephones were forbidden and even newspapers. Educated people, including my father, lost their jobs. Jewish children were expelled from German and Czech schools, and then all Jewish schools were forced to close. We all pitched in teaching Yossi what we could at home."

Chaver B became increasingly agitated, and his hands trembled. I thought more seriously of telling him to stop, but before I could say anything, he began again, and I was carried along with his memories, like being propelled by the swift current of a deep and dark river. "Every door was closing. Works by Jewish composers were forbidden; Schoenberg, Mendelssohn, and Mahler vanished from radio broadcasts and concert halls. It was even considered illegal to play Czech patriotic music. Jewish musicians couldn't perform, and not just because our instruments had been confiscated. I turned in one of my violins and hid the other, but to play publicly would have been a major offense."

"Did you play anyway?"

"Sometimes I played at home. Dvorah and Yossi would stand guard for me at the window and let me know if anyone was approaching below. But I could never play with a full sound, so I usually just ran my fingers along the fingerboard and pretended I was holding a bow with my other hand.

"For a while, I secretly met other musicians in their apartments and performed. It was against orders, but we were young and brave, or I suppose we thought we were. We would stagger our arrivals and stay overnight to avoid suspicion and comply with the curfew. But after a while, this seemed too dangerous. Some of my friends were bold enough to take off their stars, leave the ghetto, and play in clubs under a pseudonym, but I never did that."

"Did you and your family ever think of leaving Prague?" I asked him.

"Yes, that thought had crossed our minds. Those of us who had enough money and foresight were able to escape to Palestine and even South America, but by the time my family appreciated the extreme gravity of the situation, it was too late. We were caught in a trap, and the noose was becoming ever tighter around our necks."

CHAPTER XVII

Im eyn ani li, mi li,
Uch sheh ani l'atzmi li, ma ani
V'im loh achshav, matai?

If I am not for myself, who will be for me?
But when I am only for myself, what am I?
And if not now, then when?

—Rabbi Hillel, *Pirkei Avot* 1:14

Chaver B didn't look well. His face had become even paler, and he sighed as he sat down in his leather chair. "I think the lesson is over for today," he said. "It's time for me to rest."

I was relieved that he had decided to stop. This was too much information for me to assimilate, but I was more worried about him. "Will you be okay alone?" I asked. "Can I get you something before I leave?"

"I will be fine," he replied unconvincingly, but I didn't know what else I could do to help him. "And I have your wonderful cup of tea," he added as he lifted it up into the air, trying to reassure me.

"Please thank your mother for me, and thank you for bringing me her kugl."

As I walked home, I tried to absorb what Chaver B had related to me. Clearly his story was not finished, and I could easily assume that things had only gotten worse for him.

When I arrived home, my mother asked, "Did Chaver B eat anything?"

"He just drank a cup of tea," I said.

"What is one to do with him?" she bemoaned, shaking her head from side to side. "I'll have Daddy visit him tomorrow."

Chaver B didn't return to school until the following Wednesday, but I had to admit that in the meanwhile, we had a lot of fun with Chaver Lieberman as we prepared for our play, *Bontsha the Silent*, written by Itzhak Leyb Peretz, our school's namesake. The play was to be performed in Yiddish, and Chaver Lieberman was in his element. He had performed in the Yiddish theatre in Winnipeg and was more than happy to share his dramatic skills with us.

Chaver Lieberman was slight in stature. He had an olive complexion, black hair that was slicked back from his forehead and fixed in place with Brylcreem or some similar concoction, and remarkably straight white teeth. He arrived at school everyday sporting a bowtie of a variety of different colours and geometric patterns – some solid but others with stripes or polka dots. He always seemed to be in motion and was what one would call excitable. He frequently talked with his hands, as my mother would say, embellishing each conversation with a curl of the wrist or a flourish of his arm, and every day of rehearsal saw him become more and more animated. Chaver B helped us translate the Yiddish text and memorize our lines, but he said he would leave the "theatrics" up to Chaver Lieberman.

Bontsha Shvayg was the tale of a poor, luckless man who bore his trials with dignity, never complaining or asking, "Why me?" Every milestone that marked his life, even his death, passed in silence on Earth. According to the story, even the piece of wood that marked his grave was blown away by the wind and used by the gravedigger's wife to build a fire to boil potatoes for that night's dinner.

After his death, however, Bontsha ascended to heaven where he was anything but unnoticed. His arrival was heralded with great fanfare, and he was received by shofars trumpeting, a chorus of angels, and by the Judge himself. I was given the role of Bontsha's defending angel, having to argue before the Judge why Bontsha merited the finest of honours, even though it was a foregone conclusion that he would receive them.

The play was to be performed in late November at one of the Friday night gatherings called *Freitag tsu nacht*. These were regular Friday night get-togethers where adults would read and discuss one of the *Pirkei Avot*, also known as Ethics or Sayings of the Fathers, talk about upcoming events and important news, and then partake in refreshments. Richard Gold, the smartest boy in the class who all the teachers agreed had wisdom beyond his years, introduced the play.

The auditorium fell silent as Richard explained, "Tonight the grade seven class will be performing the play *Bontsha Shvayg*. This play represents one of the many gifts we have received from our Jewish education, an education that has stressed *mentshlechkayt* or citizenship. We are always reminded to 'Do unto others as you would have them do unto you,' a saying from one of our great philosophers, Rabbi Hillel."

"*Er iz geven a groyser mentsh,*" one of the guests bellowed as he clapped his hands. He was a great man.

"*Sha, shtil!*" reprimanded Mrs. Moskowitz. "*Mir darfn hern vos Richard vet zo*gn." We need to hear what Richard has to say.

"*Unshuldik mir,*" replied the man apologetically.

"We have spent seven years learning the Yiddish language—the *Mameh-loshn,* or mother tongue," Richard continued unflustered. "Over the centuries, as Jewish people in the diaspora moved from one country to another, it became a collection of words from these different lands, a language that transcended geography and served to unify a people who were already united in so many ways.

"But Yiddish, it is more than just a language," he said as he glanced around the room at the members of the audience who were clearly moved by his precocious eloquence. "It speaks of history, culture, and traditions. It's a musical language. You don't really speak Yiddish; you sing it. It's an onomatopoeic language; some words, like *kvetsh, nebesh, shlimiel, mushugeh,* and *oy vey,* barely require and sometimes even defy translation. It's a comfortable language that you can sink into like a soft chair or wrap yourself in like a warm coat. Unlike Hebrew, it makes no claims of being the language of God. It is the language of the common man."

He paused. "Tonight's play is about one such common man. We will now take a short break following which the grade seven class will present *Bontsha Shvayg.*"

We went to the classrooms and put on our costumes. They were simple: white robes and silver slippers for the angels and a golden bejewelled cloak for the Judge. Bontsha himself was dressed in rags. To denote my important role as Bontsha's defending angel, I wore a white crown with gold trim atop my smooth brown hair.

Annie and I nervously chattered to each other as we changed. The stark whiteness of Annie's robe against her pale, heart shaped face, dark eyes, and long, shiny black curls, made her look like a goddess. I examined myself in the mirror, wondering if I had that same radiant glow.

I'd grown more than five inches in the past year and was now five foot four inches tall; my arms and legs felt long and gangly. I adjusted my robe on my shoulders, but that feeling of awkwardness did not leave me. I moved closer to the mirror to inspect my eyes. That night they looked more grey than green; I wondered if that meant something.

Chaver Lieberman gave us a five minute warning, and my mind quickly turned back to the play. The important thing was to look confident, I said to myself. I stood up straight with my chin slightly raised, a stance befitting an angel with such an important job, I presumed, and walked with the rest of my class to the backstage area. We were all jittery and excited, whispering and chattering to each other. Annie took my hand in hers and squeezed it. "You'll be great," she said reassuringly, and then we both giggled.

Suddenly, Chaver B shushed us. Richard Gold was playing Father Abraham, and Chaver Lieberman directed him to move to the middle of the stage. The lights in the auditorium dimmed, and the dark-red velvet curtains opened as the voices in the audience gradually quieted. One by one, the angels in heaven hurried across the stage speaking to Father Abraham. "Did you hear? Bontsha Shvayg is coming."

"Bontsha?" said Abraham.

"You don't know?" they asked incredulously. "Bontsha has died."

When Bontsha appeared on stage, Father Abraham stretched

out his arms to greet him and embrace him. The angels, twittering with delight, encircled him, and two of them carried over a golden throne for Bontsha to sit upon and a golden crown with sparkling jewels for his head. Bontsha stood in silence, his mouth agape, eyes wide open, his face a mixture of fear and amazement. His day of judgment had arrived, and he was overwhelmed with the reception he was receiving. The court assembled, and his trial began.

I stood behind a podium to argue my case. "Your honour," I began calmly. "Here is a man who complained neither against God nor against man. His sufferings were inconceivable, yet his heart never knew hatred."

"I want facts, not interpretation. I'm not interested in flowery eloquence," the Judge called out.

"Yes, your honour," I said and began speaking more emphatically. "When Bontsha was only thirteen, his mother died. His life was taken over by a vile creature—his stepmother! In the biting cold, in the depths of winter, she forced him to chop wood outside his house, *borves*, barefoot, until his feet became as white as the driven snow and as numb as the heart of the witch who ordered him about. But he remained silent. He never complained, not even to his father.

"He did not raise his voice," I went on, my voice crescendoing with each point I made. "He had no friends; his constant companion was loneliness. He never went to school. He never knew one moment of freedom."

"Never mind the fancy rhetoric," the prosecuting angel objected.

"His father was a *shikker*, a drunkard. One night, he grabbed Bontsha by the hair and threw him out of the house into the frozen, snow," I declared dramatically, grabbing at the air with my hands and making a sweeping gesture as Bontsha's father would have done at that moment of callous baseness. "But despite his hunger, he was always silent and begged only with his eyes."

I heard people in the audience quietly sniffling at this sadness as I continued describing all the hardships of Bontsha's life in vivid detail, arguing his case passionately and fervently. "He remained silent when he was cheated, and he remained silent on his death-bed, despite his pain. He lay in complete loneliness on his cot, abandoned by his nurse and by his doctor, as he did not have the pennies to pay them. He was silent in that terrible moment just before he was about to leave this earth, and he was silent in that very moment when he finally did leave." I paused for several seconds, as if to give people a chance to say a *brochah*, a blessing. "Your Honour, I rest my case."

I felt relieved that my part was over. Now it was the prosecuting angel's turn. "Ladies and Gentlemen," he began in a harsh voice. "Ladies and Gentlemen," he repeated, this time with less bitterness. "Ladies and Gentlemen," he stated again in a softer tone, clearly overwhelmed by Bontsha's suffering. "Bontsha was always silent. Now, I too will be silent."

The angels murmured in astonishment amongst themselves, their voices waning as the Judge cleared his throat. "Bontsha, my child," he said with tenderness. "You never understood your sleeping strength. Here in Paradise, the world of truth, your silence will be rewarded. For you there is everything! Everything is yours."

Finally, Bontsha spoke. "Really?" he asked, doubtful and embarrassed.

"Really," the Judge answered. "I tell you. Everything in Paradise is yours. Choose! Take whatever you want!"

"Really?" Bontsha asked again, this time with more confidence.

"Really, really," the angels chanted in unison.

"Well, then," Bontsha said, smiling for the first time. "Well then, what I would like, Your Excellency, is to have every morning for breakfast, a hot roll with fresh butter."

A deep silence fell upon the stage. Slowly, the Judge and angels lowered their heads and sighed in disbelief. Suddenly the silence was shattered as the prosecuting angel laughed—a long, loud, caustic laugh.

The curtains were closed, and the audience applauded. The curtains were opened again, and we bowed. And then everyone went to take refreshments.

Despite our discussions in class, I found the play perplexing. Bontsha seemed both laudable and lamentable in his humility, and I struggled to reconcile this dichotomy. Was Bontsha so simple that he couldn't even imagine what riches he could have requested? Or was he so knowing that he knew that even simple things could warm the soul? Or had he been so physically impoverished that a warm roll with butter was, for him, equivalent to diamonds and rubies? These were all interesting possibilities, but why had he been so passive in life? Was he just tolerant, which is a virtue, or so weak that he could not stand up for himself?

While I was pondering these questions, a voice echoed in my head, a faint voice emanating from the inner sanctums of my mind, a voice that gradually crescendoed as it inexorably carried me back to the ice cream store in Winnipeg. I was five years old again, standing in front of the ice cream case and holding my father's hand, looking up and listening to the woman behind the counter urging me, almost commanding me to fight for what I wanted. "You should get what you want," she had admonished me, her words reverberating like a rallying call to arms.

The meaning of the play finally dawned on me. I knew at that moment that if ever I saw injustice towards myself or others, I would not be complacent and accepting like Bontsha was. I knew that I would not let it pass by unquestioningly in silence and that I would stand up to whatever iniquity confronted me. I would fight for what I wanted and for what I believed was right. What I did not know was that this would not always be easy. And as bad as his life was, there were and always would be injustices far worse than what Bontsha had endured.

CHAPTER XVIII

O, ir kleyneh lichtelech, ayereh geshichtelech,
Vekn oyf mayn peyn.
Tif in harts bavegt es zich, un mit trern fregt es zich,
Vos vet itster zayn?

Oh, you lights of mystery, you retell your history,
Your tales are tales of pain.
My heart is filled with fears, my eyes are filled with tears,
"What now?" says the haunting refrain.

—Chanukah song

As the days shortened, our town underwent a transformation. Evergreen trees with their elongated green foliage appeared in store windows and in our neighbours' homes. Adorned with trinkets and baubles, they were so exquisite and captivating, that I secretly envied this Christmas tradition.

Each night at five o'clock, the streets became ablaze with lights that stretched above the roads in colourful configurations and designs. As a young child, I had thought that some unseen being, perhaps Oz or God himself, must be visiting our community to perform such magic. But when I turned six, my father explained that it was just a worker at the electric company who had turned some switches.

The holiday Chanukah was late that year and came one week before our winter vacation. Our play had been such a resounding success that the director of the Old Folks Home asked us to perform it for the residents as part of their holiday concert. We were all excited to have this opportunity to revive our roles. We performed on a Wednesday afternoon and were equally as thrilled to miss an afternoon of class.

After the performance, I returned to school to pick up my history book, *Builders of the Old World*, that I had forgotten to take home the day before and that I needed for homework. School was still in session, and as I walked down the empty hallway, I glanced at the classrooms that I passed. Mrs. Moskowitz was standing at the front of her class, writing a lesson on the blackboard, while her students' heads bobbed up and down like ducklings in the water as they read what she had written and then copied it down in their notebooks. Mrs. Walker was sitting at her desk and reading her students a story, but I couldn't hear or see which one it was. Chaver B had come back also, and by the time I arrived, he was sitting at his desk in our empty classroom and sorting papers for the next day's class.

"Hi, Chaver B," I called to him as I walked into the room.

"Shalom, Mira. Did you forget something?" he asked pleasantly.

"Just a book for homework," I replied.

A menorah stood on the bookcase by the window, with the shamash and three candles waiting to be lit. I glanced back at Chaver B as he was placing his papers in neat piles, and I remembered the photo on the desk in his apartment of two young boys holding the shamash, the older boy's hand clutching the younger's little fingers in his as if they were one.

Ever since we'd first performed the play, the images of Bontsha and Chaver B kept merging in my mind. Perhaps Bontsha Shvayg was more than just a fictional character. Was Chaver B a modern day Bontsha, I wondered, suffering in silence, just like Bontsha had? After what he'd confided to me in his apartment, I'd wanted to learn more about his past, but my parents only brushed my questions aside, and I hadn't had another opportunity to ask Chaver B either.

I walked over to my desk in the second to last row and opened the top to retrieve my history book. As I was removing it, I looked up and asked hesitantly, "Chaver B, is now a good time for another history lesson?"

He slowly raised his head and looked at me, his face suddenly taking on a vacant expression, as though he had erased all of his emotions with a blink of his eye. "What would you like to know?" he asked me in a flat voice.

"What happened next," I answered. "After the Nazis imposed all those restrictions."

He stared at me. I didn't know if he would share anything more with me or not.

"Mira, I've told you enough," he stated somewhat sternly, but he wasn't convincing in his opposition. I sensed that perhaps he wanted to divulge more, that by telling me, he felt he might be able to relieve himself of an internal burden.

"I know there's more," I argued. "I want to know," I asserted, trying to replicate the same tone of voice I had used as Bontsha's defending angel. "And I will learn these things soon enough, anyway. After all, I'm almost thirteen," I added, although my birthday was still six months away.

He opened a book on his desk and began absently turning the pages; his ambivalence was palpable. He sighed deeply and finally spoke tentatively and slowly, and almost with a sense of bewilderment.

"Things got worse. We didn't think that things could get worse, but they always seemed to." He paused for several moments and then began again. "Suddenly, transports were being organized in Prague. A thousand people at a time were loaded onto trains and sent to 'the East,' but no one knew exactly to where. The Germans decided to convert the Czech town of Terezin, a garrison town, into a place of Jewish settlement and named it Theresienstadt, and some transports were sent there. It was presented to the world as an independent city for the Jews, but that was all illusion and propaganda. At least it was less of a mystery than 'the East' and was on Czech soil. But we all lived under the threat of transport to somewhere, and everyone knew that it was inevitable."

As he spoke, I sat down in the desk in the front row opposite him, never removing my gaze from his enigmatic face and impenetrable eyes. He turned towards the window and then spoke softly and with a sense of resignation as he once more looked at me.

"Once we registered with the Reich, we were reduced to numbers, not names. Early on, my parents and brother received notice that their numbers had come up and that they were on an early transport to some unknown destination. We didn't know to where. Because Dvorah and I were married, we had registered separately and were not given notice. We helped them pack the few items they were allowed to take and tried to buoy their spirits. I refused to even think that we might never see each other again. My heart broke for Yossi. He was only fourteen and looked terrified. I felt helpless. We talked about escaping or hiding, but time was short, and there was no one to help us. We should have thought of those things before, but our inability to fathom the unfathomable had prevented us from doing so.

"My father showed me where he had hidden some money, behind a stack of plates in one of the kitchen cupboards, in a hole in the wall concealed by a thin layer of plaster.

'Should I take anything else besides bedding and clothing?' Yossi asked me.

'I think they said not to,' I answered. Trying to sound light-hearted and optimistic, I added, 'I'm sure they'll have whatever you need.'

"I had cried so much for Moishie. With my parents and Yossi, I refused to believe I might never see them again. Or perhaps my heart was already becoming hardened.

'Don't come with us to the station,' my mother insisted. 'It is safer here. You don't need to be swept along with everyone else.'

'Tateh, Mameh,' I whispered as I placed my arms around my parents and embraced them for a long time. I turned to Yossi, tall and thin, still a boy growing into manhood, and gave him a fierce, tight hug, so tight that I could feel his heart beating against my chest and his body quivering as he bravely tried to hold back his tears.

'We will be here when you get back,' I reassured him as I looked at his downcast eyes and kissed him on the forehead. 'If not, l'shana habaah b'yerushalaim.' Next year in Jerusalem.

"Dvorah and I held the door open for them as they fumbled with their luggage before firmly gripping it, as they left the apartment and walked towards the staircase, as they turned to look at us again with their serious, grave faces before descending. They looked so weary, and their journey had not yet even begun. When we heard them reach the bottom floor, we raced to the window.

We watched them join the others, all going to some unknown place. Then they turned, looked up at us, and gave us a final wave."

"Were you able to find out where they were sent?" I asked.

"Eventually, but not right away," he replied.

"What about you?" I quickly added. "Were you able to spend the rest of the war in Prague?"

"No. I suppose that would have been good. It couldn't have been worse than what awaited us. We were safe for a while, but eventually came Dvorah's and my turn, along with her parents who had moved to Prague believing that they would be safer there than in the countryside.

"One afternoon, while at home in our apartment, we heard a faint knocking. We lived on the third floor of our building, and the knocking seemed to be coming from the first floor. It gradually became louder and louder until we heard heavy footsteps in the hallway outside our apartment and then three loud knocks on our door. We stood frozen, wondering if we should open the door or not. We stared at each other, barely breathing, but before we could decide what to do, a pink sheet of paper floated under our door into our foyer, and the knocking had already moved on to our neighbour's door and was fading into the distance.

"I ran to the window overlooking the street and saw Nazi officers going in and out of the buildings on our block, moving from one building to the next. Dvorah slowly and tentatively walked over to the pink slip and picked it up. Our 'numbers' were emblazoned on the top of the paper followed by instructions ordering us to appear two days later at a large warehouse near the train station. We could bring up to fifty kilos of belongings, including clothes, bedding, and some food. The same instructions that were given to my parents and Yossi. Perhaps we were going to the same place. I could only hope."

"Where did they send you?" I asked, eager to learn what followed.

"We were sent to Theresienstadt. The train ride took only a few hours, and we rode in regular train cars with comfortable seats. For those few hours, things seemed almost normal with the country-side flashing by us as we drove past forests and meadows under a blue sky dappled with clouds.

"When we arrived, we were processed into the ghetto, a city that normally held seven thousand people but that had a population of sixty thousand by the time we came. We were assigned to our barracks—our living quarters—and every room was filled to capacity, twelve, sometimes fifteen to a single small space."

At this point, Chaver B seemed surprisingly calmer than when I had visited him in his apartment. Perhaps the outcome had not been as bad as I'd feared.

"Were Yossi and your parents there, as you had hoped?"

"As soon as we arrived, Dvorah and I checked with the Jewish Council of Elders, the group that was our main liaison with the Nazis. They maintained lists of all those who had arrived and departed, but my parents and Yossi had not been sent there."

Just then, Chaver Lieberman gave three quick knocks on the half-open door and peered around it into the classroom. "I couldn't wait to tell you," he said while opening the door farther and walking inside, "that I just got off the phone with the director of the Old Folks Home." He raised both his hands in the air in front of him and then spread them to either side as if waving apart the Red Sea. "Everyone loved the play!" he announced excitedly. "Mira, you should be an actress, and if not, you'd make a fine lawyer," he added as he patted me on the shoulder.

"You did a fine job with the students. *Mazel tov,*" Chaver B complemented him. "The praise is well-deserved."

"Well, I just wanted to share the good news with you," he added, and as he turned around and virtually skipped out of the room, he reminded me of an ecstatic Fido when chasing a ball on Annie's skating rink. As the sound of his footsteps receded down the hallway, I quickly posed Chaver B a question before he had a chance to prematurely end his narrative for the day.

"What was life like in Theresienstadt?" I asked.

"Czechoslovakia was full of many fine musicians and composers who had been deported to Theresienstadt and who kept their music alive in the ghetto," he replied easily. "We began by surreptitiously singing in the evenings in the upper floors of our barracks. Then a piano was discovered in a cellar when some of the men were sent down to haul up sacks of potatoes. Some of us had smuggled in instruments that the guards hadn't noticed when they rummaged through our luggage on arrival. I'd taken my violin apart and hidden it in my suitcase, then glued it back together when I knew it would be safe. We would sneak into the cellar and play. But the Germans also liked their music and didn't object to our musical indulgences. In fact, they encouraged them. There was never enough food or medicine, but somehow they managed to get instruments for us."

"Where did the instruments come from?" I asked curiously.

"Some were brought in from neighbouring communities. But others came from a synagogue in Prague that the SS had set aside to be a future museum for all the confiscated instruments from Europe. And they ordered instruments to be sent to us from there."

"Don't you think it was odd that they would have stored all those beautiful instruments in a synagogue?" I asked him. "After all, they didn't even like us."

"I agree," he said. "It is ironic that they would have chosen our place of worship to be a sanctuary for these treasures. But their love of music only benefitted us. We performed; we composed. There were chamber music groups, an orchestra, a jazz band, an opera, and a theatre. Even children had their own choir, and an opera was written especially for them. If things remain as they are, I can survive, I remember thinking.

"Not just Czechs were sent to Theresienstadt," Chaver B went on. "People arrived from Germany, Austria, the Netherlands, and Denmark, and many of them were excellent musicians, too. But even Theresienstadt wasn't safe. People came in and people went out; people arrived and people left, some to Latvia, some to Minsk, but most to Auschwitz, we later learned. But at the time, no one knew to what nebulous place the transports were destined. It was all a secret."

"Auschwitz. What's that?" I wondered aloud.

Chaver B paused and looked at me with an odd expression, a mixture of disgust, pain, and stupefaction, and then he turned away.

"Auschwitz was a camp in Poland, what the Nazis called a concentration camp. They would bring prisoners there, mostly Jews, but also other people whom they considered undesirable. There was secret information from the outside about how the Nazis crowded hundreds of people into large shower rooms, filled the rooms with gas, and then left them there until they all died."

I gasped in horror and shock. I remembered Lererine Malka alluding to rumours of horrible things that happened in the camps. But she had survived, and so had Chaver B. I swallowed hard. "Were the rumours true?" I asked Chaver B, barely being able to express my words as my throat became dry and constricted.

"Were the rumours true?" he echoed. "We didn't know, but everyone who was sent away hadn't returned. They all seemed to have been swallowed up."

We sat silently. I stared at him as if waiting for an explanation. But although he was looking in my direction, he seemed to be gazing at some distant point.

"Did you ever figure out how they decided who would be sent away on the trains?" I asked.

"It didn't matter who we were. No one seemed immune. That summer, over one thousand Jewish children taken by the SS during the destruction of the Bialystok ghetto in Poland were brought to Theresienstadt, and fifty residents were chosen to be their caregivers. But less than two months later, they were all deported to 'the East,' too, and were never seen again."

Chaver B's voice drifted off, and he seemed mystified by what he had just articulated. I felt sick, tremulous, and sweaty. Chaver B hadn't said so exactly, but all those children must have been killed. His tale was becoming more sordid and more macabre. A true tale noir. I hadn't ever imagined such evil. I wasn't sure I wanted him to go on, but before I could say something, he continued.

"One day, Dvorah and her parents received their orders; they were to appear on the train platform within twenty-four hours and to bring only a few belongings. I don't know how it happened, that she would have received a slip but not me. As with my parents and brother, but this time more forcefully, I begged her not to go and tried to persuade her to hide or escape with me.

'I can't,' she said. 'If we disappear, they will harm my parents. They're too old and weak to run away with us, and I can't leave them behind.'

"I spoke to the Elders. 'There is nothing we can do,' they informed me. 'Once a name is on the list, it cannot be removed, mistake or not. Too many questions will be asked, and it won't bode well for us.'

'Then put me on the list, also,' I insisted. 'They might be upset about missing one person, but I doubt if they would care if there was another.'

"When I told Dvorah that I would be going with her, she was adamant that I stay behind. She wept and pleaded with me, even made me try to believe that we would meet again if I was placed on another transport, or when this stupid war was finally over. But I wouldn't give in. I would rather have died than live without her. And she was carrying our child. I couldn't leave her alone."

Had Chaver B had a child, like Lererine Malka? But my thoughts were interrupted as he continued.

"We arrived at the train station at seven o'clock in the evening, as directed. They made us stand on the platform all night, counting and recounting us, so as not to lose a single person. Finally we were herded onto train cars, not the relatively comfortable cars that had brought us to Theresienstadt, but cattle cars that were locked and bolted from the outside. They crammed almost one hundred fifty of us into each car. If you were lucky, there was one window with bars on it. We stood most of the way. There were two buckets at either end that functioned as latrines. The only food and water were what we'd brought with us."

I was thinking. Please stop! But at the same time, I wanted to know more. I felt myself recoiling inside, then being pulled back to the story as if I were tethered to it by a string. As Chaver B described his journey, it seemed as though I was the one on the train, but on a runaway train that was gaining momentum and that I didn't have the ability to stop.

"After more than thirty hours, the train slowed as we approached our destination," he went on. "It was almost nightfall when we arrived, but through the small window we could see the dreaded sign of Auschwitz: *ARBEIT MACHT FREI.* Work Sets You Free."

"So, the rumours were true," I unwillingly concluded. "Auschwitz was a real place after all." I paused, then fearfully asked in a hushed voice, "Was it as bad as they said?"

Chaver B didn't answer my question right away but just nodded his head in affirmation. "When the train stopped, thin, almost phantom-like men wearing loose, striped uniforms came in to get us. One of them was Czech and told us to eat our food right then and there because we wouldn't see our belongings again. Then dogs and guards came, dogs barking and guards shouting, *'Schnell, schnell! Raus! Raus!'* Quick, quick! Out, out!

"We were organized into long columns and ordered to march until we met an SS officer who told us to go either to the right or to the left. Dvorah's parents were pointed to the left, and Dvorah and I to the right. She asked one of the officers, 'When will I see my parents again?'

'Soon enough,' he replied, 'soon enough.'

"Then she and I were separated—she with the women and I with the men.

"I was ushered with the men into a building, cold and unheated. Our heads were shaved with a sharp razor and every hair..." He stopped abruptly as if reconsidering what he was about to say. "We were given clothes to wear," he resumed, "the same striped uniforms that those greeting us had worn, and wooden shoes for our feet that were either too small or too large. Then we were thrown outside to stand in the cold and dark for hours. Any question was met with a beating from a club, so we quickly learned to be silent."

"Were you able to find Dvorah?" I asked, hopeful.

"Not yet. At first, all I saw were rows and rows of long, low, wooden huts separated by fences of electrified barbed wire. It was late November, and the ground was covered with a thin layer of icy snow punctuated with patches of black earth that had managed to escape the first onslaught of winter's wrath. I could see the women's camp through the fences. The women wore an odd assortment of torn, ragged clothes, and some were even barefoot. Their faces bore no expressions. Like us, their heads had also been shaved bare. Is that where Dvorah was? I asked myself. Would I even recognize her, and would she recognize me?"

"Did you see her?" I asked. "Was she there?"

"While I was searching for her, I suddenly smelled a strange, burnt odour in the air. I turned and saw pillars of orange flames from nearby chimneys reaching upward into the dark sky. I then realized that those gaunt men in striped uniforms with vacant expressions who had greeted us on the trains and who looked scarcely human were prisoners, and I was now one of them."

Chaver B was about to continue when the bell rang indicating the end of the schoolday and jolting me back to the present. I quickly stood up and felt almost relieved. "Chaver B, I have to go home. My mother will be worried."

"Of course," he said. "I shouldn't have told you all these things. It's too much for you. There's no need for you to know."

"No, I should know them," I said. "At some point I will have to know them. But it's enough for now."

CHAPTER XIX

Happiness is a garden walled with glass:
there's no way in or out. In Paradise there are no stories,
because there are no journeys. It's loss and regret and misery and
yearning that drive the story forward, along its twisted road.

—Margaret Atwood, *The Blind Assassin*

I walked down the sidewalk flanked by tall snowbanks and towering trees with their naked branches, my feet seemingly screeching as they trod on the hard-packed snow beneath them. I clutched my history book in both arms as I made my way towards home. I could see my breath in front of me, and with each breath, I felt that I was losing a part of myself—that part of my insides had been extinguished and that these puffs of misty vapour floating in the air were all that remained. Although the day was biting cold, I felt constricted and hot in my warm coat, and I couldn't wait to reach home and take it off.

As I climbed up the four steps to our porch and opened the front door, I smelled a vegetable casserole cooking in the oven and heard my mother's voice coming from the kitchen. "How did the play go?" she called out as I was taking off my boots and coat.

"Fine," I replied absently. "I'm just going to go upstairs for a while and do my homework. Is that okay?"

"Sure," she responded. "Do you want something to eat before dinner?"

"No, thanks. I'm not hungry."

I climbed the steps to my bedroom, tightly grasping the banister as I made my way upstairs. I sat down on the edge of my bed and thought for a while about Chaver B, about what he had told me. I stood up and walked to my window. The interminable white fields laden with snow stretched before me, and clouds hung overhead—thick, grey, heavy clouds presaging a snowfall. I lay down on my bed until my mother called me for supper. Everyone seemed to be preoccupied with their own affairs at the dinner table. My father was reading the newspaper, and Sammy was holding his fork with one hand and playing with his toy matchstick car with the other, so fortunately, it was a quick meal. When it was over, I went back to my room. I tried to finish my homework, but did little more than stare at the pages and jot down a few notes.

I hadn't told anyone about what Chaver B had told me, not even Annie. Was his secret now my secret, too? I heard my mother on the phone as she spoke first to Clarice, then Pauline, and finally Miriam, and arranged dinners for Chaver B over the Christmas holiday. I wondered if perhaps they also knew his secret.

I thought a lot about what Chaver B had said. Why hadn't the rabbis of Prague unleashed the Golem when the Nazis invaded? I wondered. Wasn't he created to fight anti-Semitism?

In school we'd learned that in the sixteenth century, Rabbi Judah Loew ben Bezalel of Prague had created a Golem - a creature out of clay taken from the banks of the Vltava River - and had brought it to life by chanting mystical Hebrew incantations. The Golem was supposed to protect the Jewish community of Prague from anti-Semitic violence. But it went on a wild, uncontrollable rampage, slaying the enemies of the Jewish people and causing much destruction. Too much destruction. As Shabbos approached, the Rabbi, in an effort to stop it, began singing a psalm, the Song of the Sabbath. Immediately, almost as if hypnotized, the Golem became silent and returned to the synagogue in the ghetto. According to legend, the Rabbi then whispered in its ear, and the Golem once again turned into an inert lump of clay. Since then, it has remained in the attic of the shul, waiting to be called upon if needed.

I was outraged! What use was the Golem if it couldn't be summoned when it was really wanted? Couldn't the rabbis, with their supposed magical powers, have revived it from the attic, or wherever it had been locked up, when the Nazis invaded Prague and started deporting people?

The whole idea of the Golem seemed antithetical to Judaism, that a religion that believes that God is the Master of the Universe and condemns idolatry would have man create other creatures from dust or earth, defied reason and logic. But what did it matter, anyway? When the Golem was really needed, it wasn't there.

We spent the winter holidays visiting my grandparents in Winnipeg and stayed with my cousins. We saw three movies, and after shopping for sales, ate lunch at the Grill Room at Eaton's. During all these fun activities, I couldn't help but think of Chaver B and the horrible things that had happened during the war. We had learned a great deal about other countries in geography class. These distant places had all seemed so charming and interesting, and whenever I envisioned other children living there, I always pictured them as being content and carefree. But obviously, that was not true. Not everyone was as lucky as we were.

One night during our visit, Babbi Hannah and Zaidi Max made a party at their house for the entire family. I loved their large home. It always smelled of cabbage borscht or chicken soup or a fresh cake baking in the oven.

Zaidi Max was a broad, muscular man, solid and stoic, so stoic in fact, that he could eat garlic right out of the clove. We would watch with amazement as he rapturously devoured each mouthful while beads of perspiration appeared on his forehead.

Zaidi had a round face, not much hair except for a fringe of greyish-blond fluff encircling the back of his head, and a smooth, fair complexion with barely the trace of a wrinkle belying his seventy-six years. His round gold-rimmed spectacles, reminiscent of the Russian proletariat, concealed large puffy bags beneath his mischievous light blue eyes. His favourite game was to take off his glasses—exposing these pouchy imperfections—and from a child's perspective, converting him into a ghastly behemoth. My cousins, Sammy, and I would scurry away in complete terror to the farthest corners of his huge house, screaming at this sudden metamorphosis. All the while, Zaidi would sit in his chair and laugh at us, then cajole us to come back. "*Kumt tsurik, kinder. Zaidi iz aheymgekumen.*" Come back, children. Zaidi has come home, he'd say as he put his spectacles back on his broad nose and reverted to his usual self.

Babbi Hannah was always waiting to comfort us. She would emerge from her kitchen, her white apron tied around her swan-like neck and incongruously generous waist. She would wipe her food-stained hands on her apron and then embrace us with her long, loving arms spread out like giant wings made of soft cotton.

Her thick silver hair lay over her shoulders and was loosely contained in a net, but a few strands would always manage to escape and would inevitably brush across our faces as she leaned over to kiss us. For years I had played this game with Babbi and Zaidi, but only then had I come to realize that there were monsters in this world far more awful and horrifying than Zaidi without his glasses.

After the party, while walking back in the cold night air to my cousins' house, I looked up at the black sky. There were only a few stars visible. The moon was a crescent intermittently obscured by clouds, as if shadows were eerily drifting in front of it, auguring something loathsome and dreadful. Do we all live under the same sky, as the saying goes? I wondered. Or do we each live under a different sky? The two questions ricocheted across my brain like a ping pong ball. Back and forth. Back and forth. Which one was it? As I looked up at the hauntingly silent sky, another possibility came to me. Perhaps, I mused, we all live under an *indifferent* sky. And that was the most frightening thought of all.

CHAPTER XX

Zog nit keyn mol az du geyst dem letstn veg,
Ven himlen blayener farshteln groyeh teg.
Vayl kumen vet noch undser oysgebenkteh shaw,
Es vet a poyk ton undser trot; mir zaynen daw!

Never say you are walking your final road,
Though leaden skies conceal the days of blue.
The hour that we have longed for will appear,
Our steps will beat out like drums; We are here!

—Hirsh Glik, Yiddish partisan song from the Vilna Ghetto

School resumed on a particularly cold day in January, one of those days where the temperature dipped to 30 degrees below zero and when the lock of my dad's car froze so that he couldn't even put his key in it. As usual, when I walked into the kitchen on a weekday morning, my mother was listening to the radio. Annie's Uncle Saul, her father's brother, was a radio announcer in Winnipeg and hosted his own show every morning between seven and ten, telling us the temperature, the windchill factor, the humidity, and the chance of snow, rain, or thunderstorms, followed by the soft crooning of Doris Day or Perry Como.

Yiddish class was in the morning, and when we arrived, there was Chaver B, sitting at his desk and leafing through a book. Did he seem different? As it was so often, his face looked inscrutable, almost as if he were wearing a mask. Ironically, only at Purim had he seemed to remove it.

Even though it was cold in Ambrosia, it would soon be the holiday of trees in Israel, and we were each asked to donate fifty cents to have a tree planted there. I imagined a forest of trees with plaques attached to the trunks, with each of our names inscribed on a specific tree, but it wasn't like that. It was also time to select a piece for this year's music festival, but I just wasn't interested. I didn't mention it, and neither did Chaver B.

I visited Babbi Rachel and confided in her about my conversations with Chaver B. She tried to bolster my mood with her kitchen-table wisdom that she imparted to me in her mixed Yiddish-English lexicon.

"What do you know about the war?" I asked her.

"I had three sisters," she said, "in White Russia. They, their husbands, and all their children were murdered in the woods by the Germans. *Dos letsteh mol vos ich hob zey gezen iz geven in* 1904, before I left for Canada. We sent letters to each other, *dertseyln eyner dem tsveytn* about our *mishpoches*. But suddenly, in 1943, the letters stopped. When I left my home as a young woman, I thought I might never see them again, but I didn't think it would end this way," she sighed. "I light *yahrzeit* candles for them every year, on Yom Kippur, the holiest day of the year."

"You mean like the one Mom lights every year on Zaidi Harry's yahrzeit?"

"Of course, I light one for him, too, but on the day he died. My sisters, I don't know what day they died, what month, or for sure what year. So I just light them on Yom Kippur."

"I wonder why the yahrzeit candle is lit on the anniversary of a person's death, rather than on the day they were born. Isn't it a happier feeling to light it on someone's birthday? That would feel like we were celebrating their birth and remembering all the good things they did, not mourning their death."

"Lighting the candle is a *good* tradition," Babbi objected. "As soon as a person dies, his soul begins its ascent *tsu di andereh velt,* to the other world. When we light the yahrzeit candle, that person's soul has permission to come back to earth for twenty-four hours, the length of time the candle burns. That's why we observe yahrzeit on the day a person dies. When I light Zaidi's candle, I feel as though he is here with me."

Babbi paused, smiled, and nodded her head. Her voice then became softer and gentler as she looked into my eyes. "Whether we remember our relatives on their birthdays or on the day they left us, the important thing is to remember those who are gone. As long as someone remembers you, Miraleh, you never really die."

The year moved on with the usual round of homework, movies, violin practice, and Shabbos dinners with Chaver B. Purim that year was bittersweet. Babbi Rachel's special cookies provided me some consolation, and she tried to take my mind off recent events by teaching me how to make them.

"Someone has to carry on the tradition," she would say, "and there is no better person than you, Miraleh."

As my mother and I prepared *Shalach Manos* baskets filled with *Haman Tashen,* Babbi's cookies, and fruit to deliver to the residents of the Old Folks Home, my mother broached the subject of my conversations with Chaver B.

"Mira, Babbi told me that Chaver B has been discussing his experiences in the concentration camp with you. I think you should leave him alone. He's having a very hard time coping with his feelings about the war and everything he went through. I don't think talking to you is helpful. You remember how he was last summer. Any reminder can cause a serious setback."

"Is Daddy trying to help him?" I asked, recalling his visit to my father's office more than a year ago.

"Yes, and he's been making some progress. Slowly and in small steps. So we should do our best to help him continue in the same direction."

"Well, why don't you tell me what happened to him, then?"

"It's not up to me to tell you someone else's business. He will tell you. Eventually. But now is not the time."

"Well, you've told me personal things about Auntie Lillie and Aunt Bella," I countered.

"That's different," she said.

"How?"

"Because what happened to them occurred very long ago, and they got on with their lives."

"Isn't that what Chaver B is doing? He left Europe and came here, just like they did."

"Mira, Chaver B is a tor. . . ," she began, but she thought better of what she was about to articulate and simply said, "He's still recovering. It was only a few years ago. The things that happened in the war were so horrible, one can't even imagine them. They are not easily buried and forgotten."

Perhaps my mother was right. My mind kept returning to Chaver B's revelations on Esther, the Purim queen, and the moon—beautiful, courageous Esther and the moon embodying all her purity and goodness. Last year, when Chaver B taught us those lessons, it seemed as though his veil of sadness had started to lift and that at long last, light was making its way to his soul. Had he begun to feel that, like the moon, his life was capable of renewing itself? He had seemed almost hopeful then. But since the summer, he had lost that burgeoning sense of vitality and optimism.

He continued to come to our house every Tuesday for my violin lesson. The format of our lessons didn't change, and he still didn't pick up the violin to play. As usual, he stayed for dinner afterwards.

"I have some news," my father announced at the dining room table one Tuesday evening, as my mother walked in carrying a platter of sumptuous-smelling sliced roast beef and placed it between Chaver B and my dad. "Jacob Greenberg's medical license has been renewed."

"Isn't that wonderful!" my mom said. "All that fuss over nothing. He's such a *mentsh*, such a kind, giving person. What a shame that he had to go through all that aggravation."

"Well, Jacob was always a man who spoke his mind, so perhaps his reputation followed him."

"But he wasn't a communist, was he?" I asked my dad. I no longer felt uncomfortable discussing this in front of Chaver B, since I now knew that was not his secret. It must have been merely the presence of the RCMP that had intimidated him. Their iconic uniforms and position of power must have reminded him of the Nazis.

"No, he wasn't," he replied. "But he was always willing to call out injustice when he saw it. Did I tell you about our fight with the Manitoba legislature?"

"I don't think so," I replied.

"During the years when I applied to medical school, there was a restriction on how many Jewish students could be accepted. They allowed up to ten per year, but sometimes only five or fewer were accepted, and it had nothing to do with grades."

"How could they do that? Did they ask on the application what religion you practiced?"

"They did. And sometimes they just assumed you were Jewish by your name. Did you know I had to apply three times before they accepted me?"

"Wow! Really? And you were such a good student."

"Once we graduated, Jacob and I decided to do something about it. Actually, it was Jacob's idea. He was outraged. So we formed a committee, wrote arguments, and presented our case before the Manitoba legislature."

"And what happened?" I asked.

"We won. The quota system was abolished, and from then on, students were admitted based on merit alone."

No wonder my dad and Jacob were such firm friends. But it made me realize that there was anti-Semitism in our midst. The properties around Lake Winnipeg. The fires. Even the medical school. The idea that educated people could harbour those feelings was baffling to me. I had been so insulated at Peretz School all these years. We had learned about nations always trying to annihilate us and how we were able to fight back and renew ourselves, but we never talked about hatred so close to home. I looked at Chaver B; the stories from Manitoba paled in comparison to his tales.

Just then, the phone rang. My mother went into the kitchen to answer it and promptly returned.

"Reuven, it's for you. The hospital," she said.

My dad dabbed his mouth with his napkin, pushed his chair back, and disappeared into the kitchen. Our dinner conversation ceased, and we all sat with arms suspended and forks in midair while listening to his call. "Uh huh... sounds like appendicitis," he spoke into the telephone receiver. "I'll be right there."

"I'm sorry," he said apologetically as he hurried back into the dining room. "Maybe it's a false alarm, but if I have to do surgery, I won't be back for a while."

He glanced at his watch and took a quick sip from his glass of water; then he dashed into the front hall, grabbed his doctor's bag, and left. After dinner, I helped my mom clear the table and wash the dishes, while Chaver B played cards with Sammy. When we were almost done, my mom walked into the living room and announced, "That's enough for you, young man. Time for bed. Say good night to Chaver B."

After several protestations, Sammy finally acquiesced and trudged upstairs in front of my mother. I returned to the kitchen to finish drying the dishes. Chaver B followed me and sat down at the kitchen table. While I was putting the plates back into the cupboard, I remembered what Chaver B's father had done before he was deported—stashing money in the wall behind some dishes. I was turning over in my mind whether or not I should ask Chaver B to tell me more about the war. It had been over three months since our last conversation, and what he'd described had remained with me and continued to gnaw at me. If he was willing to talk, I was prepared to listen.

Finally, I said, "Do you remember our discussion in the classroom that afternoon after we performed *Bontsha Shvayg*? You were telling me about Auschwitz and how badly you were treated there when you first arrived. How you had to stand for hours in the cold night air. What happened after that?"

"Do your parents approve of me telling you these things?" he asked while looking directly at me.

"Babbi Rachel knows, so I'm sure that she told them," I answered and then realized that I had just told a fib. Of course, my mother and I had just discussed this very issue. I knew I was defying her. But I had to know the rest. I knew too much already to stop. Not knowing left me with a strange uneasiness. And Chaver B seemed fine. I hadn't detected any change in his mood or behaviour since he first started recounting his story to me. I still had the feeling that even though he expressed reservations about continuing our conversations, he really wanted to share his experiences with me.

"Did they finally take you to a warm place?" I prodded.

He quickly looked up at me and then cast his eyes downward, as if he, too, knew that we were entering forbidden territory. "We were finally shuttled into a barracks crowded with three-tiered bunks and told to sleep five to each tier, fifteen to a bunk. There was barely room for anyone. We still hadn't eaten. Exhausted and famished, we fell asleep. A few hours later, just before sunrise, our *kapo* woke us up and beat anyone who didn't get up fast enough. Then he commanded us to go outside and line up in columns of five."

"What are kapos?"

"The kapos were inmates who had been recruited by the SS to supervise the other prisoners. Sadly, some of them were Jewish. Their task was to carry out the will of the Nazis, and they sometimes behaved as brutally as those who gave them orders.

"While standing and waiting in the morning dawn, I suddenly heard music; an orchestra was playing marching music during roll call, and when that was finished, one by one prisoners in columns of five marched off to work. I was standing so far at the back that I could barely make out the orchestra, but as the prisoners gradually departed, I could discern the players and their instruments. Who are these musicians, and what are they doing in this appalling place? I remember asking myself.

"We had not yet been provided with our work detail and were ordered to march over to another building where numbers were tattooed on our left forearms. The same numbers were then sewn on to our shirts over the left chest. That reminded me of a Jewish superstition. Maybe you know it. It is said that if someone sews a piece of your clothing while you're wearing it, like repairing a rip, you must chew on something or your brains will be sewn up also. Of course, I had nothing to chew. And then I thought, perhaps it would be a good thing if my brain were sewn up. It might make it easier to endure this place."

"I do know that superstition," I confirmed excitedly. "Sometimes, just as I'm rushing off to school, a button falls off my blouse. My mom quickly takes out her sewing kit and has me chew a piece of bread while she sews it back on."

But Chaver B was not moved by my little anecdote. "The following day we were assigned our work detail," he resumed, as if I hadn't said anything. "The men from our barracks were to work in the mines. We worked ten hours a day and had to walk several kilometers to and from work. Food consisted of a piece of bread in the morning and a thin watery soup for lunch and dinner. That was our only liquid."

"How did you survive?"

"I don't know how," he said matter-of-factly. "After six weeks of this gruelling labour, I became thinner and thinner. I wasn't sure how much more I could bear. The rumours of gas chambers and of crematoria...where they burned..."

"I know what they are," I quickly interrupted. "You don't have to explain it. Babbi Rachel told me about them."

"Well, then you know that the tall tales were true tales after all. When I asked the kapo shortly after arriving where Dvorah's parents were, he pointed to the chimneys and said, 'That's where they went. That's where we'll all go.'"

Chaver B stood up and walked into the living room. I followed him and sat down at the dining room table facing him. I started to shiver; my hands, cold and clammy, trembled in my lap as I watched him move across the room.

"In the evenings, I would stand in front of the barbed wire fence separating us from the women's camp and look for Dvorah. My fears were assuaged. Even looking as we did, our spirits were so intertwined that we were still able to recognize each other amongst the mass of decaying humanity. Just a glimpse of her was all I needed to see me through to the next day."

I imagined the strength of their love and its power to sustain them in that wretched, abhorrent place. And it made me understand the healing capacity of love far more than any of the books I'd ever read had.

"The routine never changed," he continued, almost indifferently. "We marched off to work every morning to the strains of martial music, and returned to the camp in the evenings—sore and tired—dragging our feet to the same marching melodies, sometimes dragging the dead bodies of prisoners who had collapsed from starvation and beatings, perhaps mercifully so."

Suddenly, his voice became urgent and tense. He looked around the room randomly, and I wasn't sure if he was addressing me or some unseen audience. "We frantically searched for any scrap that might keep us alive for another day. A few drops of water, a crust of bread, a rag, a spoon, a rare piece of soap—all were ends in themselves, or else they became precious commodities that could be exchanged for other things. It was each man for himself.

"I tried to think of a way out. I had discovered that the orchestra, or *lagerkapelle* as it was called in German, was made up of camp inmates. They lived in a separate barracks, and since they played music in the mornings when we left for work and again when we returned, I assumed that was their only job.

"I didn't know how much longer I could tolerate my situation. I spoke to my kapo about playing with the orchestra, but he had no use for me and told me that my work was in the mines. And then, a few mornings later, while the orchestra was playing, I recognized one of the cellists who had played with me in Theresienstadt; I hadn't noticed him before. Had he been on the same transport with me? I furtively tried to gain his attention, but I didn't know if he saw me.

"The next morning, before marching off to the mines, someone called my name in gruff German. 'Ari Bergman. Come with me.'

"I didn't know where I was being taken or why. Had I unknowingly committed a crime or misdemeanor, and was this the call to my demise?"

My eyes widened. "You must have been so frightened," I gasped.

"By that time, I was resigned to the fact that I would die in the camp. But, to my relief, I was taken to see the *kapellmeister,* the conductor of the orchestra. When I arrived in his barracks, he handed me a violin and asked me to play. I lifted up the instrument and with sore, stiff fingers began playing a song by Kreisler, forgetting that music by Jewish composers was prohibited. But that didn't seem to bother the kapellmeister.

'Good,' he said. 'You will play for us.'"

"How wonderful!" I interjected.

"Yes, I thought so, too. Then I looked around the room filled with instruments, some hanging on pegs, others leaning against chairs or resting on the ground: violins, cellos, trumpets, clarinets, saxophones, a flute, and a tuba; there were various drums and even cymbals and accordions. How out of place this was with the rest of the camp, and it didn't seem right."

I knew what he meant by that, but I chose not to respond. "Did you meet the other musicians?" I asked. "And what about the cellist? Had you known him from Theresienstadt?"

"Yes, I had. And yes, he had told the kapellmeister about me. But that morning in the music room, there were only three prisoners besides me, all *nottenschreibers*, or copyists."

"Where were the others?" I asked Chaver B.

"All working. Much to my disappointment, except for the nottenschreibers, the musicians were not exempt from manual labour. Instead, we woke up at 4 am to set up the orchestra. After playing, we would trudge off to our assigned jobs; I still worked in the mines. We would then leave work early to prepare and play for the other prisoners as they returned. I was more exhausted than before.

"I spoke to the kapellmeister. 'I know how to transcribe and transpose music,' which was true, 'and also how to arrange and orchestrate,' which was not true, and which in fact I had never done. 'Could I not do these?' I asked him.

'There are already enough copyists,' he told me. 'We don't need anymore.'

'Oh, yes, we do,' the other copyists chimed in. 'There is too much work for just the three of us.'

"The kapellmeister walked around the room and studied the music sheets already prepared and the long list of pieces yet to be orchestrated. He glanced from the sheets to the instruments and then to the copyists. After some hesitation, he finally declared, 'Very well. You may join your fellow copyists.'"

I suddenly found myself clapping with joy.

"Yes," Chaver B said, nodding in agreement, "I felt a huge wave of relief wash over me as I was introduced into their ranks," he said. He turned and looked at me, his eyes narrowing as if pondering an important question. "And I began to believe again that perhaps people were naturally good and kind. Even there, in that wretched place, not every man was just for himself. Finally, there was camaraderie, and for a brief while, I felt safe."

He sat down at the dining room table beside me. "No longer having to work in the mines, I spent my days indoors away from the elements, arranging and writing music. We had instruments, but there were few music books, and we had to recall many marches and musical pieces from memory and write them down. I was still constantly hungry, but the food was a little better for the musicians, and without the hard manual labour, I didn't need as much nourishment."

"You were so lucky to have this break," I said.

"Yes, but even with this bit of luck, life was uncertain, incomprehensible, and unimaginable, even for those of us living through it."

"What kind of music did you play?"

"The music we played was lively and festive. The Germans made sure of that. They somehow thought that this would make our work more enjoyable and palatable, and would echo the sentiments of the camp slogan, *Arbeit Macht Frei*. But I had experienced the music from both sides, being the recipient as well as the giver, and it did no such thing. It was all a travesty and almost a crime, that music, this most transcendent and magnificent expression of the human soul, could be juxtaposed with this horrific place and such human corruption."

I could see he was upset, and he remained silent for a minute. "Did you play at any other times," I asked in a soft voice, trying to distract him somewhat, "or only in the mornings and evenings?"

"We held concerts on Sunday afternoons for the prisoners and Nazi officers. Some of us were asked to perform in the private homes of the officers, but I managed to avoid that. Sometimes a gallows would be built and an inmate would be hung for trying to escape, or for some minor offence, such as stealing a potato, and we would be ordered to play music as the prisoner approached his death. Summer, fall, winter, spring—regardless of the weather— we played and played and played. We played to stay alive, like Scheherazade spinning her tales. Occasionally we would happen to be playing as trains of deportees arrived and disembarked, as they underwent selection and marched to the gas chambers. I tried to avert my gaze from them, knowing the deception I was perpetrating and with which I felt complicit."

"But you didn't have a choice!" I declared defiantly. "You weren't ordering people to their deaths."

"You're right. I wasn't. But at times I felt like the executioner." He turned and looked at me with doleful eyes. "One day, we had just finished performing as a train of prisoners was arriving. Our platform was directly above the ramp where the prisoners walked towards the officer in charge of selection. Through all the noise— the dogs barking, the SS shouting, and the frenzied cries of parents and children as they became separated—I could hear that most of the prisoners were speaking Polish and Yiddish. It was heartbreaking to look at them, but my eyes seemed to be involuntarily drawn to the desperation in their eyes, to their confusion, to their pale faces streaked with dread and fear."

He turned away from me, clenched his right hand into a fist and raised it to his mouth. He closed his eyes, sighed deeply, and sat there, lost in his own thoughts; or perhaps he was trying not to think. After a minute, he placed his hand on the table and said, "As I glanced over the crowded ramp, I saw a familiar face. I looked again. Was that my father? He was thinner than I recalled, but yes, that was him. And beside him my mother? Where was Yossi? And what were they doing on a deportation train with Polish Jews?

"Instinctively, I ran to the fence, calling to them, '*Tateh, Mameh!*' But there was so much noise and chaos, no one could hear me. They were stooped over and almost gaunt; they looked so old and frail, I knew that they were destined for the gas chambers. Without thinking, I ran up to one of the SS guards, frantically telling him that my mother and father were in the crowd and begging him to save their lives.

'They are no good to us,' he said. 'Do you want to go with them? That I can arrange,' he sneered.

"I almost accepted his offer. What a relief it would have been to escape that hell. Even death seemed like a better alternative. But then I thought of Yossi and Dvorah. I would try to survive for them. I ran along the fence, shouting my parents' names as loudly as I could, the SS guards laughing contemptuously in the background. I kept my eyes peeled on my mother and father for as long as possible, as their line became a thin thread in the distance. And then I fell to my knees and wept; I still had a heart after all.

Perhaps it is better this way, I rationalized to myself. At least their last memory of me will be as I once was, not of the degraded animal I have become.

"Later that day, I saw the greyish-black smoke from the crematoria drift upwards into the pallid sky, and I recited the Mourner's *Kaddish*, the prayer for the dead: '*Yisgadal v'yiskadash shmey rabbaw.* May His great Name grow exalted and be sanctified... in the world that *He* created as *He* willed... He who makes peace in His heights, may He make peace, upon us and upon all Israel. Amen.' But it was like praying to the wind. No one listened and no one heard."

Chaver B seemed lost in another realm. I felt that he was barely with me in the same room; he seemed possessed. The images he described were playing out before me like a movie. But it wasn't a movie. It was his life.

He needs to stop, I told myself. I was frightened for him. He looked as motionless as when I'd come upon him in the sunflower fields the summer before. As it did then, a panic subsumed me. I should never have coaxed Chaver B into telling me more.

I climbed upstairs to look for my mother; I would have to admit my error to her. She had been right, as she always seemed to be. But she had fallen asleep beside Sammy, and I didn't want to wake her and startle her. I went back downstairs and waited, wondering what I should do, or if I should do anything.

I'll make him a cup of tea, I decided. It seemed to have had medicinal powers in the past. I quickly heated up the water and poured it into the largest cup I could find, with the tea bag resting on the bottom. I let it steep for a minute, then removed the teabag and let a sugar cube drop to the bottom.

"Chaver B, I made you a cup of tea," I said as I stirred it with a spoon and placed it down on the dining room table in front of him.

"Thank you, Miraleh," he said while turning to look at me with his dark eyes that now seemed so full of anguish. Even though he was in so much pain, I felt a tremendous rush of relief as Chaver B gradually came back to reality. It was the first time I had detected such intense emotion that was so readily identifiable in his eyes; not just a hint of one, but a feeling that was tangible. We sat silently at the table as he intermittently sipped his tea.

Finally, at ten o'clock, my father returned home from the hospital. I met him in the front hall. "I don't think Chaver B is feeling well," I said as I tried to minimize the situation I'd created.

I didn't elaborate to my father, and he didn't ask any questions. I guess he just understood. He immediately walked over to Chaver B, and after lifting up his wrist, he took his pulse. "Come, Ari," he said. "I'll drive you home." This time Chaver B didn't object.

My father helped Chaver B put on his coat. He held the front door open for him as he stepped outside. I went over to the living room window and watched them walk to the driveway, get into the car, and drive off into the dark stillness. I stared out into the nocturnal void for a long time. It seemed so harsh, so foreboding, so malevolent. There was so much to think about that I couldn't think about anything. "I'll think about it tomorrow," I said aloud. And then I went upstairs to bed.

CHAPTER XXI

Out of the huts of history's shame
I rise
Up from the past that's rooted in pain
I rise
I'm a black ocean, leaping and wide,
Welling and swelling I bear in the tide.
Leaving behind nights of terror and fear
I rise

-Maya Angelou, "Still I Rise"

Thirty days after Purim came the holiday Passover. In accordance with our dietary laws, my mother removed all *chametz* or leavened food from the house and scrubbed the counters and floors. The regular dishes were carried downstairs to the basement, and the set of dishes designated for Passover were carried upstairs and now took their place. We were only allowed to eat *matzo* - unleavened bread - during the eight days of the holiday, and on *Erev Pesach* - the eve of Passover - like Sherlock Holmes, we skulked through the house with a candle, a spoon, and a feather: a candle to uncover any wayward breadcrumbs, a feather to sweep them up, and a spoon in which to deposit them. I always liked the Passover traditions that welcomed the spring. They were comforting and reassuring. But it made me think of all the Jewish people who had died in the war. Hadn't they done the same things? Adhered to the same rituals? And to what end?

That year we had a large *seder*, our ceremonial Passover dinner. Babbi Rachel, Auntie Miriam and her family, and Annie, Kenny, and their parents came, along with Chaver B. I had decided to play violin as an accompaniment for some of the songs, and I had learned them on my own as a surprise. Sammy was thrilled not to have to sing the *"Fir Kashas"* – the "Four Questions" — solo, and everyone seemed to enjoy the change, especially Chaver B.

During the seder, we drank four cups of wine, and as usual, we set out Elijah's cup—the fifth cup of wine that no one drank, except Elijah, of course, the Prophet, who according to the Bible, ascended to heaven in a Chariot of Fire that was carried upwards by a whirlwind.

Although my dad was not religious, he thoroughly enjoyed participating in our traditions. Once the wine was poured, Sammy and I would follow him to the front hall and watch him open the door just a few inches, inviting the prophet Elijah to come and drink.

"Do you think that's wide enough?" Sammy would ask. "Will he be able to see that we've opened the door for him?"

"He will know," my dad would say. "Don't worry."

The next morning was always a time of great debate as we gathered around the dining room table, and that year was no exception. Had Elijah come? Were there any telltale signs? Was there less wine in the cup than there'd been the night before? No one expected Elijah to drink all of it. After all, there were so many homes to visit. He couldn't possibly have drunk a cup of wine at each of them. Clearly, we could have just marked the level of wine in the glass before going to bed and that would have settled the dispute, but that would have been much too easy and a lot less fun.

We invite Elijah because when he comes, the Messiah will bring complete redemption to the Jewish people, I remembered reading in my textbook. And Lererine Malka had taught us something else, too. "Inviting Elijah is like welcoming a stranger into our home," she had said, just as we had invited Chaver B.

With Passover came spring, at least according to the calendar. The mountainous snowbanks had melted and disappeared, and it was as though we were transitioning to another world, just about to begin, but one that had not quite revealed itself yet. We were on a precipice, leaving the old behind and ready to embrace the new. As I walked down the street, I noticed small purple lilac buds adorning green leafy shrubs lining our neighbours' yards. I took a breath expectantly as I passed by, believing that if I breathed in deeply enough, I could prematurely draw out the lilac blossoms' beautifully rich and heady fragrance.

In early May, I was having an extra violin lesson on Saturday in preparation for the school talent show the following week at which I would be performing. Chaver B and I had decided on the song "Csardas," which I had learned the previous year. It was bright and *freylech*, and we thought that the students would enjoy it. My mother asked if I could have the lesson at Chaver B's apartment, since she was preparing for the annual Ladies Spring Tea that would take place the next day at our home and for which she wanted the house to be pristine. She was busy baking pastries and other treats, and being quite anxious about the whole affair, she didn't want her routine interrupted. Chaver B consented.

When I walked into his apartment, I was surprised to see a music stand in the middle of his living room, especially since Chaver B had told me, on more than one occasion, that he no longer played violin or any other instrument. After I placed my music on it, we proceeded to tune my violin. Chaver B had perfect pitch, and he could tell if a note was out of tune by even the tiniest amount. We were about to begin the lesson when he realized that he had no pencil. No lesson passed without him making numerous markings and notations on my music sheets. He sifted through the drawers in his desk, but when he came up empty-handed, he announced that he would just run downstairs and buy one from the drugstore.

"I will be right back," he said.

I sat down on the sofa and patiently waited for him to return, but my patience didn't last long. They must be busy downstairs, I thought. I stood up and walked towards the window to survey who was coming in and out of the drugstore, when I again spied those three framed black-and-white photographs resting on his desk. I heard the door shut, and Chaver B walked into the apartment carrying a box of pencils. I turned towards him and simply said, "Tell me the rest. Please. I need to know."

He laid the pencils down on the kitchen table and then walked towards me. "Alright," he said, as if defeated. "Sit down." Whatever fight he'd had in him was gone.

I sat down on the sofa, and he sat down in his large, leather armchair. He said nothing more about his parents, and I didn't ask him.

He usually needed a question to help unleash his thoughts, so I began, "Things must have been a little easier for you once you joined the orchestra. Were they?"

"Yes, they were to some degree, but even though I was a musician and life was a little more bearable, I knew that I wasn't safe," he said. "Even the size of the orchestra waxed and waned. We knew that we were all condemned to death. Hitler wanted no one left behind, no one left to bear witness. The only question was when." This last remark stunned me, despite what I already knew.

"At one point, our music stands began to fall apart, and we requested new ones. A short distance from our barracks was the Terezin family camp. Families from Theresienstadt had been essentially living together for several months. Parents, children, grandparents. They were allowed to wear their own clothes, and their hair hadn't been shaved. The children were taken to a school during the day, and the adults didn't have to work. They were even allowed to play musical instruments, and the children performed their own little opera. No one knew why they were given this special status and what the point of it all was.

"One sunny morning, I saw them all being driven off in trucks, I assumed for an outing in the countryside. In the afternoon, about a dozen wooden music stands in good condition appeared in our barracks. 'Here are the music stands you requested,' announced the Nazi officer.

"I looked across at the family camp. It was silent. Beyond the fence, smoke rose from the chimneys and diffused into the blue sky. So that was it. They had all been taken to the gas chambers, and now their bodies were being burned in the crematoria. We had thought they were the lucky ones. We were beyond asking why."

I became lightheaded, and my throat tightened. I couldn't imagine people being so cruel to children, but it seemed to be a recurrent theme. I became queasy and sweaty; a great clamour of noises was ringing in my head. I could feel the blood pulsating in my veins, but I managed to calm down. Chaver B must not have noticed, because he didn't say anything, and he didn't stop.

"I worried about Dvorah," he carried on. "She was fading away, day by day. And the baby inside her? Would that lead to her end? I felt guilty and ashamed that I couldn't help her. We continued to silently communicate across the barbed wire fence. Then, I didn't see her for a few days; I feared the worst. Somehow she managed to get word to me through another inmate that she had lost the baby and had spent two nights in the infirmary, but was now back in her barracks."

I felt the tension leaving my body as he told me that Dvorah was still alive, and he seemed to echo my sentiments.

"I remember feeling relieved, almost joyful," he said. "But then I became frozen, bewildered. What kind of perverse place was I in, and what had I become that I would rejoice in the loss of my own child, even though I knew that a child could never survive here anyway? The natural order had turned upside down. Nazi officers' eyes welled up with tears as they listened to Brahms or Beethoven, but they would not shed a tear as they—with all their efficiency and exactitude—ordered and carried out the subjugation and extermination of millions of human beings."

Chaver B's expression became angry and took on a tortured quality. It was as though he was reciting a soliloquy from Shakespeare, and I decided to just let him go on. He was lost in the labyrinth of his mind, and I wondered what turn he would take next.

"I looked at my fellow prisoners, poor souls like me who were hardly human," he said in a strained voice, his facial expression now alternating between consternation, puzzlement, pain, and resignation. "Men in name only. It was hard to imagine that only a short while before, we were people with meaningful work, families, and friends, with our lives stretching before us. What *was* normal life?

Were people leading 'normal existences' elsewhere while we were barely existing here, just struggling to survive as day became night and night turned into day, over and over and over again? Our only reality was what we faced in Auschwitz. All the rest was a mirage."

He leaned his head forward and briefly cradled it in both of his hands. Then he looked up, and I could see that his eyes had once again become vacant. "Our only hope was selfishness," he said in a monotone. "Do what one has to do to make it to the end of the day, and then do it all over again the next day. Freeze your feelings. Forget about self-respect. That was the only hope. And without hope, there was no reason to wake up in the morning."

CHAPTER XXII

Where is my home, where is my home...
The garden is glorious with spring blossom,
Paradise on earth it is to see.
And this is that beautiful land,
The Czech land, my home.

—"Czech National Anthem"

Mira, I'm going to lie down for a while. Do you mind?"
Chaver B asked me.

"Of course not," I said. "Would you like me to go home?"

"No, no," he replied. "We still need to have our violin lesson. Just give me a few minutes."

I sat quietly and watched him walk into his bedroom and close the door. I went into the kitchen and poured myself a glass of water. Outside his back window, some boys were playing catch in the lane and calling each other names after one of them would make a bad throw.

Ten minutes passed. Chaver B had not yet come out of his room, and I started to worry. But then I heard his door click and saw him emerge. This time he sat down at his kitchen table, and I took the chair across from him. I allowed him to take the lead. His story seemed to be reaching its conclusion, and at this point, there was no reason for him to hold back. He needed this catharsis. I wondered if he had told anyone else about his experiences in such detail, besides me.

"Finally there was word that the Germans were losing, that the Americans were closing in from the west and the Russians from the east. If we could hang on a little longer, we would see light and salvation.

"One day, the members of the orchestra were informed that we were being transferred to another camp farther away from the front. Our instruments were not coming with us, and I wondered how I would survive without my violin. The idea of leaving our instruments behind was frightening to all of us.

"It all happened so quickly; I didn't have time to get word to Dvorah. Even though I didn't know where we were going, I wished that I could have sent her some sort of a message—something, anything."

He raised his right hand to his forehead, closed his eyes momentarily, and rubbed his temple. "We were taken to Dachau, another concentration camp but in Germany, and from there to one of its *kuferlings* or work camps, to make armaments for the war. The work was arduous and punishing, worse even than what I'd first experienced in Auschwitz, and every day saw more and more men dying.

"It's as though we were on a barren moonscape. We were ghastly, ghostly creatures so emaciated and thin, you almost expected us to rise into the air and float away. If not for the months I spent arranging music that kept me indoors, protected from the elements and with better food, I would have succumbed as well, I'm sure of it. And I nearly did.

"By springtime, there was a massive typhus epidemic that was hard to escape. I could barely keep down liquids. As thin as I was, I became even thinner. My skin hung from my bones like rags. After a while, I was too weak to even try to drink, and those around me were too weak to help themselves, let alone me. The Germans were evacuating the camp and ordered all those who were physically able to leave with them. I could hear the shots ring out as they killed the sick and infirm who were staying behind. Soon it would be my turn. Leave no one to bear witness.

"The shots came closer and closer, and then stopped. I heard a few shouts in German and then silence. The enemy was too close, and there was no time to kill the rest of us. I looked at those lying around me. I couldn't tell who was dead and who was alive. Feverish and delirious, I fell into a stupor, oblivious to all around me, until I awoke hours or perhaps days later to the touch of an American soldier's hand on my wrist. 'I've got you,' he said. 'Hang in there, pal. We've crushed those miserable scum, and you'll be safe now.'

"I recovered in a local hospital and was then sent to a facility in Sweden to convalesce. When I regained my strength, I returned to Prague, hoping that Dvorah would have done the same. Every day I went to the Jewish Agency to see if her name was on a list of survivors. You don't know how many times I dared to imagine our reuniting. Sometimes I would imagine hearing a knock at my door. I would open it, not expecting anyone in particular, and there she would be, standing in front of me. Other times I imagined we would find each other serendipitously, perhaps each arriving at the Agency at the same time to look for the other. She would be standing at the counter giving the clerk *my* name, and I, by chance, would be standing next to her, giving a different clerk *her* name. But usually in my dreams, I would see her from a distance, in a field of grass or across a room, her ethereal loveliness wafting over to me from afar. We would begin walking towards each other, slowly. Then, as our images became more distinct, we would start running, almost galloping, until we were in each other's arms, that becoming our only reality. Nothing else would matter but us."

Chaver B paused for several moments and then continued in a tremulous voice. "But her name never appeared. I later learned that as the Russians gained ground, all the prisoners were evacuated from Auschwitz and ordered to march to other camps further away from the front. She had been on one of those death marches in the brutal cold of winter and had not survived."

What about Yossi? I was about to ask, but then remained silent.

As if reading my thoughts, Chaver B continued, "My brother and parents had been on one of the transports out of Prague to the Lodz Ghetto in Poland. The residents there were used as forced labour in the factories where German uniforms and other war supplies were being made. But conditions were squalid and cramped, with no running water and little food, and many people died of malnutrition and illness. Eventually, transports from there to the camps resumed, and my parents were carried along with them, as you know. But my brother had escaped to the woods and joined the partisans. His name had not yet appeared on a list of survivors or victims, so until I heard otherwise, for me, he was still alive.

"No one else from my extended family had survived the war. So few of my colleagues and friends had survived either, an entire generation of musicians and composers erased in one breath. All those gifted musicians from Theresienstadt had been brought to

Auschwitz and gassed upon arrival, given no chance to fight for their survival. I had struggled and fought to stay alive, to be reunited with my family, to resume my life as I had known it, but now there was no one left to share it with.

"Prague no longer held any happiness for me, so I decided to leave. The Jewish Agency in Prague had a listing of job opportunities, and I chose to come here. The Agency assured me that they and other organizations would have a record of my whereabouts, and that if Yossi were still alive, he would be able to find me. Last summer, when you discovered me standing in the fields, I had just received a letter written in Yiddish from a young Polish Jew who had survived the war. His name was David. He had tracked me down here and gotten my address from the Red Cross. He had been a partisan fighter along with Yossi, and they had become good friends."

Chaver B's tone then became almost sarcastic as he repeated David's words. "He said that Yossi had spoken often of me, his older brother whom he had admired and respected so much, the future concert violinist that he was so proud of and whom he could not wait to see again. They were in the woods when the SS came upon them. A gun battle followed, and Yossi was shot. He lost a great deal of blood and survived only a few minutes. He knew he would not live long and asked David that if he survived the war, to try to find me. 'He was so sure that you would make it,' David wrote. 'I want you to know that he did not suffer long and that he did not die alone.'"

For several minutes, Chaver B said nothing, each second separated from the next by visions of horror swirling in my mind. Finally, I broke the silence. "Your violin saved you," I said, almost in a whisper.

"Perhaps," he replied. "The violin saved my life, but it didn't save the lives of others. At times I felt that I had become the enemy, lulling people to their deaths. My brother, he was a hero, and I am the one who is proud of him. He actively fought the Germans and thought not of himself. I cannot forgive myself for that, for my selfishness, for my weakness. So that is why I never play. For a long time, I could not bear to touch the violin or even look at it."

He paused and then asked me in a tone of voice he sometimes used in class, a professorial voice suddenly confident and clear, "Do you know the story of Faust?"

"No," I replied. "What is it?"

"It's a German legend. Faust is a learned and successful man who becomes disenchanted with life. So he makes a pact with a demon, Mephistopheles, and exchanges his soul for unlimited knowledge and wealth.

"That is how I sometimes feel. Just when I was about to perish, Mephistopheles stretched out his hand to me and offered me a bargain. 'Play, and you shall live, but your soul will belong to me.' And I had accepted."

Chaver B stared out the window for what seemed like a very long time. I searched my heart for words of comfort, but it was speechless. Then he stood up, walked over to his closet, and took out a violin case. He brought it over to the sofa and opened it, the violin's gleaming dark red and brown wood reflecting the sun streaming through the window. He took out the bow, tightened and rosined it, and tuned the strings. "I will play for you now," he said. And then he did.

I recognized the piece from a recording we had at home, Sibelius's violin concerto, and it harboured Chaver B's secret.

His playing captured all his pain and pathos. The melody spoke his anguish. No words were needed. There was so much sorrow and suffering in each note that my heart broke listening to it.

The violin became an extension of his soul, expressing all the pent-up feelings of his loss, of his sadness, of his torment. But it did not speak of hope for the future.

I finally knew Chaver B's secret. He was a chained spirit. He bore a humiliation of spirit that would not leave him. When he looked out at the fields, he did not see what I saw. He saw a world filled with nothing, devoid of hope, devoid of family, devoid of home, devoid of everything.

When he finished playing, he lowered his violin to his side. He looked at me with his dark eyes, eyes that were like crystalline pools through which I could see clearly to his soul, a soul that I knew was still inside him, that no one had taken away from him. Then he softly said, "You should go home now, Miraleh."

And I did.

CHAPTER XXIII

Those who can make you believe absurdities,
can make you commit atrocities.

—Voltaire, "Questions sur les Miracles"

I walked home, violin in hand, oblivious to the beautiful, warm, spring day. As I climbed up my porch steps and opened the front door, I heard my mother's voice coming from the kitchen as she talked to Clarice and Auntie Miriam who had come over to help her prepare for the tea.

"How was your lesson?" she called out as I took off my jacket and laid my violin down in the bookcase.

"Fine," I replied absently. "I'm just going to go upstairs for a while. Is that okay?"

"Sure," she responded. "Actually, I'd prefer if you stayed out of the living room and dining room today. You can play with Sammy upstairs."

"Okay," I said. "Call me if you need any help."

I spent the rest of the day in my bedroom and came down only to eat a quick meal of leftovers from Shabbos dinner. That night I had a terrible dream. I dreamt that my precious trees lining the boulevard on my street were inhabited by German soldiers—Nazi SS guards—dressed in their iconic dark grey uniforms, not flitting from tree to tree, but marching, marching in perfect step in columns of five with sunlight flashing off their shiny black helmets and dark leather boots, as they crisscrossed the boulevard and shouted words that I didn't understand. There was no ambiguity as to what they were doing and where they were going. No unknown destination.

Alongside them were dogs, big dogs, ferocious dogs, German Shepherds marching in perfect rhythm and barking. But the shouts and barks were perfectly timed. Three shouts and a bark, three shouts and a bark; very mechanical, very controlled, very exact, very sterile, very frightening. And then I looked up, and in the treetops I saw monkeys holding wooden bars to which strings were attached, each string controlling the steps and movements of every soldier and dog below. And while the monkeys manipulated the strings, they were cackling, laughing, sneering as only monkeys can do, and collectively mocking the scene below.

What had happened to these soldiers? Had they lost their will? Were they being controlled by some unidentifiable outer force? Surely these puppeteers were not messengers of God? It was impossible for me to believe that the insides of these soldiers had so curdled of their own volition, that no supernatural forces had been involved. It was almost as though they had been infected by a virus moving from person to person, from cell to cell, incorporating itself into their genes and altering them forever.

Then the dogs seemed to lose control. They tore away from their masters and started running around in a frenzy, barking incessantly. I woke up afraid and anxious. It was early morning, but the sun had not yet risen, and I heard the neighbour's dog barking outside, probably wanting to be let in from the cold night air. I felt relieved as I clutched my blanket and saw my books and stuffed animals around me.

I wouldn't bother my parents about it; they had too much on their minds. So I just lay in bed, trying to calm down until it was time to get up and help my mother prepare for the Ladies Spring Tea.

CHAPTER XXIV

Hold fast to dreams
For if dreams die,
Life is a broken-winged bird
That cannot fly.

Hold fast to dreams
For when dreams go,
Life is a barren field
Frozen with snow.

—Langston Hughes, "Dreams"

The ladies came spilling into the house, their voices rising and falling in sweet cadences, their full skirts and princess-line dresses floating and swishing about them, a mass of moving colour, like flowers in a garden gently shimmying in the wind.

My mother finally had enough confidence in me to allow me to pour tea. Pouring tea was considered an honour at such events. My mother's sterling silver tea set was placed at one end of the table—the tall, stately coffee pot, the rounded teapot with its gracefully curved spout, the matching creamer and sugar bowl all exuding regal elegance. Arranged around it were her best cups and saucers, each one with its unique design of flowers and gold trim. Only the one decorated with dark pink roses on a gold background remained in the dining room hutch, reserved for Zaidi Max when he was at our house for dinner.

As the ladies approached, I would ask, "Coffee or tea? Cream or sugar? One teaspoon or two?" The table was set with exquisite pastries and desserts made by my mother and the other ladies of the *Muter Farein*, the Ladies Auxiliary of the school. There were chocolate squares, cherry chews, marshmallow rolls, fruit tarts, and various assorted cakes and dainties all laid out in a colourful and elegant display.

Sitting at the head of the table provided an excellent vantage point to overhear the women's conversations. "*Nu, vos hert zich by dir?*" my grandmother asked Mrs. Moskowitz.

"*Gornisht.*" Nothing. "But, did you hear?" said Mrs. Moskowitz. "Mr. Levin needs an operation on his gallbladder."

"*Takeh?*" said one of the other mothers, surprised. "And Mrs. Danzker is going to visit her daughter in Saskatoon."

And there was Lererine Malka, wearing her pretty red dress, smiling and chatting along with everyone else.

I wondered how many of my other teachers had survived the concentration camps. Like Chaver B, Lererine Malka's entire family had perished in the war, even her daughter, her only child. But when thinking of her and Chaver B, it was hard to imagine that they had each endured such abomination. He was still being suffocated by his ordeal, and she seemed to have set herself free.

After the war, she had met a man in a displaced persons camp; they had fallen in love and were married. Even when she'd told my class about the war, the import of her experiences hadn't resonated with me until I'd heard Chaver B's account. Had I been too young to have appreciated the significance of her story? Was it the way she had told it to us? Or were its contents so preposterous and inconceivable that it seemed as though she was simply reading to us from another one of Peretz's tales? After all, as a fourth grader at the time, her story seemed to have had as much of an impact on me as did her grammar lessons.

The remaining few weeks of the school year dragged on. The horror of what Chaver B had told me would not leave my mind and clung to me with the tenacity of a leech. I barely remembered what we studied over the ensuing days; it was hard to concentrate.

I felt as though I had absorbed Chaver B's trauma, as though I had been there beside him in all those abhorrent, disgusting places, enduring all those horrendous things. But Chaver B bore the same inscrutable expression that he had assumed so often. Each morning, he donned his mask and taught our class as usual. Since our last meeting—when he had played his violin for me—he had reverted to that apparent emotionless self; his eyes looked more vacant than troubled. He had frozen his feelings, I realized. Just like in Auschwitz.

Occasionally I could detect a smile struggling to emerge, the suggestion of a quiver at the corner of his lips, a slight softening of the muscles of his face, like the sun evanescently peeking out from behind a cloud. But there was no playfulness about Chaver B. And his smile never reached the surface. He had become a master of concealment, presenting a composed visage full of equanimity that belied the incredible turmoil raging inside him.

Grade seven and my time at Peretz School finally came to a close. I rallied myself for all the graduation activities at the end of June, but the excitement didn't reach the level I had anticipated while watching all those who had come before me leave the school. I'd learned many things during those years at Peretz School, but in my final year, I had been given a class, private and for me alone, that I had not expected or planned to take. It didn't seem fair that I should have ended all those wonderful years in this enchanted place with such a heavy heart.

Part III

CHAPTER XXV

Oh, somewhere in this favored land the sun is shining bright,
The band is playing somewhere, and somewhere hearts are light;
And somewhere men are laughing, and somewhere
children shout,
But there is no joy in Mudville—mighty Casey has struck out.

—Ernest Lawrence Thayer, "Casey at the Bat"

Chaver B went away for the summer. My parents initially told me that he was visiting his cousin in Ottawa, but when I expressed my surprise at hearing that he indeed had a relative who was alive, and in Canada no less, a flustered look came over their faces, and I then realized that this was not the truth.

After some prodding, they informed me that Chaver B was spending the summer in a "rest home" or sanatorium just outside Winnipeg, to help him deal with his feelings. But he would be back in September, they reassured me, ready to start teaching again.

I still enjoyed playing violin, but my enthusiasm had waned over the preceding weeks, and with Chaver B being absent, I rarely picked it up.

I was waking up later and later in the mornings. At ten o'clock on a Monday morning, one week into summer vacation, my mother walked into my bedroom and pulled back the blue-checkered curtains from my window. "Mira, Annie's here. Don't you want to get up?"

I shielded my eyes from the warm sunlight streaming in, and when they finally adjusted to the brightness, I put on my slippers and went downstairs. Annie, wearing red shorts and a pale yellow sleeveless top, her black curls tumbling to her shoulders, was sitting at the kitchen table, patiently waiting for me.

I hadn't confided yet in Annie about my conversations with Chaver B. I felt bad not sharing them with her, but I was still trying to make sense of them myself, and I didn't think I could convey them to her in any kind of coherent fashion. How could I explain the whispers haunting his mind, the shadows walling him in, the ghosts refusing to leave? Besides, it was his story to tell, not mine, just as my mother had said. At times, I must have seemed more remote to Annie, but if she noticed a change in me, she never said anything.

"My brother and some of his friends are forming a baseball team," Annie excitedly told me while I was eating my breakfast of toast and marmalade and an orange cut into eight small pyramids. "There's going to be a league of thirteen to fifteen-year-olds with teams from some of the other towns. Most of the players are from my brother's class, but they need a couple more. Do you want to play?"

"I don't know," I said. "I'm not very good."

"Sure you are," she countered.

"No, I'm not. You are. Kenny's been playing catch with you in your backyard since you were three. That's the advantage of having an older brother. The only baseball I've ever played is using a bat and rubber ball at recess. I think I'll look silly."

"No, you won't," she said encouragingly. "Come on, you should play. What else are you going to do this summer?"

Annie was right. I didn't have any other obligations or specific plans. And perhaps this would shift my focus to more lighthearted thoughts. "And we have an extra glove for you," she added coaxingly, which seemed to settle the matter.

"Sure," I decided. "Why not?"

We played our first game in a neighbouring town. Two of the dads drove us in their pickup trucks. We piled into the open backs and sat on huge sacks of seeds as we rode and bounced along the fifteen miles to the game, past tall stalks of sunflowers, buds visible atop their stems, waiting to mature and open their faces to the sun. Now and then, a violet-green swallow would fly swiftly and gracefully overhead and then glide out of sight, or a flock of crows would swoop downwards, their dissonant calls breaking the distant silence. The older players chatted and joked with one another, but somewhat intimidated by the age gap, Annie and I pretty much stayed to ourselves and quietly took in their conversations and flirtations.

The game turned out to be fun. I started in the outfield, but my arm wasn't strong enough for the throw back to the infield, so Kenny told me to try second base. I only let two balls go through my legs but miraculously turned a double play. I had a single, a walk, and struck out twice. We won by one run, five to four, but no one cared much about the score.

Our next game was played at home, and for the rest of the summer we alternated between away and home games. Sammy and his friends would ride over on their bicycles to the local baseball field and cheer us on.

After the last game of the summer, Annie and I went back to her house and settled into two white wooden lawn chairs on her rear patio. Kenny's friend Chris, the third baseman, was also there, and he pulled up a chair beside us, his long legs extended in front of him and loosely crossed at the ankles. I hadn't spoken much to Chris over the summer, but I'd watched him with others, and he seemed to have an easy-going manner. That evening he was very attentive and told Annie and me what to expect in high school. We received a rundown of all the teachers—the good and the bad—complete with anecdotes that kept us all laughing.

Later that evening, Chris and I walked home together. He happened to live just a couple of blocks away from me. Although he was two years older, there was no awkwardness in our conversation. "I live down here," he said, when we came to the corner just before my house.

"It's funny we've never seen each other before this summer," I said, "at the skating rink or the park." Even if our paths had previously crossed, I wasn't sure that I would have recognized Chris. I hadn't seen him without his baseball cap all summer, and the only distinguishing features I could discern were his lazy, relaxed smile and his tall stature. He looked to be taller than my father.

"Well, I help my dad in his hardware store downtown whenever I can, so you probably wouldn't have seen me around much. And I try to help my mom at home, too. I have four younger brothers and sisters, so things can get pretty busy."

"I know your dad's store," I said. "I've been there with my mom."

"My dad said it was okay if I tried out for the basketball team this year, even though that'll mean that I won't have much time to help him out."

"Oh, I'm sure you'll make it," I said. "You're so tall. How tall are you, anyway?"

"Six-three, and I think I'm still growing," he laughed. He must have been reading my earlier thoughts, because for no apparent reason, he took off his baseball cap and ran his fingers through his sandy blond hair. He had an inviting face, slightly angular, with hazel-coloured eyes. And even though it was evening, now that his cap brim wasn't casting a shadow, I could see faint freckles dotting his nose and cheeks that I'd never previously noticed.

Just then, I saw my dad drive by in his car and pull into our driveway. He must have been called to the hospital, I thought. "I'd better go," I said quickly, suddenly feeling uncomfortable. "It's getting dark. I'll see you at school."

"See you," he said, giving me a half-wave as he turned and walked down the street towards his house.

Chris was pleasant, and although I admit our conversation lingered in my head when I returned home that evening, I didn't think about him too much after that.

I was still volunteering at the hospital. Since I was now one of the older girls, Mrs. Jones reassigned me to the gift shop. She obviously felt comfortable with her decision, as there was no trace of her head tremor when she gave me my assignment. But I missed seeing the patients on the wards and was pleased when one day she asked me to take the library cart. I passed the room where Chaver B had been the previous summer, and I suddenly started to cry. I didn't think it would have affected me the way it did. All my diversions over the past few weeks had been for naught. I decided to see if

Mrs. Singer was in the hospital; she always put me in a good mood. I looked at the board listing the patients, and yes, there she was.

I pushed my cart to her room and found her sleeping, no trace of her usual frown on her now smooth forehead. She was wearing her white cotton hospital gown and was lying on her left side. Her right arm was draped across her front, and high, sibilant sounds emanated from her chest each time she exhaled. "Mrs. Singer, how are you? It's me, Mira," I said while gently tapping her arm.

She moaned and slowly opened her eyes. "Miraleh," she said forcing a smile. "How are you, dear?"

"Do you want to play cards?" I asked.

"I'm so tired today," she replied. "Can you come back tomorrow?"

"Sure. I'll see you then." I visited the other patients and at four o'clock returned the cart to the volunteer office and went home.

I wasn't taking any chances, so the next day, rather than waiting for my assignment, I asked Mrs. Jones if it would be alright if I took the library cart again. Despite her to-and-fro head movements, she replied in the affirmative. I wheeled the cart to the third floor where Mrs. Singer was and walked into her room. Only there was another patient—a man—in her bed. I went to the front desk and reviewed the patients' names on the board tacked to the wall behind the counter, but I didn't see her name listed.

The clerk at the desk must have been new, because I hadn't seen her before. "Was Mrs. Singer discharged?" I asked.

"She died last night," the clerk replied perfunctorily.

I immediately felt the blood drain from my face and the floor come up to meet me. My vision began to close in, and it seemed as though I was looking through a tunnel. I moved towards a nearby chair, but it was taking me much longer to reach it than I had anticipated. Sherrie, one of the nurses who had overheard the conversation, quickly came over and supported me until I sat down. The clerk rushed over with a cup of cool water, and Sherrie dipped her fingertips into it and rubbed the refreshing droplets on my face. "I'm sorry, Mira," she said as she squeezed my cold, damp hand. "If I'd seen you come in, I would've told you right away. I know that you two were close."

Sherrie stayed with me until I felt better. "I'm okay now," I said after several minutes. "Thanks. But I think I'll go home."

Mrs. Jones was surprised to see me so early in the afternoon, but I told her that I wasn't feeling well and then left.

That night I discussed it with my father. "Wasn't Mrs. Singer your patient?" I asked him. "Did you know that she died last night?"

"Yes, I did," he said. "I didn't know that you knew her so well. She'd been sick for a long time," he tried to console me. "She was very broken on the inside. We did as much as we could for her."

Mrs. Singer was the first person close to me who had died. Yes, my Zaidi Harry had died, but I'd never met him, so the impact of his death was not as immediate. And I assumed he'd been old. Old people were supposed to die. Mrs. Singer was old, too, but she was my friend, and I hadn't wanted her to die.

I didn't go back to the hospital after that. It was too hard becoming close to someone only to lose them later on. Is that how Chaver B felt? That it was better not to become too close to anyone so as not to suffer pain later? Is that why he kept his distance from us, emotionally, at least? How sad, I thought, if that was true.

Summer was almost over, anyway, and I decided I would just take it easy before grade eight started in September.

CHAPTER XXVI

A bird may love a fish, but where would they
build a home together?

—Fiddler on the Roof

The principal's voice came over the loud speaker as we stood up straight at our desks, our heads slightly bowed forward, our arms dangling at our sides.

"Our Father who art in Heaven, hallowed be thy name…"

The Lord's Prayer. A Christian prayer. Each morning after the bell rang, we would begin our recitation. No one asked me if I wanted to say this prayer. I was just expected to do so. Mine was a regular public school, so I was surprised at the requirement, and no one had warned me of this daily ritual. But the prayer seemed harmless enough, and it echoed the same sentiments as did my prayers and blessings. Still, I was never comfortable saying it, never quite at ease, and it made me feel like a piece in a puzzle that was slightly irregular for the allotted space.

And so began the new school year and the new school. Sammy now walked to Peretz School with his friend Ben who knocked on our front door every morning when he came over to meet him.

Ben's blond hair was as curly as Sammy's black hair was straight, but other than this physical difference, they were similar in appearance and temperament – two happy, carefree ten-year-olds.

High school turned out to be a harsh world. I was no longer in my warm, cozy, comfortable cocoon. But after Chaver B's revelations, my world had already begun to change even before I stepped into these hallowed halls of higher learning.

There had always been something comforting in the cycle of Jewish holidays that now seemed to whiz past, sometimes barely noticed and without the lengthy prelude of preparations that accompanied them when I was at Peretz School. In fact, now it was hard to celebrate the holidays, hard to fully immerse myself in them. I went to synagogue on Rosh Hashanah and Yom Kippur, but classes continued despite my absence, and the teachers assigned homework even though I wasn't there.

The realization that I did not live in a predominantly Jewish world and that this new world was not always going to be willing to accommodate me or anyone else who was Jewish was startling and disconcerting.

When I was younger, there'd been several days during the school year when I was forced to stay home from school with a bad cold. Lying on the living room sofa and looking out our picture window, I would sometimes see the neighbourhood girls walk by in their Girl Guide uniforms - brown shirts and pleated, plaid skirts with dark brown caps and gold scarves tied around their necks. How I envied them and their cute outfits.

"Mom, can I be a Girl Guide?" I asked. "It looks like fun."

"I don't think so," she replied. "You won't know any of the girls, and besides, they meet in a church."

"So," I said, "what does that matter?"

"It's just better that you don't," she said.

And that was that. I wished she would have let me, though. I would have been better prepared for life.

Richard Gold and I had been put in a special class called Major Work Class, which was exactly what it turned out to be—major work. I missed my old friends, especially Annie. Although we all attended the same school, our paths rarely crossed.

During the previous May, just before graduation, the seventh graders had been given a special test, and Richard and I were the only ones who earned a high enough grade to attain entrance to the class. I wished I hadn't done so well.

The work seemed relentless and was exhausting. I was always doing homework. Before dinner, after dinner, and on weekends. We were perpetually being assigned research projects that turned the visits to the library, which I'd once eagerly anticipated, into something I dreaded. And never-ending tests. Not only that, but the other students were just not friendly, to say the least, bordering on hostile. When I asked one classmate a question about the homework, she simply said, "Go figure it out for yourself."

Chaver B had returned from Winnipeg and resumed teaching. He again joined us for Shabbos dinners, and although he seemed slightly more relaxed and less guarded, this alteration in his demeanor was barely perceptible, the change in his eyes subtle. Our violin lessons also resumed on Tuesday afternoons at five o'clock, but with so much homework, my violin playing suffered. Some days I couldn't even find the time to practice, and when I did, I usually rushed through my exercises and pieces.

"What's the matter, Mira?" Chaver B asked at one of my lessons.

"It is now three weeks in a row that you seem distracted. Is something wrong?"

"I'm sorry," I said contritely. "I just have so much school work." Then I added, "You know, no matter how hard I work, I keep hearing these voices in my head telling me to work even harder."

"Really?" he said without changing his expression. "That's interesting. Well, this week, why don't you just work on the same exercises and songs. Nothing new."

The next night after dinner, my father and mother sat down with me in the living room. "Mira, how would you like to go into the regular class with Annie and your other friends?"

"Do you mean that?" I virtually screamed. "Oh, thank you, thank you!" I jumped up, ran over, and hugged them. "I was so afraid of disappointing you!" Although all the schoolwork had taken my mind off darker thoughts, I'm not sure it had been worth it. But Chaver B had rescued me. Obviously, he had related to my parents what I'd told him. And although I might have been upset that he had betrayed my confidence, it was comforting to know that he cared enough about me to intervene.

"And why don't you try some extracurricular activities," suggested my mother. "You always liked to act. There must be a drama club at school."

Although the idea of escaping into someone else's skin, or rather psyche, seemed very appealing, at this point in time I felt I needed something emotionally light and with a less complicated objective. Sometimes I felt that I was already an actor in a play, and I wasn't sure that I liked the part I'd been given.

The school was holding tryouts for the junior high girls' basketball team. The league had just started the year before, and the team had done quite well. Perhaps the fact that Chris played basketball had subconsciously influenced me, even though I hadn't seen him since the summer.

All those years of playing violin must have enhanced my hand-eye coordination, because I made the team. My father was not pleased and thought it was a waste of time. "Does it teach you anything?" he asked. "All you have to do is run up and down the court and throw the ball into the basket, or swat it out of your opponent's hands."

"That's not allowed," I said. I tried to defend the game as best I could. "And, we have plays and strategies."

Despite his disapproval, I found the games cathartic, and contrary to what one might expect given the physical exertion, the games were energizing. And they definitely took my mind off everything else. Playing point guard and setting up most of the plays made me feel that I was choreographing a dance, a dance of cooperation and mutual purpose. For a short time, I felt as though I had control over my own destiny. Once in a while, I felt the exhilarating thrill of throwing the ball and watching it swish through the hoop. Yes, sometimes things did go according to plan.

Even Chaver B came to my games. And they seemed to energize him almost as much as they did me. I could see him in the bleachers, clapping and cheering for our team. Once, out of the corner of my eye, I even saw him stand up and wave when I made a basket.

His sojourn to Winnipeg last summer had helped him after all, and his emotional palette seemed to have expanded. Since his return, he had gradually become more at ease with himself and engaged in life—less constrained, less repressed—not consistently, but often enough that it was noticeable. Of course, he was no longer my schoolteacher, so I only saw him at my violin lessons and at Shabbos dinners. But he contributed more to conversations than he had previously and was quite free about voicing his opinions.

My mother even began inviting other guests to the dinners, including eligible single ladies. But learning from her first mistake, as she viewed it, she never invited just one woman and Chaver B; there would always be other acquaintances or family, like Babbi Rachel and Auntie Miriam and her family. I was too busy now to eavesdrop on the mah-jong games to gather additional information, but as far as I knew, no romances had materialized.

Chris had also come to watch me play basketball. One day after school, just as I was leaving for home, he appeared beside me. "Hey, Mira. Can I walk home with you?"

"Sure," I replied. "I'd like the company."

"I watched some of your games," he said. "You look like a natural."

Basketball season ended, but our walks home together continued. Chris turned off before reaching my house, and I hadn't mentioned him to my parents. One day in June, he asked me if I would accompany him to the final school dance. Of course, I accepted.

I waited until the following evening to tell my parents. I was sitting at the dining room table after dinner and finishing my homework. My father was reclining on the sofa reading the newspaper, while my mother sat in one of the floral wingback armchairs and was just starting a new novel that was very thick and that would likely take her weeks to read, especially with the summer holidays approaching, and Sammy and I home from school. I looked up from my notebook and casually announced, "Someone's invited me to the school dance."

My father lowered his newspaper, and my mother glanced up from her book with a look of both surprise and amusement.

"Really?" she said. "How nice. Who is he?"

"He's a tenth grader," I answered.

"A tenth grader?" she repeated, her expression suddenly becoming mildly concerned.

"And what's his name?"

"Chris," I answered, trying to sound nonchalant. "His father owns the hardware store downtown." I needn't have added that second bit of unsolicited information. They knew Chris's dad, but it was obvious that Chris wasn't Jewish, regardless of who his parents were. No Jewish boy was ever named Christopher or Nicholas or Luke or John with an *h*.

My parents became very alarmed. I had never mentioned him before, and they almost forbade me from going since they knew nothing about him.

"What!" my mom blurted out, clearly not filtering her emotions before speaking. "You're not going to go with him, are you?"

"Of course I am. Why not?" I countered. "He's very nice."

"He may be very nice," she said dramatically, "but he's not Jewish."

"So, I'm not going to marry him," I replied insolently. "We're just going to the dance together."

My mother was silent, but I knew exactly what was going on in her mind. "That's what you think," I could hear her say as she envisioned me following the path of Aunt Bella.

"Well, he's a friend of Kenny's, if that makes you feel any better. We played baseball together last summer," I offered hopefully.

Chris was Protestant. I don't think it had ever crossed my parents' minds before that I might be friends with a boy who wasn't Jewish, and I hadn't realized how much it would upset them. It was the first time I had ever had a major disagreement with them.

I could feel the blood rushing up to my face and boiling under my skin as the discussion became more impassioned. "I think you're both being very silly," I said. "Chris is very sweet. We're just friends, and he's always been very polite and considerate. And there is no logical reason in the world why I shouldn't be able to go to the dance with him!"

"Well, you both come from different worlds," my mom said. "Those kinds of things never turn out well." I could have asked her what she meant by that, but I didn't need to.

Although I had addressed both my mother and my father in my arguments, my mother had provided most of the objections. My father, in fact, had been quite reticent. Finally he joined in and said in his most diplomatic manner, "I agree with your mother. I don't think it's a good idea, but since you've already accepted, you can go with him. It would be rude of you to decline now."

Initially I hadn't expected such a furor over Chris's invitation, but when my father actually acquiesced, I was quite stunned. My mother seemed to be equally shocked. Her face remained stern and her eyes angry, but she said nothing. Over the years, my parents had mastered the intricate dance of parental disagreement. If they were at odds with one other, they never argued in front of us. And it wasn't always my father who made the final decision. But for whatever reason, this time he had prevailed.

For the first time in my life, I saw my parents as being closed-minded and narrow. But in some ways, they were right. Chris and I moved in the same world at school. But outside of that environment, our experiences were in many ways quite different. Or were they?

Although our Jewish community was an insular world, it was not exclusionary, except when it came to marriage. Anyway, I still couldn't understand what all the fuss was about. After all, I had only just turned fourteen.

CHAPTER XXVII

Efsher oych veln di verter,
Dervartn zich ven af dem licht
Veln in shaw in basherter
Tseblien zich oych umgericht?

Perhaps these words will endure,
And live to see the light loom
And in the destined hour
Will unexpectedly bloom?

—Abraham Sutzkever, "Grains of Wheat"

One evening, a couple of weeks later, I was sitting in the living room finishing my homework when I overheard my parents talking in the kitchen.

"Ari will be going to New York this summer," said my dad, "to work at the Yiddish Institute."

"New York!" exclaimed my mom. "How did this come about?"

"Chaver Lieberman had a meeting with all the teachers at the school. Apparently, the Institute has received a large shipment of Yiddish books from Europe that survived the war, and they need people to sort and catalogue them. Ari decided to go. He's already written to them. It's all arranged."

"Where will he stay?"

"They'll be billeting everyone in people's homes. And he'll be paid for his services."

"Do you think that's a good idea?" asked my mother with obvious concern. "He'll have to take the train all the way to New York; that's a two or three-day trip. Don't you think that will revive unpleasant memories?"

"Claire, he can't avoid trains his entire life. And he already took a train from Montreal to Winnipeg when he first arrived in Canada."

"I don't know," said my mom. "I can't see it doing any good. He's bound to come across a book he read as a child, or even an actual copy that belonged to someone he knew, with their name inscribed in it. I think it's a mistake."

"Look, he can't stay here all summer. There will be too much time for him to think. He needs to keep busy."

"You should tell him not to go."

"I can't do that," replied my father. "He's an adult."

"But you're his doctor, and you can tell him that it's a bad idea— even order him to stay here. We'll find something else for him to do."

"Look, he has to make his own decisions. I'm sure he looked at all the pros and cons and thought it would be worthwhile. He has to make a life for himself. That's part of his healing process. We all try to make the best decisions we can with the information at hand, and that's what he's doing."

"You sound as though you're talking about a child."

"There's a child in all of us," said my father. "Some more than others."

Two weeks after Chaver B left, we received a letter from him, filled with all the excitement of starting a new endeavour.

July 7, 1951

Dear Reuven, Claire, Mira, and Sammy,

The task before us is enormous. There are more than just books here. There are posters announcing Jewish films, concerts, plays, and sporting events. Unpublished plays and poems. And they have come from all over Europe.

It wasn't enough that the Nazis wanted to destroy all the Jewish people. They wanted to extinguish every last trace of our culture, too. So many books were burned or shipped to local paper mills for recycling.

Many of the books and papers that have survived are damaged and will need to be restored before we can even begin to study their depths. And the stories we hear of the lengths people took to hide these works and salvage them from destruction are staggering—stealing them from libraries and hiding them under their clothing as they walked down the streets, plastering them inside walls, storing them in cellars and underneath floorboards, or leaving them with good-hearted Gentile friends, all at risk to their own lives.

Everyone here has been very generous. I am staying with a lovely family, much like yours, and they are showing me the wonderful sights of New York City. I will tell you all about it on my return.

Mit libshaft,
Ari

While Chaver B was doing important work, I was enjoying my summer days thoroughly, unfettered and without reservation. I had discovered romance novels, and the library seemed to have no shortage of them. *Pride and Prejudice, Forever Amber,* they were captivating. The willow tree in the nearby park, with its elegant flowing branches, was the perfect setting for enjoying them. I would prop myself up against its sturdy trunk, sit under the canopy of weeping foliage, and read and read as the leaves of the tree shushed around me, seemingly commenting on what I had just read.

Annie and I and Kenny and Chris continued to play on the baseball team. Chris's and my relationship remained casual, and my parents took no steps to prevent us from seeing each other. A group of us would often meet in the evenings and walk downtown for ice cream or to see a movie. Annie's house remained the centre of our activities, where we had barbecues and would sometimes light a bonfire in a clearing behind her house. The hours of sunshine each day were many, and we took unmitigated pleasure in every minute of the sun's radiant glow.

My family continued to go to the beach on weekends, and on one particular Sunday, Annie and her family joined us. Annie's Uncle Saul, the radio announcer, was visiting from Winnipeg. I'd met him before; he was difficult to forget with his deep, resonant voice and ready smile.

"I have something to tell you," Annie said as we walked on the wet sand along the shore, the waves licking at our feet and washing away our footprints as soon as we made them.

"Hmm, sounds important," I replied. "What is it?"

"Every July, my Uncle Saul comes to visit. He comes at other times of the year, too, but when he comes in July, he doesn't bring my aunt or my cousins; he comes by himself. Doesn't that seem odd to you?"

"Maybe he wants to spend time alone with your dad, like when they were kids," I offered.

"That's not it," she said. "Whenever he comes, he and my dad take a drive for the afternoon. They never take Kenny and me, and they never tell us where they're going. But this time, while they were gone, I asked my mom."

"What did she say?" I asked expectantly.

"It seems that I have another aunt."

"Another aunt?" I echoed. "What do you mean?"

"My dad always told me that there were only two children in his family, him and Uncle Saul. But it turns out there's a sister, Sara, the youngest."

"What happened to her?"

"Well, my mom said that when Sara was eighteen years old, my dad and Uncle Saul found her pacing in her room, wringing her hands, talking nonstop but talking to no one. Later they realized that she was seeing and hearing people who were saying upsetting things to her and telling her to do things that were wrong. Somehow my dad and uncle managed to calm her down. They took her to the doctor right away, and he gave her a sedative. But when she woke up, she acted the same way. They hospitalized her in a mental institution, but because she didn't get better, the doctors did an operation called a frontal lobotomy, where they destroyed nerves in part of her brain in order to control her behaviour. My mom says that she changed dramatically after the surgery; she was no longer the sister they had all known. They eventually moved her out of the institution, and now she lives in a boarding house in Wasaga, about thirty miles from here, where the owner looks after her."

"And you've never met her?"

"Nope."

"Why would your parents keep her a secret?" I asked. "Only see her once a year? And not tell you and Kenny? It's as though they're denying she even exists."

Annie was clearly upset and confused. Why would her parents have behaved in this fashion? Clearly they must have felt that they were protecting her and Kenny, but from what? It seemed that parents often did that—at least mine did—and now it seemed Annie's did, too. Not outrightly lie, except for the time my mom and dad told me that Chaver B would be going to Ottawa for the summer, but rather withhold information that they feel might be difficult for children to comprehend and make sense of. Why did adults underestimate the intelligence of children and their depth of understanding and empathy? Only Chaver B hadn't. He had confided in me and told me his innermost thoughts. He had let me look deep into his soul; for however brief it was, it was enough time to have glimpsed his essence and to have forged an irrevocable connection with him.

"Does Kenny know?" I asked.

"My mom told him later that afternoon, before my dad and uncle came back, but she asked us not to say anything to our dad for the time being."

Our conversation was interrupted when we heard someone shouting our names. We turned around and saw Sammy and his friend Ben running over to us. Annie and I had been so involved in our conversation that we hadn't realized how far along the shore we'd walked.

"Mom sent us to find you. She's worried," Sammy said breathlessly.

"Well, you can go back and tell her you found us. We'll be right there."

When we rejoined the others, Annie's Uncle Saul had taken out his guitar and started to play and sing some campfire songs. A crowd quickly assembled, and within a few minutes our troubling thoughts had dissipated, and all we could think about was the blue sky, warm sun, and refreshing water.

The following week, our baseball game was being played in Wasaga, the same town where Annie's Aunt Sara lived.

"I'm going to visit her," Annie told me as we sat on my front lawn, running our hands over the blades of grass and watching the parade of puffy clouds drift overhead.

"Are you going to tell your mom?"

"No," she stated defiantly.

"Do you know Sara's address?"

"Nope," she answered seemingly unperturbed, but then she began twisting a strand of dark curls around her finger, something she'd recently started doing whenever she felt nervous.

"Well, if you don't tell your mom, how are you going to find her?" I asked in a worried tone.

"Wasaga is a small town. There can't be *that* many boarding houses."

"But there won't be any time. Usually we go home right after the game's over."

"I'll just have to take my chances," Annie said matter-of-factly.

The next Wednesday we rode in the pickup truck to our game. The day was hot and dry, windless and sluggish, a day where you just wanted to sit in the shade and drink a glass of cool lemonade. Even the birds remained hushed in the trees. Luckily, there were too many players, so not everyone was needed. Annie, Kenny, and I volunteered to sit out. We informed the team that we would be walking downtown and would be back in about an hour, or at the latest, before the game was over.

Wasaga was smaller than Ambrosia. Downtown consisted of only two blocks. I suggested that we ask at the drugstore for the names of boarding houses. Annie's aunt probably took some medications, so maybe the pharmacist would know where she lived.

The pharmacist was a tall, thin, middle-aged man with closely cropped light brown hair and a bump in his nose above which sat a pair of round dark brown spectacles with thick lenses that magnified his eyes to twice their size. He was busy behind his counter when we arrived, studiously measuring out a powder and adding it to a thick white liquid.

"Sure, I know Sara," he said affably, after Annie asked him if he'd heard of her. "She lives over at Mrs. Stadnyk's boarding house. Just walk to the corner, turn left on to Landsdowne Avenue, and it's two blocks down. There's a huge white screened-in veranda in front. You can't miss it."

As we left the store, I asked Annie and Kenny if they were still committed to their plan. "Are you sure you want to go? You can change your minds if you want to."

"Positive," they replied without hesitation.

We found the house easily, a two-storey, white wood-framed house with a front yard edged with marigolds. Annie and Kenny walked up to the front screen door and boldly knocked, while I stayed a few steps behind them. A pleasant, stout woman with a kind, open, round face and chin-length curly brown hair answered the door.

"Mrs. Stadnyk," Annie said. "We've come to see Sara. I'm her niece, Annie, and this is my brother, Kenny, and my friend Mira," she added while turning towards me.

"Well, isn't that nice," Mrs. Stadnyk replied in a singsong voice. "I'm sure Sara will be happy to see you. She doesn't get many visitors, but just last week her brothers came. When it rains, it pours! Come in," she said welcomingly while holding the screen door open for us. "She's right here, sitting in the living room."

We entered the house. Mrs. Stadnyk led us into the living room off to the left of the front hall. The room smelled of liniment and was dimly lit, the curtains having been drawn to keep out the afternoon heat.

"Sara, you have some visitors," Mrs. Stadnyk said in a gay voice. "Your niece and nephew."

I expected Annie and Kenny to be reserved and shy, almost fearful, but they weren't. They had come on a mission, and they were going to complete it exactly as they had planned. They immediately walked over to Sara and stood in front of her, while I remained standing at the opposite end of the room.

"Aunt Sara," Kenny said, "I'm your nephew, Joseph's son, and this is my sister, Annie."

Sara was a large woman. She was sitting in the corner of Mrs. Stadnyk's floral sofa, her back rounded, head bent forward, eyes focused on her thick hands that were resting in her lap. I thought she resembled Annie's Uncle Saul. She had the same high cheekbones and square jaw, the same slight curvature of the nose, but her straight shoulder length hair was already completely grey, whereas his black hair was only just starting to grey at the temples.

I'm sure Annie and Kenny were expecting some sort of a welcome, but Sara gave very little. She raised her pale, dull eyes to look at them when they introduced themselves, but there was no smile, no handshake. She uttered a few words of response in a monotone, but offered nothing spontaneously.

For a minute, the air was filled with a heavy silence as Annie and Kenny studied Sara. I could only imagine how surprised they were at what they had encountered. Despite what their mother had told them, I was sure that this was not the Sara they had anticipated. Annie sat down on the sofa beside her, and Mrs. Stadnyk brought over a folding chair so that Kenny could also sit near her on the other side. Annie took Sara's left hand in her own, while Kenny placed his hand on Sara's right forearm, periodically patting it as they spoke.

They carried on a seemingly one-sided conversation, telling Sara how old they were, where they lived, what they were studying in school, why they were in Wasaga, and anything else they could think of to fill the painful, silent void.

"She doesn't say much since the operation," volunteered Mrs. Stadnyk, "but I think she understands everything, and I'm sure she's happy that you came. Before you go, why don't you have some milk with these chocolate chip cookies that I just baked," she said while placing a tray on the coffee table in front of the sofa.

After forty minutes, we said goodbye and made our way back to the baseball field. I was impressed at how calm Annie and Kenny had been, but after walking half a block, Annie's lower lip began to quiver, and her eyes filled with tears; she scrunched them shut, stood still, and sobbed, wet tears flowing down her cheeks as her whole body convulsed with pain and sorrow. Kenny put his arms around her and hugged her until she quieted down.

"It's so sad," she said, wiping her eyes with her shirt sleeve. "What happened to her? It's hard to imagine that she's my father's and Uncle Saul's sister. She hardly said anything. Did she even hear anything we said? Is this all because of the surgery?"

I tried to comfort her. "Mrs. Stadnyk said that she heard and understood." But I wondered if that was true. Chaver B had a similar vacant look in his eyes sometimes, but his was more of an incoherent look, and I often wondered what he was thinking about and if he heard what I'd said. His was either a willful vacancy, commanding himself not to think, or else he was so full of swirling emotions that it was impossible to discern what he was feeling. With Sara, it was more like looking into a dry well. What had Chaver B said about survival in the concentration camp? The only way to survive was to freeze your feelings. He would have gladly sewn up his brain to withstand such torment if he'd only been able to do that. Had Sara had that same sense of desperation?

I tried to imagine being so overwhelmed with negative feelings, intolerable feelings, that I would want to shut myself down so as not to feel anything. Could Sara cry at the ending of a sad movie? Could she laugh at a funny joke? Could she take joy at the sight of a rainbow or take pleasure in the refreshing waters of a cool lake? Could she love someone? Could she hate someone? Could she feel *anything*?

Despite what Mrs. Stadnyk had said, Sara seemed vacuous, an empty hull with a heart to pump blood, lungs to move air in and out of her body, arms to touch and grab things, and legs that allowed her to stand and walk. And a brain that helped her do all of these things, all of these things except feel, and even reason. It was as though her soul had been exorcised.

By the time we returned to the baseball field, the game was in the eighth inning. Chris asked us if we wanted to play, but we declined. We were somber on the way home and didn't even try to join in with the others. As we bumped and bounced along the road, I wondered what Annie's Aunt Sara was once like and what had caused her to change so drastically that she needed to have such an extreme operation in order to control her thoughts and behaviour. Had she been so out of control to warrant being reduced to this emotionally arid being who seemed indifferent to everything around her? Had her family and her doctors realized what would become of her when they agreed to the operation?

I imagined Sara's brain being filled with a cacophony of harsh, dissonant, deafening sounds that were agonizing to listen to. Was it better to endure such horrible discord or to cut it out and deprive yourself of everything else at the same time? How tragic to believe that the latter was the better alternative, or perhaps the only choice. Sewing up one's brain, cutting out one's brain; it was all tantamount to the same thing.

The event had been troubling, and I was eagerly anticipating Chaver B's return in the middle of August. Based on his letter to us, we assumed that he would be in good spirits. But he came back despondent and moody. Even when visiting our home, he seemed lost in his own thoughts, only tenuously connected to his surroundings. My mother had been right; perhaps my father should have listened to her. Just like when the mah-jong ladies had tried to play matchmaker, her intuition had prevailed.

For a while, my father wasn't sure if Chaver B would be well enough to return to teaching in September. There were many nighttime meetings around our kitchen table between Chaver B and my parents. These gatherings took place after my brother and I had gone to bed or were otherwise occupied. Although the adults tried to speak quietly or even cryptically, we could still hear or at least intuit what they were saying. And there was no use speaking in Yiddish, since Sammy and I both understood it.

As my mother had predicted, his experience in New York had been more painful than therapeutic. "It wasn't just the books," I overheard Chaver B saying, "with their torn pages and defaced letters. It was what they stood for—remnants of all those once vibrant communities that are now gone, forever."

But his nightly conversations with my parents proved to be cathartic, and with each passing day, seemed to restore his rather tenuous equilibrium. By Labour Day, he looked like the old Chaver B, or was it the new Chaver B? I couldn't really decide. But whichever it was, he looked like he'd recovered from his setback and was ready to start a new school year.

CHAPTER XXVIII

Music is...a higher revelation
than all Wisdom and Philosophy.

—Ludwig van Beethoven

G rade nine was about to commence. I felt less enthusiastic
about the start of school than I had in previous years. School
was beginning to feel a little more like drudgery, and the expectations were higher. But I was looking forward to walking home
with Chris, playing basketball, and starting violin lessons again.
Despite Chaver B's ambivalence towards the violin, he seemed
more comfortable with himself when he came over to teach than
he did at other times. And even when he wasn't the most sociable, I
still enjoyed his company. I also decided to join the school orchestra that year and would be playing first violin.

"This year I'm going to teach you about the sonata form,"
Chaver B announced at my first lesson of the year. "This is important," he continued in a professorial manner, "because this form is
the foundation of symphonies, string quartets, and concertos.

"Sonatas are pieces that follow a certain pattern," he explained.
"They declare their themes in the first section, which is called the

exposition. This is followed by the middle section or development, where the themes are explored and expanded. Then there is a recapitulation, a repetition of the themes leading to a resolution. This is the final section."

He put on a recording of a sonata to illustrate his points.

"The themes or main ideas in the first section contrast with one another. They are played in different keys and have different tonal qualities," he continued as I struggled to follow along with the record. "But the important ingredient is tension, tension between the themes.

"In the middle section, or development," he went on, "it is as though the themes are talking to one another, thrashing out ideas, agreeing, disagreeing, conflicting with each other, and even changing. By the time we reach the recapitulation, the final section, the same themes are again presented, but with a fresh perspective. If the conflict between them cannot be resolved," he added, "sometimes the piece will end with a coda or a tailpiece to provide a sense of closure. But a coda is not necessary. Not all sonatas end with one."

I must have had a confused look on my face, for then he added, "I know that this is more complex than the Baroque music that you like so much, Mira, with its more organized rhythms and structures."

Chaver B was right. I did like Baroque music. Bach, Vivaldi. It all seemed so straightforward and controlled, and offered a sense of security. Those pieces had more than one theme, too, but their themes were more harmonious and uniform throughout and glided into one another more seamlessly.

I had difficulty understanding all the points that Chaver B was trying to explain. But some things did resonate. At times I felt that he was talking about himself, or to himself. The sonata form almost seemed like a metaphor for his life. He needed to take his "themes"—all his issues, his qualities, his history, and their inherent tension—and examine them, explore them, and rearrange them. He needed to resolve his internal "tonal conflict," and play all his "themes" in the same key, just as is done in the recapitulation. He needed to reach a new balance between the conflicting aspects of his life—one that would make him happy.

What had Chaver B said? "One of the most important parts of the sonata is the transition, where the main argument ends and the resolution emerges. Most composers precede this point with a lengthy passage of mounting tension."

Chaver B had not yet reached that transition point, I presumed. He was still somewhere in the development, arguing, thinking, rationalizing. And his tension seemed to be ever-increasing. I wanted to help him come to his resolution, but I didn't know how. I guess it was something he would have to figure out on his own.

If I couldn't help him attain a new equilibrium, I thought, at least I wanted to be there when he finally did reach it, so I could witness the sense of relief on his face and see his dark eyes sparkle.

After our discussion, or rather Chaver B's lecture, he assigned me one of Beethoven's sonatas. Sonatas certainly weren't my favourite type of composition. Somehow, their melodies didn't send me on flights of imaginative fancy as many other pieces had. But the sonata taught me some of life's most valuable lessons. Its form and structure created a guide for how to confront issues, how to navigate conflict, and how to come to terms with all life's disparate elements.

CHAPTER XXIX

You must remember always to give, of everything you have.
You must give foolishly even. You must be extravagant.
You must give to all who come into your life...
And the more you give, the more you will have to give.

—William Saroyan, *The Human Comedy*

The Days of Awe came early that year, and well before the end of September, we had already built our *sukkah*. The weeks after Labour Day had been unseasonably warm, and as soon as Sammy and I returned home from school, we would quickly change into shorts and race outside to enjoy the last bits of sunshine. I would tend to the flowers in our front yard, while Sammy and Ben would join other children at the local playground.

And something else unusual happened. Having a cold during the school year was routine. Since we spent most of our time indoors, the germs seemed to fly from one student to another like wildfire. But although the weather had not yet turned, I developed my first cold before September was even over.

One morning in the middle of science class, my throat became sore, and I felt nauseous. With fifteen minutes remaining before the end of the period, I tried to persevere. But the teacher noticed how unwell I was and asked, "Mira, are you alright? You look so pale."

As I tried to answer, my teeth started chattering, and I was barely able to reply. She hurriedly assigned the class a chapter to read and then accompanied me to the nurse's office. Feeling unsteady and weak, I quickly lay down on the cot as the nurse popped a thermometer into my mouth. "One hundred four!" she declared a minute later. "I'd better call your father."

After fifteen minutes, he arrived. With the nurse's help, he walked me down the hall to the school entrance and out to the car. When we arrived home, my mother's pallor matched my own, and my father's joviality seemed forced and unnatural. Their more than usual concern for me was obvious. But why? After all, I'd had so many colds and flus while growing up. I was perplexed why this one seemed to frighten them so much. My mom had already prepared my bed. The down comforter had been removed from the linen chest. The pillow had been especially fluffed up and the sheets turned down awaiting my arrival.

Their fears were assuaged when after two days, the fever gradually dissipated and when by the end of the week, I was able to resume my activities.

One week later, Sammy woke up in the middle of the night with a throbbing headache and feeling hot and sweaty. "Don't worry," I told him the next morning as I peeked into his bedroom. "You probably have what I had. You'll feel better in a few days."

But Sammy didn't get better. Two days later he couldn't move his right leg. And then his left arm. My father knew right away what it was. Polio.

Polio wasn't new to our communities. There had already been four epidemics of the virus in the previous twenty-five years. But with so much else going on in the world over the past decade, it seemed to insidiously sneak in again like a sly thief, an unwanted visitor catching us off guard.

"The polio virus infects the nervous system," my father explained to me. "Not only are people struck indiscriminately, but each person is affected in a random and individual way. How the virus decides exactly where in the nervous system to deposit itself, up or down, right or left, is a mystery."

For two weeks Sammy was quarantined in the hospital and not allowed any visitors except for my mother and father. But I would sneak into the hospital anyway and wave to him through the window of his door, as he looked up at me with his big brown eyes and tried to muster a smile. I ate most of my meals at my Auntie Miriam's house and stayed there until my parents picked me up on their way home from the hospital. Basketball season was soon to start, but I decided to forego it. That decision came easily.

The waiting was excruciating. Would Sammy continue to worsen? Would he have trouble swallowing or breathing and need the iron lung, that monstrous, cylindrical, metal contraption that helped patients breathe? I could hear its whine coming from the rooms of patients as I walked down the hospital hallways, each whine and groan allowing their lungs to expand and fill with air and keep them alive. I wondered about my dad. How could he go on treating his patients when his own son lay there so sick? I felt sorry for Babbi Rachel, Zaidi Max, and Babbi Hannah. Never had they thought that they might outlive their own grandson.

We were all so distraught. A number of students at all the schools were sick, but no one else in Sammy's grade six class, other than him.

But Sammy was spared the worst. After two weeks, his condition was no longer considered critical, and he started his long course of physiotherapy. Every day after school, I would visit him in the hospital and sit by his bedside. I must have read him every *Hardy Boys* book there was, or so it seemed, adding as much dramatic flair to each passage that I could. Sometimes Chris would come with me and fill Sammy in on how the hockey teams were doing and which players had scored the most goals. Chaver B visited, too, and brought Sammy a shiny red race car as a gift.

After two months, Sammy was discharged to continue his recuperation at home. He needed help to walk and could barely use his left arm. "It will take time," my father said, "and don't expect him to recover fully. He probably won't." But no one had the heart to tell Sammy that. If things didn't get better, I guess he would eventually figure it out for himself.

Why was Sammy given this terrible burden? He was so sweet and silly, and he always made us laugh. It weighed on me that Sammy had been dealt a blow that he did not deserve, even though he always did what he was told and followed whatever rules he was supposed to, religious and otherwise.

"There are some things that are out of our control that we simply have to accept," said my father. "If we choose life, then we have to accept the good and the bad. It's the things that we have the power to change that we need to fight for."

Over the next few months, Sammy did improve. But deficits remained. We tried to hide our own angst from him and gushed over the many presents he received from family and friends. He would be missing the remainder of the school year, so his teachers had prepared special homework for him, which kept both him and us occupied during the long, cold, winter months, as we tried to help him learn his lessons.

Chris came over to our house a few times a week, and when the weather finally warmed up and the days lengthened, he took Sammy outside to play catch. Sammy would sit on a chair on the lawn, and Chris would crouch down and throw the ball to him. "Don't be a baby," he would say. "You're better than your left arm. You're the boss of it," he encouraged.

One day in May, Chris came over wearing his team basketball jacket zipped up to his neck, which was rather surprising since it was a balmy day and the temperature hovered around seventy-five degrees. He held his left arm awkwardly bent at the elbow and across his chest, so I wondered if perhaps he'd injured it. While slowly undoing the zipper with his right hand, faint whimpering could be heard, and the heads of two tiny kittens poked through the opening.

"My cousin's cat just had a litter," Chris informed us. "The kittens were looking for homes, and I thought they'd cheer up Sammy." That was an understatement! These most enchanting creatures seemed to cheer up everyone.

The kittens, two tabbies, a brother and a sister, were adorable. Their fur was varying shades of grey with black streaks framing their eyes and cheeks. The grey metamorphosed into a soft, fine beige over their abdomens, and when they cleaned themselves, it looked as though they were licking cotton candy. Their ears perched upright at the tops of their heads seemed much too large for their tiny bodies. In short, they were fluffy delights.

Sammy quickly named them Daisy and Sylvester. "Daisy's a sweet name," I said, "but why did you pick Sylvester? Isn't Sylvester the cat who could never catch the bird? Don't you want your cat to be smarter than that?"

"I like the name," he said. "It sounds distinguished. And I'm going to call him Syl for short."

"Okay, but don't think I'm always going to let you have your way," I teased him.

It didn't matter what you called them, anyway. They played, they fought, they licked each other up, and they were always consistent in their affection towards us. Their presence was a good counterpoint for Sammy. He'd grown accustomed to everyone hovering over him, but now he could be the caregiver. Since the kittens still had to learn how to use the litter box, he certainly had his work cut out for him.

Chris continued to come over regularly. "Hey, Sammy," he'd say when he greeted him, his lazy smile always brightening Sammy's days. He and Sammy were so sweet to watch together. Sammy clearly idolized Chris, and not just because he was so tall. He was much nicer to Sammy than I had ever been. Sure, I'd taught Sammy things, like how to tie his shoelaces and how to do long division. And I'd played with him when he was bored, read him bedtime stories, and let him tag along with me and my friends. But Chris was just genuinely nice to him. Of course, I loved Sammy; he was my little brother. But little brothers are also supposed to be teased and occasionally tormented by their older siblings. At least, I thought so, anyway. Even my parents stopped complaining that Chris wasn't Jewish. Loyal and kind, his generous heart had won over their parochial sensibilities.

Chris and I had become good friends over the preceding few months, and we shared a lot of our time and a lot of our feelings with each other. We exchanged stories about our religions and traditions and found more commonalities than differences. But sometimes, when we walked home together or found the same jokes funny, I couldn't stop feeling that I was being disloyal to Chaver B. He had helped me when I didn't even know that I'd needed help, and sometimes I felt that I had only made things worse for him. Often when talking with Chris, it seemed that I was betraying Chaver B, and I felt guilty.

I hadn't seen much of Chaver B lately. Since Sammy had gotten sick, I'd missed many violin lessons, and he'd been at our house for Shabbos dinner only occasionally. He declined several of my mother's invitations, telling her that we should worry only about ourselves for the time being, and that he would be just fine. And of course, he added, to please let him know if there was anything he could do to help.

In the middle of May, we had four days of continuous drenching rain. By Sunday afternoon, it finally stopped.

"You must feel as cooped up as I do," I said to Sammy. "C'mon, let's go outside."

The temperature was in the fifties. I helped Sammy put on his black rubber boots and a light-weight blue jacket and walked him to the lawn at the back of our house. "I should bring you something dry to sit on," I said when I realized how wet the garden chairs were. I quickly ran into the house and carried out a folding metal chair, placed it on the red brick patio, and supported Sammy while he walked across the wet ground and sat down.

"I feel so free!" I exclaimed as I stood in front of him and looked up at the now blue sky with its few remaining pale grey clouds. "Want to dance?" I asked him, but without waiting for a reply, I grabbed his hands in mine. I winced when I felt how much weaker his grip was on the left and saw how much thinner his left hand looked compared to his right. But I swiftly dismissed these thoughts, because I knew that if I dwelled on them, I would only start to cry, and the last thing I wanted to do was to cry in front of Sammy. I quickly moved his arms from side to side and started to dance.

"What shall we dance to?" I asked. "How about 'Shall We Dance?' from *The King and I?*" This was one of the newer musicals being performed, and my mom had just purchased the record featuring the original Broadway cast.

"Okay," he said. We started singing, and Sammy gamely moved his good leg to the beat of the song, but he had trouble keeping time, and I could see that he felt uncomfortable.

"You're doing great. Watch this," I said as I let go of his hands, and with my arms extended to either side, I started twirling around on the damp grass. In the meantime, a dark purplish-grey cloud had moved in, and it started to drizzle.

"Oh, no! It's raining again!" I shouted, but unperturbed, I kept spinning. "This is what it must feel like when you're drunk," I said a little breathlessly as I gained momentum. It was so liberating to be outdoors that the harder it rained, the faster I twirled, faster and faster, until I lost control and landed on the wet, muddy grass, right on to my backside. I must have looked very silly, because I hadn't heard Sammy laugh so hard in a long time. I laughed, too, and it felt exhilarating.

My mother had seen us through the kitchen window and excitedly ran outside without even putting on a raincoat or taking an umbrella. "Mira, what are you doing? Sammy will get sick, and you will too," she scolded me. "Come into the house." I picked myself up off the ground, and she linked her arm through Sammy's and walked him inside and into the kitchen.

"Mira was so funny. Did you see her, mom?" Sammy said while she was drying his hair with a towel.

My mom's eyebrows furrowed, and her lips tightened into a thin line. "I saw her," she said flatly with a tinge of sharpness in her voice. I was certain that she was about to reprimand me some more, until she looked at Sammy and saw his face lit up in a huge grin.

My dad had been reading the newspaper in the living room and upon hearing the commotion, joined us in the kitchen. He took one look at Sammy and me and smiled. "Don't worry," he said, calmly defusing the situation. "A little rain never hurt anyone. They'll be fine."

I went upstairs to clean up and change my clothes. My mom gave Sammy a warm bath and dressed him in his pajamas, even though we hadn't yet eaten dinner. Later in the evening, I heard Sammy humming "Shall We Dance?" to himself as he played with his train set in the living room. And while I was lying in bed trying to fall asleep that night, I sensed a new calmness pervading the house.

Ninth grade passed. The days had seemed interminable when Sammy was so sick; I couldn't recall a year ever feeling so long. But then, before I knew it, the spring rains had come, rinsing the world and leaving behind their sweet scent, like the soft smell of a newborn baby.

June arrived, and like the previous year, Chris and I went to the final school dance together. He walked me home, and as we stood outside my front door saying goodnight to each other, his blond hair illuminated by the glow of the porch light above, he bent over and gently touched his lips to mine. His kiss was as soothing as a summer breeze. I had just turned fifteen. I guess that's what he'd been waiting for.

"Mira," he said, "I'm going to work on my uncle's farm this summer. My dad wants me to earn some money. I'll be leaving next week."

I was surprised and disappointed. Chris had told me that he was going to work in his father's hardware store downtown.

"Why the sudden change?" I asked.

"My uncle just lost a farmhand, so he asked me to help out. I'll see you when I get back," he reassured me as he took my hand in his and laced his fingers through mine.

I was worried about Sammy. I would miss Chris, but I knew that Sammy would miss him terribly. I stayed home over the summer to help my mom as much as she needed. And I didn't play baseball either. Annie was away at overnight camp for a couple of weeks, and I didn't want to play without her. Instead, I resumed my old reading habits and became a frequent visitor at the library.

CHAPTER XXX

Once upon a time, a girl with moonlight in her eyes,
Put her hand in mine and said she loved me so,
But that was once upon a time, very long ago.

—Charles Strouse and Lee Adams,
"Once Upon a Time"

Chaver B was also staying in town for the summer, so I thought that would be a good opportunity for me to resume regular violin lessons, now that things had calmed down at home. My father had secured a job for him with a local builder.

"Really?" I asked my mom one afternoon while I was helping her iron clothes in the laundry room in the basement. "Construction? Does he know anything about that?"

"Your father thinks it's better if he has an activity over the summer," she said. "Something to occupy his days. Apparently, as a young teenager, his father had insisted that during the summer months he learn some practical skills, so he worked with a carpenter making furniture."

A couple of times per week, my mom would prepare sandwiches for him and have me bring them over on my bike to his worksite. Now that I knew the secret of his left arm—that in fact he had no physical infirmity—I was no longer surprised to see him pick up large pieces of lumber or saw them into smaller pieces.

Over the next few weeks, Chaver B seemed to undergo a physical transformation. He usually wore short-sleeved shirts at the construction site, and while I watched him nailing wooden boards into place and applying drywall, I couldn't help but notice that his arms had become muscular and solid, his hands rougher, and that his face and arms had developed a deep tan, partially obscuring the numbers tattooed on his left forearm.

"Thank you, Mira," he would say as I'd hand him sandwiches and a drink. I usually stayed for a while, and we sat on a bench under a leafy elm tree and chatted while he ate.

"How is Sammy?" he always asked. Had I heard from Chris? Was I still going to play basketball next year? "You're good," he would say. "You should play again," he suggested, alluding to my hiatus from the sport when Sammy had been ill. "And furthermore, you enjoy it."

One day, after watching him nail a wooden beam across a ceiling, I said, "I'm surprised your father encouraged you to do carpentry. Wasn't he afraid that you'd injure your hands and not be able to play the violin anymore?"

"My father was a mathematician, but his logic often defied me," he replied. "Don't your parents sometimes make decisions that seem unnatural? *Gey veys.* Go figure. Isn't that how you say it in English?"

I smiled and laughed, and no further answer was needed.

On one particularly fine afternoon in mid-July, I bicycled over to Chaver B's worksite to bring him his lunch. It was a perfect summer day. The sky was a flawless crystalline blue. The warm sunshine enveloped me and made every part of me tingle. A light breeze stirred the leaves in the trees as a red-breasted robin scurried across the grass in fits and starts, searching for his next meal.

While riding over, I had noticed a patch of white, like snow, at the edge of a grassy field. Surprised that this bit of snow would have escaped the spring thaw and lasted well into summer, I stopped at the side of the road to examine it and discovered that it was a patch of wildflowers—small, silvery leaves forming a groundcover, adorned with little white flowers in clusters, like the toes of a pussy cat. They were heavenly. If there's a God, I thought, surely this day would be one of his finest creations.

"Do you believe in God?" I asked Chaver B as he sat down beside me on the bench. I immediately realized that the question was tactless, because what I was really wondering was how could Chaver B believe in God after all he'd been through. But I quickly tried to conceal my true thoughts by adding, "My father doesn't."

Chaver B looked at me quizzically and smiled easily. "Well, your mind has been busy on your summer vacation," he said while unwrapping his sandwich. "Yes, I believe in God, but I don't understand him. I don't understand how he thinks, how he makes decisions. I've thought a lot about this. But I would never not believe in him. It would be a desecration of the memory of all those who died simply because they were Jewish."

I imagined God sitting on a gilded throne at an ornately carved wooden desk with a huge sheet of paper spread out in front of him filled with notes and schematic diagrams as he wove his intricate plots, some breathtaking, many, it seemed, diabolical.

"And what about you? Do you believe in God?" he asked me.

"I don't know," I confessed. "Sometimes I do. But I'm just not sure. I don't know why he would have let Sammy get sick. I can't imagine what plan that would be a part of. So, I guess I agree with you. He is hard to understand."

After that, I was more careful in what questions I asked Chaver B. I tried to speak of generalities and neutral subjects. But somehow, most topics seemed to relate back to the war and his life before it started. I suppose it's impossible to erase all of one's past experiences, and perhaps Chaver B didn't want to. How could he? His life before the war had been happy.

I tread gently. I asked him about where he found the coins that he periodically showed Sammy, because I knew that collecting them was one of his hobbies. As soon as I asked the question, I regretted it, for surely, he had brought some of them with him from Europe. But he simply said that he had saved some from his travels and had visited coin shops when he was in Winnipeg and New York. I was curious about the Yiddish books he'd come across in New York, but I dared not ask about them. Instead, I told him about the books I'd taken out from the library and asked him if he'd read any of them.

"You speak and read English so well," I said. "Where did you learn it?"

"I studied English in school in Prague," he replied. "The rest I just picked up from reading a lot, and of course, from speaking it here."

I considered Chaver B an intellectual and welcomed his insights. I had just finished reading *Battle Cry*, a novel about marines fighting in the South Pacific during World War II. Although the story didn't deal with Europe directly, I decided it best to avoid discussing it. I'd started reading *The Human Comedy*, about a boy, Homer, and his family who lived in Ithaca, a fictional town in California, probably similar to Ambrosia, I imagined. Initially I thought it would be harmless, but when I realized that Homer's brother had died in the war and that his wounded war buddy was coming to Ithaca to meet Homer and his family, even that book seemed too risky. I certainly didn't think I could discuss a romantic novel with Chaver B. It made me feel uncomfortable. I didn't have any romantic notions about him, did I? So why did I feel the colour rush to my face when I thought about it?

Over the summer months, I resumed my violin lessons on Tuesday afternoons, and without having to contend with schoolwork, I had plenty of time to practice. Lately, Chaver B had taken to humming the melodies of new pieces for me. He assigned me my first concerto, or rather a part of one—just one movement.

His teaching style also changed somewhat. Unlike Mrs. Morgenstern, Chaver B rarely made physical contact with me during the lessons. As well as playing her own violin to demonstrate, Mrs. Morgenstern had been very physical, almost aggressive. If she hadn't liked the way I held my bow arm, she grabbed my forearm and lifted it up usually to a more horizontal position, and if I played out of tune, rather than saying anything, she took my finger and placed it on the correct spot on the fingerboard; surprisingly, she was usually accurate.

Chaver B's approach, on the other hand, was almost antithetical to hers. He was all words. But lately, he would gently touch my elbow when instructing me how to hold my bow, or lightly touch my finger on the fingerboard when showing me how to play vibrato. And those swift, deft, almost fleeting movements never failed to send a tingling through me and make my pulse flutter.

As before, after the lessons were over, he stayed for dinner; but now, rather than simply talking with my parents, he also played checkers with Sammy and taught him to play chess. Chaver B and Sammy had always played cards, but now this was particularly challenging for Sammy, because for most games he had to be fairly ambidextrous, holding some cards with one hand, picking up cards with the other, and sorting and stacking that usually required the use of both hands simultaneously. Chaver B was very patient and intuitive. He recognized Sammy's limits and would let him manage on his own until he sensed that Sammy was becoming frustrated. Chaver B would then quietly intervene before Sammy even knew that he was becoming upset.

In the middle of my violin lesson during the last week of August, I heard someone enter the house through the back screen door and then heard whispering. After the lesson ended, I walked into the kitchen, and there was Chris sitting at the table, drinking lemonade, and talking to my mom.

"Chris, you're back!" I cried out as I rushed over and hugged him. "When did you get home?"

"Just this afternoon," he answered. "I didn't mean to interrupt your violin lesson."

"Don't worry. You didn't. We already finished," I reassured him. "Does Sammy know you're here?"

"Not yet. Where is he?"

"He's over at Ben's house," my mom interjected. "I have to pick him up in a few minutes."

"I'd be happy to get him," Chris offered. "Is he able to walk home?"

"Sammy's doing very well," my mom said emphatically. "You'll be surprised to see how much progress he's made. He's managing with his crutches, and he just got a new leg brace," she continued with a broad smile. "And Ben just lives down the block. Being able to walk there has been great motivation for him. Would you like to stay for dinner, Chris?" she added. "Chaver B is staying."

With my excitement on seeing Chris, I had forgotten about Chaver B. I turned around to look for him and saw him framed in the doorway between the dining room and the kitchen. With his usual politeness and quiet consideration for others, he had chosen to detach himself from the scene unfolding in front of him. Looking at him standing by himself made me feel that I had been a bad friend, forsaking one friend for the other.

"Thanks, Mrs. Adler," said Chris, "but my mom's expecting me at home."

Chris and I left together to pick up Sammy. I noticed that Chris's blond hair had become even lighter and his freckles darker from having spent so much time outdoors over the summer. Sammy was ecstatic to see him and couldn't stop talking as he showed Chris his new skills and prowess with his crutches, which he announced he would soon no longer need. When we arrived back home, Chris said goodbye and promised Sammy that he would come by soon to play catch with him.

On a warm summer evening two days before the start of school, Chris and I were walking back home from the ice cream store downtown.

"Mira, I can't see you anymore," he said suddenly.

"What do you mean?" I asked. "Why not?"

"My parents won't let me." He hesitated, then said, "I'm only allowed to date girls of my own faith."

"But they hardly know me!" I retorted incredulously. "Do they even know what kind of person I am or what I think about? I don't understand. I thought you said that our religions didn't matter, as long as we liked each other."

I shouldn't have been surprised. During the entire time Chris and I were friends, he had rarely invited me to his house. It turned out that my parents were more open-minded than his. Even Babbi Rachel liked Chris and had accepted him. "He is a nice boy," she would say. "A kind person, *un er iz aza sheyner.*" And he is so handsome.

"Babbi, that's not why I like him."

"I know…*Ich veys, ober es iz nisht geferlech.*" Not so terrible that he is, she would nod with a twinkle in her eye and wave her hand knowingly. "The most important thing is that he is good to you. But you're too young to think about marriage anyway."

I was surprised that Chris had gone along with his parents. He had disappointed me. I guess we didn't have as much in common as I thought we did. As kind and considerate a person as he was, I knew that I could never love someone who didn't have the desire and the courage to stand up for his own beliefs and convictions.

CHAPTER XXXI

Look at how a single candle can both defy
and define the darkness.

—Anne Frank

I was lying on the sofa in our living room, reflecting on my recent conversation with Chris and making plans for the new year ahead. On the wall across from the sofa, above a *demi-lune* table in a satinwood veneer, hung a painting of a grassy field and gently outlined white farmhouse in the distance, flanked by low bushes in front and towering trees behind it. And in the forefront, a brook. A man knee-deep in grass and holding a fishing pole stood beside it, his string dangling in the water. Four ducklings with dark green heads circled in front of him just beyond reach of his line, their movements making round ripples that diminished in intensity and then disappeared when the last ripple reached the shore. Beyond the ducks, the sun shimmered off the water's surface, the fisherman's line cast in its glow.

The brook travelled for a short distance and then wound around a bend. I couldn't see what was there. The brook beckoned me to follow it, to find out what lay around the corner, like the future calling to me but always just beyond my reach, just beyond my grasp.

The details in the picture were so clear that the painting was almost like a photograph. Yet each time I looked at that painting, I was certain I could see the fisherman's rod move up and down as he attempted to attract his prey. A *trompe-l'oeil*, no doubt. I tried to convince myself that this scene had no life, but despite my protestations, I felt as though I could almost jump into that picture, that world, and travel an uncharted journey if I willed myself to do so.

I was about to dip my toes into the water when my mother's voice called to me from the kitchen, "Mira, don't you think you should go to bed? First day of school tomorrow."

Grade ten began. Miss Miller, the music teacher, asked me to be concertmistress of the school orchestra, which meant that I would be the lead violinist and sit just to the left of her as she conducted. Chaver B was pleased, and the news seemed to elevate his spirits.

"Concertmistress," he said, raising his eyebrows and nodding his head. *"Zeyer gut, Mira."*

He came to the house more frequently, spending extra time with me to go over pieces for the orchestra. Chaver B was now Sammy's teacher at Peretz School, too, so there was no shortage of talk about him. It was Chaver B this and Chaver B that. I knew that he would watch out for Sammy. It was almost like having an extra parent or brother, only not quite. More like something in between.

Although Sammy's left arm had regained a great deal of its strength, he still walked with a limp. With his new leg brace, he no longer needed crutches, but my mom was concerned about how he would navigate the winter snow and ice over the few blocks to and from school. She had even learned to drive, and my dad had bought a second-hand car for her, a teal blue sedan, so that she could take Sammy to all his physiotherapy appointments and pick him up after school until he became stronger.

That year we were studying Canadian history again, for the third time, having already done so in grades five and eight. Our history teacher, Mr. Margolis, remarkable for his rotund body and affable nature, was always ready to challenge us. His approach to teaching was rather unorthodox; classes often began with impromptu discussions, and he preferred not to follow events in chronological order but rather to intersperse history with what was currently going on in the news.

True to form, rather than beginning with the early explorers whose expeditions we had already learned about extensively in previous grades, we began the year studying the Great Depression leading into World War II and its aftermath. The history lessons usually extended into dinner conversations at home. After all, my parents had lived through these important periods in our past, and I was anxious to hear their perspectives. My father had volunteered to join the army, but because he was a medical practitioner in a small community, the army wouldn't accept him.

"Did that disappoint you?" I asked him.

"It did initially," he admitted. "Many of my buddies had joined the army or the airforce and were going overseas. I felt that I was shirking my responsibilities as a citizen, but the army assured me that the work I would be doing at home was also important. On the other hand, I felt relieved. I would've missed mom so much, and you and Sammy, too. Sammy was just a baby at the time. And in the end, some of my friends never came back. We never know what life has in store for us."

Our discussions were usually quite dynamic. My mother, who typically didn't readily offer her opinions when it came to politics, did not hesitate when it came to discussing Canada's policy on immigration during those years.

"Prime Minister Mackenzie King was an anti-Semite," she said without reservation. "Everyone knew that. He refused to accept Jewish immigrants from Germany and elsewhere in Europe, even after *Kristallnacht*," she said.

"Even the Americans weren't always welcoming," added my father. "They turned away a ship full of Jewish immigrants trying to escape Nazi persecution and sent them back to Europe, many to their deaths."

I had trouble believing that this information was true. Could these civilized nations have acted so callously and without regard for human suffering? I glossed over the chapters in my history textbook but could find no mention of Canada's immigration policy during the war. I could have discussed the issue with Mr. Margolis, but I preferred to research it on my own first.

The next weekend, I visited the library. Chaver B was there, sitting at one of the tables and reading a book. I wasn't surprised to see him. I was actually surprised that I hadn't run into him more often, since I knew from our conversations over the summer that he was an avid reader and often frequented the library. But there he was, sitting alone, engrossed in the words on the pages in front of him. Alone but not alone. I walked over and gently touched him on his shoulder. He looked up, nodded, and smiled.

I approached the librarian and asked her if she could provide me with a good reference on the subject of Canadian immigration in wartime. "I'm not aware of a book that specifically addresses your question," she said, "but since the war didn't end that long ago, you might be better off looking at old newspaper articles or previous issues of *Maclean's*."

"That seems overwhelming. Where would I even start? Which newspaper should I look at and from which date?" I asked her. It seemed an impossible task.

"We have files downstairs prepared by our staff addressing certain topics. Why don't I see if there's one addressing Canada's policy on immigration during the war?" she suggested.

She returned ten minutes later carrying a manila folder. Inside were newspaper clippings from the *Winnipeg Free Press* and the *Globe and Mail*. Some were articles and some, editorials. I turned the pages, one after the other.

My parents had been right in all respects. Mackenzie King had allowed in far fewer Jewish refugees during the Nazi regime than were admitted by the United States and some other countries. Some of the articles supported Mackenzie King, stating that his actions only reflected the prevailing anti-Semitic sentiments of the times, as if that was an acceptable excuse. Canada had been under a lot of economic stress from the Depression and didn't need to be burdened with desperate refugees, was another rationale. And there were so many of them! Where would it end? It seemed that no one really wanted the Jews. "None is too many" is how one politician phrased it.

One of the articles also confirmed that indeed the United States had turned away a ship full of Jewish immigrants fleeing persecution. The *St. Louis*. In Florida. In the spring of 1939. I felt as though a stone had sunk in my heart. I looked over at Chaver B sitting by himself in a straight-backed wooden chair at a round wooden table with his book open in front of him. At that moment he seemed to embody all the people who had suffered during the war, those who had survived and those who had not.

I was too stunned to feel anything. Or was I feeling so many emotions that I couldn't disentangle one from the other? Disappointment, disbelief, shock, anger, intense sadness. Was there no end to this evil in the world? Did my wonderful world stop at the borders of Ambrosia, or was there evil here, too? Evil and heartbreak that I just never saw before, or saw but ignored? Even when I'd watched the soldiers returning to Ambrosia after the war, they'd all looked so happy that I didn't associate the war with the terrible things that had gone on there. What was truth? What I believed to be true and what seemed to be true were not coinciding.

That day I felt like Alice in Wonderland, that I had fallen down the rabbit hole into a bewildering, inexplicable, and at times, terrifying world.

I walked home, pushing my way through the piles of fall leaves that littered the path and scuttled in front of me. Usually I would swish my feet through them and delight in their variegated beauty, but that day they were no more than impediments to reaching my destination. I marched into the house and straight into the kitchen where my mother was cooking dinner.

"You're right!" I almost shouted. "Everything you told me was true!" I spent the remainder of the evening sitting on the sofa in the living room, with Daisy curled up on my lap and Sylvester resting on the floor and nudging my feet, while I ruminated over what I had learned.

That night, I lay in bed and tried to fall asleep. My eyes slowly closed, and I felt myself drifting into a strange and unfamiliar world. As I tried to separate illusion from reality, I became enveloped by a dark emptiness. There was nothing above me, below me, or beside me. Was I floating? I couldn't even tell; there was nothing to help orient myself. I felt lost, aimless, without boundaries or direction. I felt alone, solitary, without a connection to anyone or anything. And worst of all, no one seemed to be coming to show me the way out of this darkness.

CHAPTER XXXII

The magi, as you know, were wise men—wonderfully wise
men—who brought gifts to the Babe in the manger.

—O. Henry, *The Gift of the Magi*

Fall quickly turned into winter that year. It was the middle of
November, and already the snow was three feet deep and the
winds were howling across the fields. Chaver B was over at our
house that Saturday afternoon to give me an extra violin lesson.
Annie and I had planned to go to the movies in the evening, but
during my lesson, she called and told my mother that she had
developed a sore throat and wouldn't be able to go.

"Why don't you go with Chaver B?" my mother innocently
asked. "Ari," she continued while turning towards him, "I'm sure
you'd enjoy it. They're showing *Singing in the Rain*. Reuven and I
saw it last weekend, and it was wonderful."

I was embarrassed at my mom's suggestion. Had they seen me
blushing? I turned away and busied myself fluffing up pillows on
the sofa until I sensed that my complexion had returned to its
usual colour. But if Chaver B had noticed anything, he effortlessly

defused the situation. "I would be honoured," he said. "What time does it start?"

"Seven o'clock," I was able to answer.

It was already five, so Chaver B stayed for dinner. Afterwards, we walked together to the theatre downtown, and he bought popcorn for me at the concession stand. As my mother had said, the movie *was* wonderful with the actors dancing over sofas and Gene Kelly with his umbrella twirling and splashing in the rain. But despite these almost acrobatic feats and the exciting story, I was distracted by Chaver B's presence. At times, I was more aware of the sound of his breathing and his laughter than of what was unfolding on the screen. I had never heard him laugh so heartily before. It was a warm, full sound, and I imagined him as a child, laughing and joking with his friends. I envisioned Moishie, his dog, jumping up to greet him when he returned home. Moishie would be standing on his hind legs, his front paws against Chaver B's chest, as Chaver B would rub his head affectionately and say, "See, I told you I'd be back."

Our arms brushed as he repositioned himself in his seat. And although I had seen his hands thousands of times before, they never looked quite as they did that night under the flickering light and dancing shadows of the changing picture in front of me—strong, secure, safe.

After the movie ended, he insisted on walking me home, even though he lived downtown. "You don't have to," I told him. "I'll be fine walking alone."

"No, no, I'll make sure you get home safely. And I like to walk," he said as we started towards my house. "The cold air is cleansing. It numbs me. And I don't think of other things. Just the moment I'm in. Like being here with you."

I wasn't sure how to interpret what he'd just said. The streets were quiet. I felt alone with him in the universe. It seemed to be just the two of us and the night sky.

When we arrived at my house, he held the door open for me. I asked him if he wanted to come in to warm up, but he declined. "Thank you, Mira. Good night," he said, and then he turned, walked down the steps, and disappeared into the darkness.

The house was still. My parents had left on the lights on the porch and in the front hall, but everyone seemed to already be asleep. The house was so unnaturally quiet that it seemed foreign. I felt almost dazed as I took off my coat and hat and hung them up in the closet.

As I walked towards the staircase, I seemed to be moving in slow motion. Had something just happened between Chaver B and me? It was almost as though a spell had been cast. We'd already moved beyond being just teacher and student; that change had happened long ago. We were friends, good friends, but now, were we something more?

"How was the movie?" my mom asked the following morning. "Did Ari like it?"

"I think so," I said. "Do you think he's ever going to get married again?" I asked. "Do you think he can ever love someone as much as he loved Dvorah?"

"Well, he has a girlfriend," she replied. "Elaine. You remember her. She was here for dinner a couple of months ago."

Yes, I did remember her. She was also a teacher, but taught at the public elementary school on the other side of town. My mother had invited her and Chaver B over to our house for Friday night dinner on a couple of occasions. I wondered why he hadn't spent Saturday evening with her, but before I had a chance to ask any more questions, my mom informed me that Elaine had been busy attending a concert at her school. Well, that seemed to settle any speculations I had from the previous night. No wonder he's been in a good mood. He must like her, I thought.

Elaine was going to visit her family in Calgary for the winter holidays and had asked Chaver B to join her. They would be going by train. The winter holidays could be a lonely time for him in Ambrosia without the structure of school to brighten the days, and my parents agreed that it would be a good diversion for him, to see another city and meet new people.

"Are they serious?" I heard my mother discussing it with her mah-jong group. "She's certainly interested, but is he?"

I had trouble envisioning Chaver B with Elaine. She didn't seem to be his type. She was pretty enough, almost as pretty as Dvorah had been, but she seemed to totally dominate him, like a mother hen. He probably did need mothering, I agreed, but when I'd seen them together, she appeared to be suffocating him with her well-meaning attention. She certainly didn't understand him the way I did.

One week after the holidays, I casually asked my mom if Chaver B had enjoyed his trip. "He's no longer seeing Elaine," she said, "so I suppose the trip was not a great success."

"What happened?" I asked.

"I guess she just wasn't right for him," she replied. "Sometimes you have to spend a lot of concentrated time with someone to really know what they're like and how well the two of you get along."

My mood seemed to lighten; I wasn't sure why. I felt weightless and otherworldly, like one of the clouds skimming across the sky overhead, and a smile formed itself on my lips. I looked out the living room window at the freshly fallen snow covering the earth like a white velvet blanket. As I walked upstairs to my bedroom to start doing my homework, a song filtered through my brain, inching its way into my consciousness note by note. It was "Salut d'Amour".

I felt different. And I couldn't stop thinking of Chaver B. He seemed to be everywhere. When I brushed my hair in the morning and chose my clothes for the day, I thought of him. How would I look to him if we happened to meet?

Two days later, on a typically freezing January afternoon, Chaver B came over for my violin lesson. I took more pains than usual getting ready and decided to wear my dark-navy pleated plaid skirt with matching stockings and royal blue sweater. I watched him walk down the snow-covered sidewalk on my boulevard, turn into my yard, and climb up the steps to the front porch.

As usual, my mother greeted him at the door and let him inside. She took his black wool coat and hung it up in the hall closet and laid his brown fur hat on the entryway table. His summer tan had faded a while ago, but he had not lost the weight he had put on doing construction work. His clothes no longer hung on him like remnants from another soul, and he had finally bought some new ones that suited him much better. Today he wore a maroon pullover sweater with a checkered shirt underneath. The creases at the corners of his eyes lent him an air of distinction, and he seemed to be gazing at me with an intensity I had not previously seen. I looked into his dark eyes, trying to discern what he was thinking, as I had done so many times before. How do you know if someone likes you or how they like you? I thought. Just because you like someone, I cautioned myself, it doesn't mean they like you back.

Even though things had not gone well with Elaine, he seemed relaxed and almost happy, and his eyes held a certain serenity. "I have a surprise for you," he said. He pulled some sheet music out of his brown leather bag. "I want you to learn this piece. It is by Mendelssohn. I played this for my debut with the Prague Philharmonic Orchestra. And I will play it for you now, so you know what it sounds like," he said, as he took my violin and bow into his hands.

This was the first time Chaver B had played for me or for anyone else since that revealing day almost three years ago. This time he played Mendelssohn's First Violin Concerto. Like the Sibelius, it was also in a minor key, but unlike Sibelius's unrelenting plaintive passages, some of Mendelssohn's soaring melodies contained moments of brightness, and its third movement began with a light cascading of notes as if twittering birds were heralding the arrival of spring.

Chaver B's playing was magical and moving. His hand and the bow seemed to merge into one. It was almost as if it was his own hand gliding over the strings, caressing them, guiding them, encouraging them to voice their thoughts. At times, the bow seemed like a magic wand; with a slight alteration in pressure or position, he could change the mood instantly. He seemed so at one with the violin, I wondered how he could have forsaken it all these years, despite what he'd been through. As I listened to him play, I was once more struck by the power of the violin. It contained the song of the human heart.

Sammy had left his bedroom and was sitting at the top of the stairs listening, while my mother stood in the doorway to the kitchen, motionless, one hand clutching a dish towel, the other hand pressing against the doorframe, as if for support. When he finished, my mother was about to applaud, but caught herself and silently returned to the kitchen rather than risk breaking the spell. Sammy did the same and quietly returned to his room.

"Don't you think this concerto is too difficult for me?" I asked softly. "I'm not sure I'm ready for it."

"You won't learn it all at once," he replied. "I don't expect you to. Just bit by bit. We'll start with the easier sections, and then, when you've learned the appropriate technique, you'll add some more. It may take years for you to be able to play it the way you want to. It will be a goal of yours. To master it and make it your own."

I accepted this gift matter-of-factly. I didn't tell Chaver B how beautiful his playing had been or how happy I was that he had played the violin again. I didn't say that his face seemed to have taken on an almost ethereal glow. I didn't admit that I was honoured that he had such faith in my abilities. I just carried on with the lesson as if it was routine, trying not to think too much about how handsome he looked and about all the feelings churning inside of me. But when the lesson was over, I laid my violin down in its case, took Chaver B's hand in mine, and kissed it.

"Thank you," I said, and then I turned and went upstairs.

Before going to sleep, I stood by my bedroom window just as the icy patterns were beginning to form on the windowpanes, bewilderingly elaborate patterns, as if an invisible artist was sweeping his brush across the glass creating a panorama of frost and ice. It was a new moon, a moon that would continue to wax every day over the next fortnight, each day becoming a little bit larger and rounder. What would the moon's expression be this time? Would he have that same indecipherable look, his mouth forming his defining "O" as if he were shocked, questioning, warning us of something, or about to speak? Or would the corners of his mouth curl upward, his eyes narrow and begin to smile? Perhaps this time he would look different.

That night I slipped into sleep with a lightness of heart, anticipating the new day ahead. I woke up the next morning feeling invigorated, and although I couldn't recall any, I was certain that I'd just had a night full of the sweetest dreams.

Chaver B had developed a cold and didn't come for Shabbos dinner that week. I could hardly wait for the next lesson when I would see him again. The days went by slowly.

The following Tuesday, while waiting for him to arrive, I organized my music on the stand. Restless, I went back and forth to the living room window to see if he was coming down the street. He was late. Perhaps he had an errand and would be coming from the opposite direction, I thought.

"Still not here?" asked my mom, coming from the kitchen.

"No, not yet," I replied. "I wonder why he's late."

I planted myself by the window and continued to search the street. A light snow was falling, the street lamps illuminating each delicate snowflake as it silently drifted downwards. My mother returned to the kitchen, and I could hear her dialing the phone and then in a tense voice speak to Mrs. Rempel, my father's receptionist.

"Yes, please interrupt him," she said. "It's important."

I don't remember what euphemism my parents used to describe Chaver B's death, *alev ha'sholem*.

After my mother called my dad's office, my father checked with Mrs. Rempel about the urgency of the waiting patients' appointments, and then after assuring himself that there were no dire problems, he politely excused himself and said he had an emergency to attend to and left.

He arrived at Chaver B's apartment and knocked several times—each knock louder than the previous—but no one answered, and the door was locked. He quickly went downstairs to the drugstore and found Mr. Clark, the pharmacist and owner of the building, who had an extra key. Upon opening the door, they were confronted with the unmistakable smell of gas. Mr. Clark ran to the living room window and opened it, then checked the stovetop in the kitchen and turned off the burning elements. My father raced to Chaver B's bedroom and found him lying in his bed. There was nothing more they could do.

CHAPTER XXXIII

A voice said, Look me in the stars
And tell me truly, men of earth,
If all the soul-and-body scars
Were not too much to pay for birth.

—Robert Frost, "A Question"

"Was it me?" I asked my mother. "Did I remind him too much of his past? If he hadn't met me, he might still be alive."

"You can't take responsibility for someone else's actions," my mother tried to reassure me. "Only your own. You're just a young girl learning to play the violin. I think teaching you gave him pleasure. His burden was too great."

In Jewish tradition, a person who commits suicide cannot be buried with his fellow Jews. It seemed so unfair to me, that a person who felt so alone in life would be so alone in death, too. Almost self-fulfilling. An outcast in life and an outcast in death. My father changed the death certificate to read *Cause of death: heart attack*.

"The man suffered enough," he said. "Does he need to be shamed also? What was his crime?"

I guess it's alright to lie sometimes. I remembered a discussion we'd had in *Chumash* class. Is it permissible to lie? Ever? We all agreed that it's okay to lie so as not to hurt someone's feelings. Everyone must lie at some point in their lives, I assumed. I tried to imagine a world where everyone told the truth all of the time. It seemed both laughable and awful.

Are lies absolute, I wondered, or does the degree of the lie matter? A white lie versus a black lie. I thought of the times I told Chaver B I'd practiced violin everyday and hadn't. Was that a sin? Chaver B telling the kapellmeister he could orchestrate music, when he never had. My father telling the RCMP that he no longer had the letters that his friend Jacob had sent him when he assuredly did. What about my other lies? There were other times I hadn't told the truth. What about them? It was easier to think of the lies of others rather than my own.

And was there some sort of hierarchy for all lies? A lie to avoid disappointment from your parents as opposed to a lie to prevent you from going to prison? Would the ultimate punishment be the same for both lies? And was the lie judged separately from the act you were concealing? How would Bontsha's judge have ruled? What would be God's verdict?

The *Talmud* says that it's alright to lie in order to save an innocent person. "Truth is a high value," says the *Talmud*, "but the saving of innocent life is a higher one." We could no longer save Chaver B's life, but we could at least save his soul.

The next day I awoke to a clear, bright sky, not atypical for a prairie winter. In accordance with Jewish tradition, the funeral was held that morning. Although I was already fifteen, my parents felt that

I was too young to attend, but I announced at the breakfast table that I would be going because Chaver B was my friend, and I would not let him down. . . again. My parents' eyes met, and to my surprise, they consented. A service was held inside the shul. The rabbi and several others, including my father, said a few words and recited prayers. Then the guests filed out and drove to the cemetery.

The earth was so hard that I don't know how the gravediggers were able to dig a hole so deep, but they had. We all stood there in the bitter cold, little clouds of vapour seeming to appear magically in front of us as we recited the Mourner's *Kaddish* and said goodbye to Chaver B. Lererine Malka and many of the other teachers from Peretz School were there, but some had to stay behind to look after the children. Mr. Clark, the owner of the drugstore who together with my father had found Chaver B the day before, came. Almost all the parents from my old class and Sammy's class were present and other townspeople as well. Even Chris was there, although I hadn't told him what had happened.

Was there justice in the world after all? I wondered. Would I hear shofars trumpeting as with Bontsha, or see Chaver B being carried off in a chariot of fire into the unbounded sky, like Elijah? But I heard no trumpets and saw no chariots.

Chaver B had been an orphan in the most elemental and purest sense of the word. No living relatives. No one with the same blood pulsing in his veins. To me, that seemed the epitome of loneliness.

He had come to our community looking for peace, and it had eluded him. The past had remained inside him, and he had not been able to relinquish it. It had been his constant companion, indelibly imprinted on his mind and in his heart. He had been helpless to fight the painful disquietude and desolation within him.

He had seemed so happy in recent months, as though he was

finally feeling comfortable with himself and with life. Was that because he'd already made his decision? Perhaps he had resolved his inner conflict, his internal struggle, and it had left him with a sense of tranquility. Was this his recapitulation? Was this the resolution he had finally come to?

"I wish we could have done more," lamented my mother when we returned home from the cemetery. "Such a *guteh neshama*," she continued, almost talking to herself. "Such a good soul. We took him into our community and couldn't help him. That is our burden now."

Her guard had finally come down. No longer stoic, she lowered her head into her lap and wept. I had never seen my mother cry before. She looked like the same wounded bird Chaver B had sometimes been. Vulnerable herself, she was no longer able to protect me from what was true in this world. Too much had happened, and I had seen too much.

I suppose I should have been upset or frightened at seeing my mother cry like that. Instead, I felt a tenderness and intense closeness with her, unlike anything I had experienced before. I sat down beside her and put my head on her shoulder. We threw our arms around each other and became as one, weeping uncontrollably for our lost friend.

I sat thinking. At times religion can be a comfort. At other times it can be harsh. The chanting of the prayers at the funeral provided some solace, but all the events leading up to Chaver B's death exposed the harsh realities that religion can engender. All the hope and hurt of religion.

Sometimes we are not perfect. We are made in God's image. Does that mean that God sometimes loses his way and makes mistakes too? I wondered. It seems that He clearly had.

Later that evening, I looked at my music stand with my music resting on it and envisioned Chaver B as a young man before the war, his future life awaiting him like a cadenza to be improvised, a cadenza with flourishing sweeps and arpeggiated passages unencumbered by adherence to strict rhythm and metre, a cadenza to be played with masterful technique and great virtuosity. Instead it had come to this, a final tragic coda.

I glanced at my violin and wondered if I would ever play again. I couldn't imagine another teacher making the music seem so exciting, so real, as Chaver B had. We'll see, I thought, we'll see.

During those few years since I first met Chaver B, I had crossed from innocence to experience. It was a stepwise crossing, as though someone had taken my hand and led me from one signpost to another, awakening my consciousness to the existential questions of what life was about. Life no longer seemed simple or certain. I eventually realized that I had, in fact, had an epiphany, an epiphany that not only was there randomness in life that we could not control, but that there was depravity in this world so enormous that it was almost fantastical, so enormous that the veneer of civilization that covers our souls is not always able to contain it.

Coda

CHAPTER XXXIV

Teach us to number our days,
so we may gain a heart of wisdom.

—*Psalms* 90:12

Today I lie on the grass outside my home, watching the clouds as I have done so many times before. Today they are racing to an unknown destination, clouds galloping, like the days passing by ever faster and faster.

Time may pass, but what happens stays within us. I am older now, but I still vividly remember those years during which Chaver B was my teacher and my friend. And although I now live in arguably one of the most beautiful places on earth, when I think of beauty and wonder, my mind first goes to those halcyon days of my childhood on the windswept prairies, and then inevitably turns to those transformative days where under a cerulean sky, my understanding of life was crystallized. I looked out my window and saw things I had neither expected nor wanted to see.

I did not recover from Chaver B's death quickly. Actually, I don't think I've ever recovered. I do know that after his passing, whatever joy I experienced was never as joyous as it should have been. And herein I learned another paradox; the exquisite radiance and aching agony of love.

It wasn't until years later, on a summer's day much like today, that I realized that Chaver B had given me the Mendelssohn concerto as a parting gift. He had given it to me, this beautiful bittersweet concerto in the minor key, as though it was a part of himself. His spirit, his soul, would be in every note that I played.

All those hours, days, months, and years that I would spend perfecting it, I would be thinking of him and connected to him. And that's what he wanted. As long as someone is thinking about you, you never die. That's what Babbi Rachel had told me. Chaver B had given me that concerto so I would never forget him..... How could he possibly have thought that I would *ever* forget him?

I tried to play the violin again, but couldn't. The memory of his playing was too haunting. But it was more than that. Each time I picked up the violin, I regretted that I'd never told him I loved him. In truth, I have never told anyone. That is my secret and my sorrow.

After graduating from university, I became a teacher, like Chaver B. I joined the organization CUSO, Canadian University Service Overseas, and taught English in communities in Africa. While abroad, I met my husband, an American who was working in the Peace Corps.

Passionate about our work and each other, one day, almost on a whim, we were married in an African village on the shores of the Indian Ocean. The village women wove a garland of flowers for my hair and gave me a flowing white cotton dress as a wedding present. The waves lapping against the shore sang our wedding song, and the wind blowing off the ocean played with our hair and clothes as we said our vows. By the time the ceremony was over, the wind suddenly dissipated, and I couldn't help but think that it had been gathering all the good wishes from our loved ones and was delivering them to us on that day. Its task complete, the wind could then rest. Perhaps Chaver B had sent a message also. "He is the right one for you," I could hear him say. Afterwards, we drank wine made from the sap of the coconut palm. It tasted like the sweet nectar of the gods.

Upon our return home, we had a religious ceremony under a *Chupah* (wedding canopy) in Ambrosia, and then settled in California where my husband is from. Over the years, I have continued to hang on to my traditions and heritage. They are such an integral part of me; I could not imagine a life without them. And I try to teach them to my children and imbue them with all the positive attributes that religion has to offer. Because if I didn't have these traditions, I would create others to take their place, to carry me on the rhythms of life and mark the passing of time.

It is understandable why people invented a God to explain the natural phenomena around them. But in so doing, man has spent much of his existence trying to rationalize the actions of an unseen entity that probably has never and does not now exist. A way of putting order to disorder.

"If you're such a nonbeliever," my friends ask me, "why do you still fast on *Yom Kippur?*"

"Hedging my bets," I reply. "Hedging my bets."

A few months ago, as I was rummaging through my attic looking for an old costume of Queen Esther for Purim, I came across an unmarked box sealed with tape and tied up with string. I eagerly cut the string with scissors and ripped off the tape, anticipating that inside I would find the silver tiara and light blue chiffon dress that I was searching for.

As I opened the box, a familiar scent floated towards me. It was the same musty smell of the books in the library in Ambrosia, books that had been sitting on shelves for a very long time, patiently waiting for someone to pick them up and turn their pages. An assortment of volumes and notepads lay in the box, and on top rested the first violin book Chaver B had given to me. I picked it up, slowly leafed through the pages, and found "Humoresque" on page seventeen. Immediately I was eleven years old again, standing in my living room in front of my music stand, listening to Chaver B weave his fanciful tale as I became the girl in his story, skipping down the street on a hot summer day and refreshing myself with ice cream— feeling its soft coolness as it touched my lips, my whole body being overcome with its soothing pleasantness. As I ate my ice cream, a voice echoed in my head in almost perfect counterpoint to the song, telling me to fight for what I believed in.

I was awoken from my reverie by a patter on the roof, like a soft drumbeat, and I realized that it had started to rain. Soft, lyrical sounds floated towards me from the open window, and when I looked outside, there were children laughing and singing on their way home from school, their heads tilted upwards and mouths wide open as they tried to catch the raindrops falling from the sky.

I looked back into the box; there lay a copy of "Csardas" and of course, "Salut d'Amour". Underneath I spied my book of sonatas and smiled as I picked it up, remembering how I forced myself to practice those pieces; more drudgery than passion to my way of thinking. I turned the pages and saw Chaver B's markings; there were so many, many more than on my other songs. As I closed the book and turned to place it down on the table beside me, a small white envelope fell from its pages and floated on to the floor. I bent over to pick it up and was surprised to read my name on its front. *"Far Mira"* it said in Yiddish script. I turned the envelope over in my hands to see if anything else was written on it, but nothing was. I stared at the neat blue letters and immediately recognized the handwriting. After all, how many times had Chaver B written on the blackboard in class and made us copy down his notes?

I was afraid to open it. When had he written it, and why had I not seen it before? My throat tightened, and I could feel my heart beating inside me and hear it pounding in my ears as I anticipated what lay inside. The only way to calm myself was to open the envelope and read its contents. I carefully opened the flap, trying to preserve as much of the integrity of the envelope as I could, and slowly removed the one sheet of plain white paper inside that was neatly folded into thirds.

January 22, 1953

Tayereh Mira,

I write this letter not knowing if you will ever read it, but hoping that someday you will. What can I say to you? That next week I may not be here? That this will probably be the last time we will see each other? I am not writing to explain my actions or to defend my choices. You know too much already, and I think you will understand.

*You are a beautiful child. I could never burden you
with my pain. It wouldn't be fair to you. You deserve a
life that is carefree and untroubled, a life full of sweet,
soaring melodies. There is too much inside me that I
cannot rid myself of, and I fear that it has overtaken me
like a cancer. It is too painful to feel. Even happiness
is agony.*

*I am grateful for all the good things that life has given
me, including you. Thank you for your friendship and
your kindness.*

Mit libeh,

Ari

I had never expected to read such a letter. How like Chaver B
to put it in my book of sonatas. He knew I rarely opened it, and
that way, I was unlikely to see it for weeks, or as it turned out, years.
But then there was the chance I might never have seen it.

But also how fitting. I was right. The sonata was a metaphor for
his life. He had come to his resolution and shared it with me.

I didn't cry. Should I be crying? I didn't feel like crying. Rather,
I felt a sense of relief. I had meant something to him. He had said
goodbye to me after all, and I felt happy.

As I stood there, my eyes fixated on Chaver B's words, I heard a
voice from below becoming louder and louder as it drowned out
my inner thoughts, a voice calling out, "Mom, where are you? Are
you home?"

I walked downstairs to the kitchen and greeted my son. As he lay his books down on the table, he told me what he'd learned about in school that day. Civil wars in Africa. Perpetual fighting in the Middle East. Terrorists lurking everywhere. I wondered if the world had changed at all over the decades and centuries and millennia, or if in fact there is "nothing new under the sun," and it is only the external trappings that are different.

My major focus now is nurturing and raising my family as best as I know how, but I wonder if I have lived up to the example of Queen Esther even in a small way, or if that task still lies before me. Or if no matter what I do, there will always be some battle awaiting my help. Over the years, I have written articles in my local newspaper championing women's rights and decrying injustices that I saw in my community. Should I be content to fight these small battles at home, or should I be thinking of something larger and grander? There seems to be no shortage of causes to consume my energies.

Lately, I find myself daydreaming. After all, daydreams can be so lovely. In an instant I can conjure up another place and time that insulates me from the harshness around me. In the light of day, I dream of pleasant things, gentle things, beautiful things. I dream of melodies all played in a major key. I dream of the child in me and pray that it will never become a forgotten secret. I dream of good lives for my children and for all the children of the world. I dream of the many people in my life who have touched me in a meaningful way. And of course, I dream of Chaver B.

THE END

AUTHOR'S NOTE

*P*rairie Sonata is a work of historical fiction. Ambrosia is a fictional town. Peretz School, however, was a real place.

Although several sources were consulted for historical accuracy, any errors are my own. The references I used in writing this book include *The Tin Ring* by Zdenka Fantlova, *Music in Terezin* by Joza Karas, *Terezin Requiem* by Josef Bor, *Holocaust Journey, Travelling in Search of the Past* by Martin Gilbert, *Night* by Eli Wiesel, *The Drowned and the Saved* by Primo Levi, *Music of Another World* by Szymon Laks, *Playing for Time* by Fania Fenelon, *The Story of the Writings* by Joseph Rosner, *Coming of Age, A History of the Jewish People of Manitoba* by Allan Levine, *The Forgotten Secret* by Robert Pack, and *Great Jewish Short Stories*, edited by Saul Bellow. Other sources I consulted were Chabad.org, *Encyclopedia Britannica*, and The United States Holocaust Museum.

ACKNOWLEDGMENTS

I would like to extend great thanks to all those who selflessly helped me with the creation of this book: To my husband, Arnold, for his willingness to listen and for his invaluable ideas. To my sister, Myrna, my initial and tireless cheerleader, who was always willing to read whatever version I offered her and for her great insights. To my son, David, for his wonderful encouragement, and for seeing things in my story that even I didn't see. To my son, Richard, for allowing me to sit through his many years of violin lessons and for exposing me to such beautiful music. And to my son, Kenny, who with a few suggestions helped me transform my early chapters and make my book all the better. To all those who read my story and offered their suggestions, thank you: my brother, Hersh, and sister-in-law, Arna; my daughters-in-law, Kathryn and Chloe; and my good friend, Marilyn. I would also like to thank my good friend, Sheva, for her help with some of the Yiddish translations.

I would like to thank the following who provided me with editorial advice and who were generous with their ideas: Marcy Dermansky, Roland Merullo, David Corbett, Brooke Warner, and my editor at Friesen Press, Melissa McCoubrey.

Lastly, I would like to remember all my teachers at Peretz School who taught us as if we were all *zeyereh eygeneh kinder,* their own children.

DISCUSSION AND
STUDY GUIDE

1. *Prairie Sonata* is in part a coming-of-age story. Discuss Mira's passage from innocence to experience.

2. A major lesson Mira learns while growing up is that one should stand up for one's beliefs. Discuss the various instances when Mira learns this lesson and how it is reinforced throughout the novel. Provide examples of how she demonstrates what she has learned, or perhaps you may feel that she has not lived up to her own expectations. Take a stand and support your argument.

3. The novel is filled with descriptions of nature. These descriptions serve to provide a setting for the story, but also have other purposes. The changing of the seasons marks the passage of time as Mira grows up. The weather sometimes parallels the moods of the characters. At other times, it is seemingly at odds with what is occurring in the novel. Often, the landscape and the natural surroundings become characters in themselves. Please choose at least one of the above,

provide examples, and discuss how the author employs her descriptions of nature to enhance the story.

4.   Music is an integral element of the book. Like nature, at times it also becomes its own character. Chaver B imbues the pieces that he teaches Mira with personal qualities. Mira uses music to define her world. Provide examples and discuss how music shapes the novel.

5.   Moon imagery is used throughout the novel. The moon is described as being a symbol of light and renewal. The Jewish calendar is a lunar calendar, and Mira refers to the Jewish holidays as being gifts that the moon brings. At times, the characters are compared to the Man in the Moon. Provide specific examples and discuss.

6.   The idea of Survival of the Fittest is a biological term that originated from Darwin's theory of evolution, but which was actually coined by Herbert Spencer, a biologist and anthropologist, in reference to Darwin's theory of natural selection. Mira first uses this term in reference to her teachers, Mrs. Pirsnansky and Mrs. Campbell. Discuss other characters to whom this term would apply.

7.   Chaver B is a complex individual. During one of the violin lessons, he teaches Mira about the sonata form. Mira believes that the sonata form is a metaphor for his life. Do you agree? If so, discuss how Chaver B's life follows the sonata pattern. Does Mira's personal journey from innocence to experience also follow the pattern of a sonata? If you were to divide the

book into the parts of a sonata, where would you start each section, and why?

8. When Chaver B is first introduced to Mira's class, she immediately views him as an intriguing and mysterious character. She spends at least the first half of the novel trying to figure out who the "real" Chaver B is. Who do you think the "real" Chaver B is? Discuss the various facets of his personality. How do forces throughout our lives change who we are and what we later become?

9. Most people who were deported to the concentration camps in World War II died there, either in the gas chambers, from disease, malnutrition, abuse, or sometimes at their own hands. Why did some survive? Was it because of luck, because of their wits, on pure determination, or because of something else? Why do you think Chaver B survived? Discuss Chaver B's ambivalent feelings towards the violin in relation to this question.

10. Some people remain steadfast in their religious beliefs throughout their lives, but many people question the value of religion and the existence of God. Mira grows up in a household where her mother believes in God but her father doesn't. Although she attends a Jewish school, it is a secular school that teaches about Jewish history, literature, and traditions; there is little emphasis on prayers and rituals. She learns primarily Yiddish, the language of the common man, not Hebrew, the language of the Bible. Discuss how Mira's

religious beliefs evolve and what she ultimately comes to believe as an adult.

11. Both Chaver B and Mira had seemingly safe and secure childhoods, but then are confronted with the evil that exists in society. One of the tenets of *kashrus* is that Jewish people eat meat only from animals with split hooves. This is to be a daily reminder that each of us has the ability to choose between good and evil.

    Chaver B's awareness of the magnitude of evil in the world came on quickly and with great force in the shape of the rapid rise of Nazism. Mira's growing awareness was more subtle and insidious. Discuss how over time, Mira becomes aware of the evil that lurks in her community close to home and her reaction to how people make their choices between right and wrong.

12. The author devotes an entire chapter to paradoxes. What other paradoxes do you see in the world? Discuss.

13. Many people in Mira's community are depicted as being caring and loving, regardless of their religion or faith. Discuss the value of community as expressed in the novel.

14. Discuss Mira's relationship with her parents, her brother, her grandparents, her friends, and other characters in the novel. What does she learn from each of them?

15. The holiday *Purim* looms large in the book and brings together some of the novel's themes. Discuss Purim in relation to these themes, to Mira, and to Chaver B.

16. Each chapter is prefaced by a quote. Choose one quote and discuss how it foreshadows and highlights events in that particular chapter and how it relates to the novel as a whole.

17. The themes woven throughout *Prairie Sonata* are timely and timeless. They transcend age, gender, nationality, race, and religion. Discuss one theme and how it relates to the world today.

CPSIA information can be obtained
at www.ICGtesting.com
Printed in the USA
FSHW010143270921
85034FS